FAIRYTAIL FARM

ALI SPOONER

Also by Ali Spooner

Single Books
Sullivan's Trace
The Blank White Page
From the Cradle to the Stone
Holy Water and Whiskey Scars
The Ghost of East Texas
The Trophy Wives Club
The Bee Charmer
Forever Home
Ruined
Back in the Saddle
Open Your Heart
South of Heaven
Shotgun Rider
The Settlement
Love's Playlist
Cowgirl Up
Twisted Lives
The Epitaph
Terminal Event
Bailey's Run

Erotica
The Wolf and The Unicorn

Series
The Island Series
Neptune's Ring
Venus Rising

The Hunter Series
The Devil's Tree
Bound

Sasha Thibodaux Series
Sugarland
Bayou Justice
Line of Sight

Strong Southern Women Series
Diamond Dreams
Gator Girlz
True North
Footprints

Cast Iron Farm Series
The Mountain Whispers
The Star Child
Soul on Fire
The Sky People
Turn the Page

Songwriters Series
Six Strings and a Dream
Midnight in Nashville
Out and Loud

Co-authored with Annette Mori

Humbug- The Ultimate Lesbian Christmas Carol
Heart Strings Attached
Free to Love
Trouble in Paradise

Co-Authored with K.L. Gallagher

Hat Trick

FAIRYTAIL FARM

ALI SPOONER

Affinity
Rainbow Publications

2025

Fairytail Farm
© 2025 by Ali Spooner

Affinity E-Book Press NZ LTD.
Canterbury, New Zealand

Edition First

ISBN: 978-1-99-104096-1 (paperback)
ISBN: 978-1-99-104097-8 (EPUB)
ISBN: 978-1-99-104098-5 (PDF)
ISBN: 978-1-99-104099-2 (KINDLE)

Editor: Angela Koenig
Proof Editor: Lisa M
Cover Design: Irish Dragon Designs
Production Design: Affinity Publication Services

ACKNOWLEDGMENTS

I thank my fans for following my stories and providing great feedback and encouragement. Writing wouldn't be so much fun without you. Thanks to Affinity, Irish Dragon, for the cover art and the team of editors and readers who continue to help me grow as a writer.

DEDICATION

When my publisher and I discussed this story, she suggested we attempt something new with this book and agreed to incorporate photos of the reader's pets. The covers will include pictures from readers, and each chapter will feature images of two fur babies. I reached out on Facebook requesting photographs of fur babies, and I was overwhelmed by the response. Over one hundred photos were received within the first two days, but unfortunately, I couldn't include all of them. People also included heartwarming stories to share their experiences with rescues and furry family members. Enough to inspire another book. Our community loves animals, and I laughed and cried when reading some of the stories. I tried to keep a list of everyone who sent in images, but if I've missed anyone, please know that I appreciate your generosity in submitting your babies. Thank you all for submitting and making this project memorable.

SPECIAL THANKS TO

Front Cover

Beagle-Gordon (Chris Paynter)
Shepherd-Max (Dana Holmes)
Bassett -Zeke (Cindy Huff)
Calico-Danae – (Kate Rupley)
Doxy-Zeke (Deborah Dodge Hankin)
Kit Kat (Nicole Morrison Clark)

Back cover

Ray Ray (Elaine Roth Nichols)

Chapters in order

Athena (Audrey Hanagan) Hemi (Ladyhawke)Charlie
(Audrey Rupley)
Artemis (Cheyenne Bowman) Fluffy (Deanna Gross)
Calliope (Barbra Dennis) Riley (Chey Springer)
Chaos (Lisa Stafford) Archie (Mary McNeely)
Cora (Valerie Dunne) Zoey (Robin Haspiel)
Belle (Dawn Meyers Ward) Pinky (Shyla Allison)
Chris (Sefton Dof) Monrow (Paige Kinney)
The Twins (Julie Meachen) Husky (Devon Englerth)
Belle (Kate Ripley) Finlay (Nicole Morris Clark)
Umiko (Heather Anderson) Goldi (Chris and McGee)
Raye the bag lady (JM Dragon) Barney (Iris Faulkner)
Lucipurr (Kelly Duran) Roku (Chris Van Grundy)
Sadie (Donna Ashe) Shiloh (Emily Cubbage)
Mercury (AC Miller) Elli (Chris Paynter)
Kenidi (Paige Kinney) Sherpard (Donna Gross)
Yaya (Deb Vickery) Micro (Rosie Stetler)
Shakira(Robin Haspiel) Tio (Renee Whiteside Taylor)

Katie (Julie Meachen) Tucker (Dana Holmes)
Juliet (Brittany Wilson) Maxwell (He enjoyed his happily
ever after)

About the author/other Books (Ali's pets)

Casper and Punkin & Baby Cruz
Maggie and Oreo & Rascal
Coal and Easter
Kiwi

TABLE OF CONTENTS

CHAPTER ONE

Athena (Audrey Hanagan) Hemi (Ladyhawke)

Dr. Hillary "Hill" McCall sat behind her desk and smiled at the elderly woman facing her, holding a small mixed-breed pup. "What Can I do for you today, Mrs. Thompson? It's not time for Boscoe's checkup yet."

The woman's blue eyes sparkled as her hand stroked the small dog's head. "No, Boscoe's doing fine, but I want to discuss a proposal with you."

"Is everything okay?"

"Things are well, Hill. I have learned of a secret project you have started, and I want in on it," she explained. "My banker told me that you bought the old Tyson chicken farm and some acreage with the intention to have a place for abandoned or unwanted pets. Is this true?"

Hill smiled. "It is, but it must not be a secret any longer. I have bought the location as a retirement project for Alice and me. She is finally retiring from teaching this year, and we've always dreamed of a place to allow all animals to be loved and well taken care of through the remainder of their lives."

"That's a beautiful dream." Mrs. Thompson had tears in her eyes.

Hill nodded. "Alice doesn't know about it yet, so mum's the word. I want it to be a total surprise for her."

"I understand. As I said, I have a proposal for you." Mrs. Thompson looked down at Boscoe. "I'm not healthy these days, and Boscoe is still a young dog. I want to ensure he will be adequately cared for after I'm gone. I want him to live out his days on your farm, and I'm prepared to pay for his care in advance."

"That's not necessary, Mrs. Thompson," Hill replied. "We would love to care for Boscoe when the time comes."

"An undertaking of that size will not be cheap to maintain with the quality of care I know you will insist on, so I'd like to help. I've drafted a proposal for you to review and included a check to fund a foundation enabling you to maintain the facility for many years. I never had children, and my family has all gone before me, so I would like to help you create a very needed program in our small town." She handed Hill a thick envelope.

"Your donation will be graciously accepted. I will still work at the clinic several days a week to provide some income, and I have a few other ideas, but donations will be critical for the program's long-term success."

"I understand you're busy, so please review my proposal when you can, and we will make this dream come true." Mrs. Thompson stood to leave. "I know you would care for Boscoe without hesitation, and you are precisely the person I feel most comfortable with to care for his needs." Mrs. Thompson stood and started for the door.

"Thank you for trusting me, Mrs. Thompson," Hill said as she walked to the door with Mrs. Thompson.

"I trust you implicitly," she remarked and left the office.

Hill closed the door behind her and returned to her desk to open the envelope Mrs. Thomas had handed her. She had been the clinic's primary veterinarian for over twenty years and witnessed far too many abused or abandoned animals. Mrs. Thompson was a wealthy woman and could afford a generous donation, but Hill had no idea what she was about to receive. A check was paperclipped to the top of the proposal, and Hill's eyes opened wide when she saw the amount. She reached up and pinched her cheek. "This has got to be a dream." She began reading the proposal, and Hill was still in shock when her receptionist announced her next patient. She slipped the envelope into her desk drawer and left to greet her next patient.

†

Hill's mind reeled with excitement as she read through the proposal a second time. Mrs. Thompson had included a check for two million dollars, with five hundred thousand to be utilized to pay off the property and fund remodeling of the buildings. The rest would be invested, providing ongoing income to purchase needed goods and supplies.

It would take two hundred thousand to pay off the mortgage. Hill had already contracted a fencing company to build large runs and modify the chicken houses to handle cats and dogs separately. The third building she would use as a clinic and quarantine for new animals upon arrival. A small section was also built into a living area for an on-site staff she hoped to afford. The previous day, she had received an estimate to install a solar power system to heat and cool the buildings, but she had no idea how she would cover the expense. Now she did. She could also purchase a backup generator to support all three buildings.

Mrs. Thompson's only requirements were that Boscoe would live out his days on the farm, and the only animals euthanized would be those too sick or injured to survive. Hill had no quarrel with either of those demands. She hated to fail an ill or injured animal, but she would not allow them to suffer needlessly.

Hill was lost in thought when her telephone buzzed.

"Alice is on line one for you," the receptionist announced.

"Hey, sweetheart, I was just about to call you. I want to take you to dinner tonight after I show you something. Great, I'll be home by five. Love you." Hill hung up the phone and placed the proposal in her bag.

"I'll see you in the morning, Gretchen," she told the receptionist on her way out. "Dr. Cindy is on call tonight."

"Got it, Doc. Have a good night."

"You too, Gretchen."

†

Hill drove to the edge of town and turned down a long driveway. When she pulled onto the property, employees of the fence company were still working on the runs. She walked inside to review the progress on the build-out and was pleased to see the interior work completed.

"You guys have made tremendous progress," she told Tom, the work crew supervisor.

"We hope to have everything else finished by the end of the week."

"Thank you."

"I love what you are doing here," Tom told her. "If there is anything I can do to help, please let me know. I'm a big animal lover, too."

"Trust me, I will," Hill said, then walked to the next building.

The cat enclosures were complete and would safely house a hundred cats. Hill hoped they would successfully adopt out some of the animals, but she wanted to be prepared to accommodate as many as possible.

Tom caught her before they left. "Do you have an idea for the name of this place?"

Hill nodded and smiled. "I do. I plan to call it Fairytail Farm: Home to Happily Ever Afters."

"I love that. Would you mind if I made a sign for you for the front of the property?"

"Knock your socks off," Hill replied. "Just let me know how much."

"No, ma'am, this one's on me. My contribution to the farm."

"Thanks, Tom." Hill walked out to her car as the men left. It had grown much later than she thought. She pulled out her phone for a quick text.

I'm on my way. See you soon. Love you.
Love you too. Be careful.

Hill stopped halfway back to the road. There was a large, cleared area that would fit nicely into her plan. She smiled and drove home to pick up Alice. She hadn't planned to share the farm with her yet, but with the generosity from Mrs. Thompson, there was no way she could keep it a secret. Her face hurt from smiling so hard, and there was no way she could keep her excitement contained and hidden from Alice.

†

Hill took Alice in her arms and kissed her. "Are you starving?"

Alice looked at her wife with a quizzical look. "No, I'm good for a bit. What has you so amped up? Did you drink a pot of coffee this afternoon?"

6

Hill shook her head. "Just one cup, but it was a big cup." She grinned and reached for Alice's hand. "I've got something to share with you, and I can't wait any longer. Come while it's still light out."

Hill closed the door behind Alice, trotted to the driver's side, and climbed in.

"Are you going to give me a clue or keep me in the dark here?" Alice asked.

Hill backed out of their driveway. "It won't be a long wait." Her cheeks ached as she smiled at Alice.

"I haven't seen you this excited in years. You don't have a new woman on the side, do ya? I know you've been working later than usual lately," Alice teased.

"Yes, I have been working late. You should know by now that you are the only woman for me." Hill sighed. "I've been working hard on a new project, but it's been worth every second of the long hours." She reached over and took Alice's hand in hers. "I pray you won't be disappointed."

"As excited as you are, I seriously doubt you could disappoint me." Alice lifted Hill's hand to her mouth and kissed it.

Hill drove several miles from their home and turned on her turn signal. Alice looked at her. "The old chicken farm?"

When the buildings came into view, Hill pulled to a stop. "It used to be the Tyson chicken farm years ago, but now it will be Fairytail Farm."

"What?" Alice asked.

"Fairytail Farm. A forever home to hard-to-adopt cats and dogs that are overrunning the shelter. I know we've thought about creating a place once you retired. I have been working on this as a surprise for you."

"Well, you certainly have surprised me. I had no clue what you were up to." Alice smiled. "Show me."

†

After Hill finished giving her a tour of the buildings, she stopped talking and looked at Alice to see her reaction. "Well, what do you think?"

"You have done a fabulous job here. It will be a haven for many animals. How are we able to afford this?"

"I have been putting money aside for this project, and the bank loaned me the money for the property. I plan to still work a day or two a week at the clinic to help with revenue, but something happened today that rocked my world."

Darkness had fallen around them, and Hill opened the door for Alice. "I had a visit from Mrs. Thompson and Boscoe this afternoon."

"Was everything okay with Boscoe?"

"Yes, he is in perfect health and is a young dog. Mrs. Thompson learned about the project from the banker and offered me a proposal that was too good to pass on." Hill pulled the envelope out of her bag. "She wants to start a foundation for the care of unwanted animals at Fairytail Farm with a permanent forever home for Boscoe once she passes." With hands shaking from excitement, Hill pulled out the check, turned on the interior light, and passed it to Alice.

"Are you freaking kidding me?" Alice's hand covered her mouth. She looked at Hill in shock. "Two million dollars?"

"Five hundred to pay off the mortgage and retrofitting projects, and the rest will be invested to provide operating revenue for the future. I had to pinch myself when I saw the check for the first time."

"This is incredible. We've dreamed of this for so long. I will retire at the school year's end in a couple of months. Will we be ready to open?"

"Probably before then, but we can go slow. We don't need to fill the capacity right away. I have one other idea I'd like to discuss with you." Hill drove back toward the road, stopped at the vacant field, and turned on her bright lights. "I thought of another method to generate some revenue. This spot is cleared except for a few shade trees and is mostly level. We could pour some concrete RV pads and run water and solar power to create a woman-only campground. We could charge by the night, or if someone has limited funds, they can perform some work to cover the cost of the campsite."

When Alice looked at her, Hill could see tears glistening in her eyes. "You have put a lot of thought and effort into this project. I have just one request."

"Anything you want," Hill told her.

"I get to drive the tractor to mow all this grass." Alice chuckled. "You know I love tractors."

"We have a total of one hundred acres, much of which is wooded with a trail back to the lake. You can mow to your heart's desire." Hill dimmed her lights and started the drive to town. "I'm glad you approve, but I want to take you on a trip after you retire to celebrate."

"That's very sweet of you, but honestly, I'd rather stay and work with the animals. We can take a break once we get things running smoothly. I don't think we could relax and enjoy our time together with the project in its infancy."

Hill nodded, agreeing with Alice's assessment. "You will get a retirement trip, though. You deserve it after teaching all those years."

"I'm sure the farm will be running well by next spring, and we can sneak off for a trip. It will give us time to decide where we want to travel." She squeezed Hill's hand. "Thank you for making this dream come true."

"We need to thank Mrs. Thompson. Her generosity has dramatically reduced the stress of maintaining this project. I will still go to the clinic, but the investments, donations, and campground should keep us operational."

"The campground is a great vision. Solar and water will be inexpensive, and the concrete pads won't be all that expensive. If we do some advertising, the campground will pay for itself in a year or less."

Hill ran her hand through her hair. "That will need to be your project. I don't have a clue about how to create a website or internet ads."

"I have several students who would welcome the challenge of creating the website and business page for some extra cash." Alice chuckled. "They could probably do it half asleep."

Hill sighed with relief. "That beats me losing sleep over trying to figure it out." She looked at Alice. "Steak okay with you? I think we need to celebrate."

"Perfect," Alice replied, tucking the check and envelope back into Hill's bag.

"We'll need to meet with Mrs. Thompson to finalize the foundation soon. I will contact her tomorrow and set a meeting with her after school."

Hill was lost in her thoughts as she stared at the menu before her. Luckily, Alice ordered for both of them, allowing Hill to dream.

Charlie (Audrey Rupley)

CHAPTER TWO

Artemis (Cheyenne Bowman)

Several weeks passed, and the first animals were brought in from the shelter. Hill stayed busy giving each of them a thorough examination and treating ailments. She had given the last cat a vaccine when the van from the shelter arrived. Dan, one of the techs, carefully led a large German Shepherd into the dog compound. The dog stood as tall as Dan's waist, and Hill frowned at the thick rubber muzzle he wore.

"Is the muzzle necessary?"

Dan nodded and let out a deep sigh. "Unfortunately. He has been aggressive with other animals and humans since he arrived three days ago. We don't have much of a history for him, either. When we opened the clinic, he was found muzzled and tied to a pole outside the door. All we know is the name if his collar is correct."

Hill looked down at the collar. "T Rex," she read aloud. "You'll just be Rex here." She heard a low growl. "Was he examined?"

"After being sedated. Rex is strong, and it took two of us to sedate him. The Doc said he is in excellent health, about four years old, but too aggressive to be adopted. She hoped you would take him in to keep him from being euthanized."

Hill smiled at him. "That's what we're all about here. Let's give him a private run. We've only taken a few dogs in so far." Hill opened a gate, and Dan walked through with Rex and carefully removed the leash and muzzle before rushing out of the run. Rex snapped at him but fortunately missed Dan's backside by an inch. "I wonder why he is so angry?"

"I don't know," Dan answered. "He's a handsome dog but also dangerous." He clipped the leash into the clasp of the gate to secure it. "If anyone can teach him to trust and love again, it would be you, Doc."

"I'll give it my best shot, but I can't promise miracles. Thanks for bringing Rex out, Dan."

"You're welcome. What you're doing here is great. Can I come to volunteer sometime?"

"As often as you wish," Hill replied. "Have a great night."

Hill watched him leave and then filled the kibble and water in Rex's run. She turned a five-gallon bucket over and sat next to the run. "Welcome home, Rex. I hope we will become friends." Hill watched him pace back and forth at the end of the run. "I wish I knew your history to explain your anger. You look like you've been cared for and aren't physically injured." Hill let out a sigh. She knew there were many other types of abuse animals experienced and prayed she could discover his triggers.

Hill hadn't realized how long she sat observing Rex until she heard Jess enter the compound. She looked up to see the young woman walking toward her. She stood and stretched stiff muscles. Jess was a young college student aspiring to become a vet. She had interned with Hill at the clinic. "Hey, Jess. How was class today."

"Hey, Doc. It was good. I've found I love anatomy."

"That's good if you plan to go to vet school. You will need to know very much about anatomy."

Jess looked into the run. "Who's this handsome fellow?"

"This is Rex. Dan dropped him off this afternoon."

"I'll make him a name tag for his kennel."

"You need to put up a bite warning, too. Rex has to be muzzled for aggression."

Jess looked at the full containers. "Has he eaten or drank anything yet?"

Hill shook her head. "Nope, he hasn't stopped pacing since he arrived."

"I'll watch him closely tonight," Jess replied. "I'll be up studying for a while."

"Hopefully, he will settle in once the lights go low. How are you doing in the apartment? Is it comfortable enough for you?"

"It's perfect, Doc. Thank you for this opportunity. Any other new arrivals?"

"A few more cats. Everyone has been examined and fed for the evening."

"Thanks. I think I'll fix something to eat and make rounds before I start studying," Jess said. "Are you heading out soon?"

Hill locked eyes with Rex for several seconds and then picked up the bucket. "Yeah. The sandwich I had for lunch is long gone. I'll lock up here as I leave. Oh yeah, Alice called to confirm we have our first campground rental this weekend."

"That will be interesting," Jess said.

"I hope so. Goodnight, Jess."

"Night, Doc."

"Goodnight, Rex," Hill said and locked the front door behind her.

†

Alice poured Hill a glass of wine when she walked into the house. "Dinner will be ready soon. How was your day?"

"It was good. We had a few arrivals today, primarily cats, but one beautiful, angry shepherd."

"That sounds interesting. Do tell."

"Dan said they found him tied to a pole at the clinic three days ago. He's super aggressive with humans and animals.

15

Came in muzzled and nearly took a chunk of Dan's cute butt before he escaped the run."

"So, no history to explain his behavior?"

"None, and he's a beautiful dog. Maybe we can do something with him," Hill said, sipping wine. "How was your day?"

"It was busy. We've gotten a ton of emails about the campground. I think your idea is going to work out well. Our first two guests will arrive tomorrow. I wouldn't be surprised if we had a full schedule this summer."

Hill sat next to her. "Tomorrow is your last day of school. Are you ready?"

"You know, I've loved teaching, but I'm ready for a new adventure with you," Alice answered.

"Good. The grass needs mowing," Hill teased.

"I'll start on it Saturday morning. After our guests are up and moving." Alice chuckled. "I need to welcome them at five tomorrow night and ensure they get settled."

"Then dinner out to celebrate retirement?"

"I could be convinced." Alice smiled. "Tomorrow is just a half day, and I've already packed up my classroom."

Hill smiled. She was positive Alice didn't know about the luncheon they had planned for her after the students left. Alice hoped for a low-emotion exit, but her principal and fellow teachers had other ideas. Hill would join them at noon to celebrate.

†

Jess finished her dinner and made rounds through the two compounds. The cats were curled up on various perches, and only one small black cat woke to greet her. A young tom stretched lazily and trotted over to her. "Hello there, handsome," Jess said as she reached inside to scratch his chin. *I wonder if Doc Hill would mind if I picked out a companion for some company? I bet she wouldn't, and you would make a good friend. I'll ask her tomorrow before I go to class.* "Would you like to share a home with me?" The kitten answered with loud purrs as he nuzzled her hand. "I'll take that as a yes." Jess checked all their food and water before exiting and walking to the dog compound.

They had only taken in five dogs so far, and she checked on each of them as she made her way down to Rex's pen. Toby, a small beagle, was a bundle of pure joy. Jess couldn't figure out why he wasn't adopted. Maybe he was too old at six for most families looking for puppies. She was sure he would make a good companion for someone. When she reached Rex, she found his food undisturbed and frowned. "You are in a safe place, and we will love you if you allow us," she whispered. "Doc and I will take excellent care of you, but you need to eat." Jess knelt at the doorway as she talked to Rex. He had stopped pacing and was stretched out midway into the run, eyeing her warily. "No one will hurt you here, so you can trust us." Jess thought she saw a brief thump of a tail as she talked to him with a soothing voice. "We won't give up on you. It's time to study, but I'll be back later to check on you."

Jess locked the door to the compound and returned to her apartment. Doc Hill had provided an apartment in exchange for her living on the premises and working with the animals. She would assist Doc in the small clinic and learn valuable skills that would help her with her studies. Doc also provided financial assistance to cover her tuition and a stipend to cover her living expenses. There was no way Jess could do enough to repay Hill for her kindness and generosity, but she would do everything possible to make Fairytail Farm a success. She settled at her desk and opened her laptop to review her notes for the big test she had the following day.

†

"That was a fantastic dinner," Hill told Alice.

Alice smiled as she stood to clear the table. "I'll store the rest in the fridge for you to take for lunch tomorrow."

"That sounds perfect," Hill replied, carrying dishes to the kitchen. She wouldn't be at the farm for lunch, but she was certain Jess would enjoy the leftovers.

"I've got this if you want to shower, and then we can see what's on television," Alice suggested as she took the dishes from Hill.

Hill playfully sniffed at her pits. "Do I smell bad?"

"No, silly. A hot shower and some comfy clothes will make you feel better."

Hill hugged Alice from behind as she rinsed the dishes. She nuzzled her neck and whispered, "I can think of other things to make me feel better too."

Alice turned in her arms and kissed her deeply. "That is definitely on my list of probabilities tonight." Her hands landed on Hill's butt cheeks and gave them a squeeze. "I won't be long in here."

Hill kissed her softly before leaving for the shower.

†

Alice's hand landed on her chest. She could feel her heart pounding. Even after all these years, Hill could make her feel like a teenager. They had met at a college party, and she felt an immediate attraction to Hill, but they were already both with partners when they met. It wasn't until their junior year that they both found themselves single at the same time. Hill had asked her on a date, and that began a beautiful partnership that had lasted more than twenty years.

Hill had come home from her practice one night and made a marriage proposal in their backyard under a blanket of stars. She remembered the tremor in Hill's voice when she dropped to a knee and asked Alice to be her wife. They had lived as partners for years, but Hill insisted that now that it was legal, she wanted the formal and legal commitment they deserved as a loving couple.

After finishing the kitchen cleanup, Alice smiled at the memory and poured two glasses of wine. She could hear Hill singing in the shower when she entered the bedroom and stopped to listen. Hill was singing along with Wynona on the radio, and they didn't sound half bad as they belted out, "*No one else on earth.*" Alice placed their wine on a nightstand and lit candles before undressing and climbing between the bed covers.

She was sitting propped against the headboard, sipping wine, when Hill entered the room.

†

Hill could feel her cheek muscles turn into a smile when she entered the room and found Alice waiting for her. She placed her robe on the back of a chair and climbed onto the bed. "You are even more beautiful today than when we first met," she told Alice as she accepted the glass of wine.

"You are so sweet, but I really think we need to have your eyes checked." Alice chuckled.

"There is nothing wrong with my vision," Hill replied, touching her glass to Alice's. "It's perfect in every way, just like you."

"You've always said the sweetest things to make me feel so loved," Alice stated.

"The night is still young," Hill answered. "Let me put my words into action." She took Alice's wine glass and set the pair on the nightstand.

Hill's fingers traced Alice's face. She loved the tiny crow's feet wrinkles around her eyes that sparkled when she laughed. Hill kissed each of them softly. "I love every single inch of you."

"Even when there are more inches than before?" Alice asked.

"I wouldn't change anything about you, my love."

Their lovemaking was slow and tender, as they both had grown to love. There was no need to rush in a fever of passion for either of them, much preferring a slow rediscovery of one another's body as hands and mouths touched every sensitive spot.

Completely sated, Alice curled up in Hill's arms, and they dozed until Hill crept from the bed to blow out the candles. She returned to the bed and snuggled into Alice's back as they melted into each other and sleep claimed them for the night.

†

Jess studied for several hours, and when she felt comfortable about memorizing the material, she walked into the small kitchen for a snack. She found a small bag of peanut butter-filled pretzel bites and walked into the dog compound to check on Rex. He still hadn't eaten but moved closer to the front of the enclosure. Jess sat down on the floor and watched him as she nibbled on her snack. Rex watched her every movement, and she saw his tongue lick his lips as she munched on the sweet treat.

"They are delicious," she told him. "Would you like one?" Jess held a small treat through the opening of the gate. "This will have to be our secret." She watched as Rex crawled forward several feet, dragging his body across the floor. "That's a good start," Jess praised. "Will you come a little closer?" She tossed the treat into the run halfway between them and waited patiently.

Rex looked at her and then the treat as he considered moving forward. Jess popped another treat into her mouth and moaned loudly. She smiled when she saw his ears perk up at the sound. "They really are good." Jess watched him deliberate for several minutes without moving forward. "Well, I have a big test tomorrow, so I'm going to get some rest. I hope you have a good night." She stood and walked away slowly. Jess smiled when she heard the crunch of the treat coming from Rex's run. "Good boy," she whispered, pressing the lock to secure the building.

Fluffy (Deanna Gross)

CHAPTER THREE

Calliope (Barbra Dennis)

"Happy Retirement Day," Hill said when Alice entered the kitchen.

"Thank you. You didn't have to cook breakfast," Alice said as she poured a cup of coffee.

Hill flipped an egg in the pan. "I know, but this is a big day for you, and I wanted to start it with a good breakfast." Hill moved the fried egg to a plate with several slices of bacon and toast. "Would you care for some juice?"

"No, I'm good, thank you. This looks delicious."

Hill cracked another egg for the frying pan. "I know we usually eat breakfast together on the weekends, but from now on, we can share it together if we wish."

"I could get really spoiled," Alice said as she carried her plate to the table.

Hill turned to smile at her wife. "That's the plan. We will both have full days now that we are retired, but the least we can do is take time for us to start every day."

Hill finished cooking her egg and joined Alice at the table.

"You cook the best eggs," Alice said as she sopped up the broken yoke with her toast. "Mine always come out rubbery."

"I've had lots of practice, and I will cook them for you anytime you wish."

"Thank you. Do you have a busy morning?"

"Not that I'm aware of. We may get another delivery from the shelter today, but nothing urgent."

"I'll come out after school ends to make sure everything is all set for our first campers. I already have a folder with the contract and charges. It should go smoothly."

"I have no doubt it will. How long are our guests booked?"

"For three days. They sound like a lovely couple from Ohio, camping on their way to see grandkids in Florida."

"That sounds good. It will give us a good critique of services to see if we need to add anything."

Alice took a sip of coffee. "We are getting a lot of hits to the website. I hope that's a sign of good things to come."

"Have faith. We've built it, and they will come," Hill joked. "Even if we don't see much traffic, we will still have enough funds to keep everything going."

Alice looked at her watch. "Good Lord, where did the time go. I don't need to be late on my last day. Thanks for breakfast."

"Go, and I will clean up and see you later today. Love you," Hill said as Alice bent down for a kiss. "Enjoy your final day. I know it's kind of bittersweet for you." Hill could see tears pooling in Alice's eyes.

"It is, but I'm ready for time with you. I'll see you as soon as I can."

†

It was still early when Hill finished cleaning the kitchen, but she was eager to check on Rex. She grabbed her truck keys and walked outside into a beautiful late spring morning. The drive to the farm had become automatic, and she pushed the opener to the front gate, leaving it open during the day. Jess and any campers would have access to a code if they wanted to leave at night, but as a general rule, the gate was closed when the sun went down.

Hill was surprised to find Jess in the dog compound when she entered. "You're up early," she said.

"Morning, Doc. I have an early exam, and I'm done until the summer semester starts in a month."

"Any plans for a vacation?"

"Nope. I will stay busy around here and maybe get a jump on the summer reading assignments."

"Don't hesitate if you need some time off for a break between semesters. Maybe a weekend trip to the beach or something."

"Are you trying to get rid of me, Doc?"

"Heavens, no, but you do need time to recharge. The work only gets harder as you go. You need time to be a young adult and have fun too."

Hill frowned when she saw Rex's food bowl still full. "He didn't eat last night?"

Jess beamed with a smile. "He ate sometime after midnight. I've already refilled him this morning."

"Speaking of food. Alice sent me leftovers for lunch, but I won't be here to eat them. I thought you wouldn't mind some chicken and dumplings."

"Not at all. Where are you going to be?"

"Today is retirement day for Alice, so they are planning a surprise luncheon after school for her that I'm attending."

"Tell her congratulations for me."

"You can tell her yourself. She'll be out this afternoon to welcome our campground guests. She'll be on the tractor tomorrow cutting grass, so I hope you don't have plans to sleep late."

"My body isn't built for sleeping late. I'm usually up by seven on the weekends." Jess glanced at the clock. "I'd better get moving. I'll see you later this morning."

"Good luck with your exam. If I miss you, I'll return with Alice after lunch."

"Have fun," Jess said and walked swiftly to her car.

Hill turned back to Rex, who remained in the back portion of his run. "That's a good start. Keep eating, and we'll build from there."

†

Hill checked on all the animals before opening the gate to let the smaller dogs out for a run and exercise. Rex was in a separate area, but Hill opened his gate to allow him to see other dogs playing and being happy with their new home. She watched him looking out from the entrance as she played fetch with Toby and several small dogs.

An alert came across her watch that someone had entered the front gate. She stopped playing to see a van pull to a stop, and a young woman stepped out. Hill did not recognize the woman, and she exited the run to greet the new arrival.

"Hello," she called out as the woman entered.

"Good morning. Are you Doc Hill?"

"Yes, I am. How can I help you."

"My name is Anita Jones, and I'm the social worker and manager of the Spring Hill home for girls. We have ten girls, from eight years old to our oldest, seventeen, living in our foster care program. I'm sure you know the school year ends today, and I'm looking for some summer volunteer activities for several of our girls. One of them, Haley, heard about your program from a teacher, and she's interested in helping out this summer."

Hill ushered her inside the dog compound. "I would gladly consider some younger volunteers. Playing with these guys wears me out."

"Four of the girls want to sign up as volunteers," Anita said. "Do you have tasks they could help with for a few hours during the week? We are only a mile from here, so I would transport them."

"What do you know of our program?" Hill asked.

Anita blushed. "Not much, I'm afraid. I've just now heard about your project."

"Fairytail Farm is a forever home for dogs and cats that have remained unadopted, and many have special needs. Our mission is to provide them love and care until they can be adopted by someone special or until the end of their lives. Many of our animals have been abused, and only wish to be loved and cared for by someone."

"That sounds similar to our mission with the girls. Most have been in foster care situations that haven't worked out well, and they need to learn to trust and love again. Haley, our seventeen-year-old, is the odd case. She's been with us for almost six months. Her entire family was killed in a vehicle accident, and she had no remaining family, so after a lengthy hospital stay to recuperate from her injuries, she was given into our care until she ages out next year at eighteen."

"Then what happens?"

"Unfortunately, she will be on her own. She's a very bright child, and we are working on getting grants or a scholarship for her at the local university."

"Four girls?" Hill confirmed.

"Yes, two want to work with cats and two with dogs."

"They could help keep the environments clean, food containers filled, water fresh, and provide love to some animals that could use it." Hill swung her arm. "I hope one of them has a good arm. These guys love to play fetch."

"Maggie would be perfect for that. She plays on the high school softball team and wants to work with Haley with the dogs. She's fifteen. The others are a pair of twins who are twelve, Lisa and Lara, who are totally wild about cats."

"Sounds like we have some volunteers. When can I meet them?"

"Would tomorrow be too soon?"

Hill smiled. "Tomorrow would be perfect. Around ten?"

Anita nodded. "We will be here. I can't wait to tell the girls."

"We will be more than happy for them to volunteer as much as they would like over the summer and on weekends once school starts in the fall. I'm sure we can work out a schedule."

"Once we start, I can have the girls bring sack lunches with them."

"Have them bring them tomorrow, and we can get started right away. Unless that's not in your schedule." Hill saw Anita smile, and for a second, she thought she would hug her.

Instead, she took a step back. "Tomorrow will be great. I know four girls who will be extremely excited."

"I'll see you tomorrow then," Hill replied.

"Thank you." Anita walked back to the van.

"Well, that was an interesting visit," Hill spoke aloud. When she turned around, Rex watched her in front of his run. "What do you think about meeting some young friends tomorrow?" His coffee-brown eyes stared back at her until he turned away." Hill felt his sadness. "You don't know it yet, but we will become good friends."

Hill left the dogs in the run as she walked to her office and checked emails and voice messages. Dan from the shelter had another delivery he wanted to make, and Hill responded it would have to be after three so she could be sure to be here to welcome the new arrivals. It only took Dan a minute to respond with a thumbs up emoji.

†

Hill had made a cup of coffee and was sitting at her desk when Jess bounced in. "That was fast."

"I blew right through that exam. I feel confident I did well. How has your morning been so far?"

"Very interesting. Take a seat, and I'll bring you up to speed."

Hill explained about the visit from Anita and the four girls from the group home who wanted to volunteer.

"I think that's great. The girls probably need love and kindness as much as the animals."

Hill shouldn't have been surprised by Jess' comment, but she was. "That's very intuitive of you."

"I went to high school with a girl that lived there, and she told me several bad stories about living with foster families. She lived at the group home until she aged out, and now she's in her second year of college."

"That's good to hear. One of the girls is seventeen and lost her entire family in an accident, so she will be aging out next year."

"That's sad," Jess replied.

"Dan will be making another delivery this afternoon around three. I didn't think to ask if they were dogs or cats."

"Speaking of cats. Would you mind if I adopted the little black tom? I would pay for all of his food and care."

"No, you won't. He will still be on the premises, so we will ensure he's cared for. You might want to pick up some toys and special treats the next time you're in town. We have plenty of litter and extra pans here."

"Thanks, Doc."

"Have you named him yet?"

Jess nodded. "I call him Buster. We play at night while the older cats crash."

"Well, if you've named him, he's yours." Hill saw the smile on Jess' face. "The girls will be here at ten tomorrow to start volunteering. Can you help me with their training?"

"Absolutely. Any change with Rex?"

"He stayed at the entrance of his run to watch the other dogs playing for a while. He didn't venture out to explore. I thought I'd leave the gate open to see if he will."

"It's such a pretty day out. Maybe he will. What time are you heading into the school?"

"I need to leave by eleven thirty. Do you need something?"

"No, I was going to heat up your leftovers, and then I'll play with the dogs."

"Good. Toby nearly wore me out playing fetch. We need to get one of those ball launchers." Hill laughed.

"He does love to play. Is there anything I need to do while you're gone?"

"Call Dan to see who he is bringing us. You may need to set up more feeders if he's bringing dogs."

"I'm all over it. You might want to hit the road, Doc," Jess teased. "You're in stealth mode, remember."

"That's true. I'll see you later today, Jess. Enjoy lunch. They were outstanding last night."

Jess nodded and walked toward her apartment.

†

Hill finished her coffee and stepped into the bathroom to freshen up. She was excited for Alice but aware she was leaving much of her past behind at the school. They would enjoy the summer together, and if it appeared Alice missed teaching, Hill thought she might suggest some substitute teaching. *Only time will tell.*

Hill drove to town and parked a block away from the school to avoid detection. She was instructed to arrive at the cafeteria at noon and came with five minutes to spare. James Thomas, the principal, greeted her when she arrived.

"I'm so glad you could join us today, Doc."

"I wouldn't miss it for the world."

"She's already had a full day of emotions as students stopped by her classroom to wish her well. She even broke out a box of tissues."

"Today is a day she has looked forward to and dreaded for months," Hill told him. "I'm still not one hundred percent sure she's ready to stop teaching, but we'll see."

"I'd take her back in a heartbeat, even if it's only on a substitute basis."

"That's always an option. Is there anything I can help with?"

"Yes, will you bring Alice here?"

Hill smiled. "I can tell her I'm here to help with her boxes and parked behind the cafeteria."

"Devious. I love it. See you soon."

†

Alice was stacking her boxes on a cart when Hill entered. She turned around, and Hill could see the redness in her eyes from crying. Hill walked over to her and pulled her into a hug.

"What are you doing here?"

"I thought I would come and help you load your boxes. My truck is parked behind the cafeteria," Hill answered.

"That's very sweet. I didn't realize how much I had accumulated over the years."

"That's no problem. I've got plenty of room in my truck." Hill smiled. "Are you sure you want to do this?"

"Yes, I'm ready," Alice replied.

"Let's break you out of this joint then. Open the door, and I'll bring the cart."

Alice smiled and held the door open for Hill. When they reached the cafeteria, Alice was surprised to find all the teachers and staff were present to see her off. She looked back at Hill, who nodded to her to enter the room.

†

Many tears were shed during the beautiful retirement celebration, and when Alice decided it was time to exit, Hill loaded the boxes in the back seat of her truck.

33

"I'll meet you at the house to unload the boxes, then you can ride to the farm with me if you like."

"I'd like that very much. Thank you for being here today."

"It was very much my pleasure. I wouldn't have missed it for anything. I have some good news to share with you on our ride."

"That's always fun to hear. I'll see you at home."

†

Hill carried the boxes into the house while Alice got her folder for the campground guests.

"You know you can share the office with me at the farm if you'd like. We could get a small desk and set you up in no time."

"I'd like that, and it makes good sense to be on site."

"We will make it happen then," Hill said, holding the door open for Alice. She told her about the group home social worker visit and the agreement to have four girls as volunteers.

"I love that idea, and I think both the kids and animals will benefit from visiting. I've had students from the home in my classes who have all been wonderful young ladies. Very eager to learn and attentive in class. I believe one of them went on to college."

"She did, and a seventeen-year-old will be volunteering who ages out of the home next year. The social worker said they were trying to get grants or scholarships for her to go to college."

Alice reached over and took Hill's hand. "Maybe we could help with that. We've got plenty of room in the house, and we could offer her a part-time job at the farm to help with expenses."

"That's a great idea. We could also consider adding another apartment at the farm if she and Jess get along well."

"That too," Alice replied.

†

When they arrived at the farm, they were surprised that the campers had arrived early. Jess was talking to them and pointing out various locations. "Looks like our junior park ranger is on the job," Hill teased.

"That's funny." Alice chuckled. "Let's go meet our guests."

Hill took Alice's hand as they walked over to the small group. Alice introduced them, and Betsy and Lou were welcomed to the farm.

"I hope you don't mind we were early. We were so excited to get here. My foot got a little heavy on the gas. Lou and I love what you're doing here and couldn't wait to see the farm."

"Do you want to get set up first or take a tour?" Hill asked.

Betsy and Lou shared a look. "A tour, please."

Hill, Alice, and Jess showed the guests around the property. "We have a developing trail back to a small lake, and there are kayaks and canoes you can use or fish if you'd prefer." Hill pointed toward the bathhouse. "We had some downed trees, so we cut the wood for the fire pit. It's stored in the small shed next to the bathhouse."

Jess was surprised to hear Toby howl when they entered the dog compound. She looked at Hill with a funny expression. "I've never heard him do that."

"This is Toby. He's a beagle and is about six years old. He's very affectionate, but most people want a puppy, not an older dog," Jess explained.

"He's a handsome boy," Lou said as she bent down to greet Toby.

"Will you allow us to help around here?" Betsy asked.

"We have an exchange program, so you can work instead of paying the campground fee," Alice explained.

Lou shook her head. "Oh, no, we will still pay the fee, which is extremely low, but we'd love to help. Maybe take someone for a walk or help with cleaning or feeding?"

"We have a group of young ladies coming out to volunteer tomorrow morning, but you are more than welcome to join us," Hill said. "Alice plans on cutting grass tomorrow, but she's agreed to start later in the morning."

"No worries. We are both early risers," Betsy said.

Hill turned when she heard a vehicle approach. She looked at Jess. "Our day is about to get busy. We have some new arrivals that need exams and settling in. It was nice to meet you. Welcome to Fairytail Farm."

Hill and Jess left the group to meet Dan. "What do you have for us today?" Hill asked.

"A mixed bunch. Several dogs and a few cats. One that needs some close attention that was hit by a car and has a broken leg. She's young and otherwise healthy, so there was no need to euthanize her."

"She will need to be in a crate until that leg heals," Hill said as Dan handed Jess the carrier with the cat.

"You can keep this carrier," Dan offered.

Jess peered inside to find an orange tabby looking back at her with big yellow eyes. "Does she have a name?"

"Doc has been calling her Gabby, but you can change it if you like," Dan answered.

"Gabby it is then." Jess looked at Hill.

"Go ahead. I see it in your eyes, but you must explain Gabby to Buster," Hill teased. "There is plenty of room for two in the apartment. Just remember Gabby needs to rest in the carrier until her leg heals."

"Thanks, Doc."

†

Alice looked at Lou and Betsy. "Let's get you checked in so you can get set up. They walked to the campground, and Alice pointed out another small building. "If you need water hoses or extension cords, several are in there."

"I can't get over how beautiful this place is," Lou said as she stretched.

"Thanks. It has been a dream of ours for a while. I just retired from teaching today, so I hope the campground will take off. That's my management part while Hill and Jess tend to the animals."

"Congratulations on your retirement. I retired from teaching last year and can't say I've missed it. Lou and I have traveled and been able to do so much more together."

"You are our first guests, so you can pick any spots," Alice said.

"I like the one close to the fire pit," Lou said.

"Number three it is then," Alice said.

"We entered our payment online, but is there any deposit we need to cover?" Betsy asked.

"No, the payment includes all the services," Alice explained.

"You really are underpricing your service," Lou said with a frown. "You could easily charge double and still be reasonable."

Alice shook her head. "Honestly, the campground was an afterthought and a way to help offset some of the expenses, but we want to make it reasonable for any woman or women that need a stopover. We have sweat equity options for those who can't afford the fees to provide some work in exchange for site fees." She gave them the folder with instructions and the gate code after having them sign the necessary paperwork. "Jess is a college student who lives on site, and we have included our cell numbers if you need anything."

Lou shook her head. "This place is amazing. Is there any issue with reserving a spot for our return trip?"

"Not at all. Just give me your dates, and I'll book you in. Hill and I will be here for several hours, so make yourselves at home and let us know if you need anything."

"I'd like to take a peek at that lake," Lou said. "After we get set up."

Alice smiled. "Like I said, make yourselves at home."

"Thanks," Betsy called out as Alice turned to leave.

†

Hill looked over Gabby's paperwork. "She's all good if you want to take her to the apartment and get her set up. I can get started on the new arrival exams."

38

"I won't be long," Jess promised.

"No worries, my other assistant is on her way," Hill said, nodding to Alice. "Can you help with the new arrivals while Jess settles Gabby?"

"I'd love to," Alice said with a smile. "Our guests are getting settled in too."

"Perfect. We have three cats and four new dogs to examine. Let's get to it," Hill said.

"Cats or dogs first?" Alice asked.

"Let's start with the cats." Hill picked up a tiger-striped cat, and they walked to the clinic.

†

Jess arrived when they were examining the last cat. "Did you get Gabby settled?"

Jess nodded. "I already had a litter pan and food set up for Buster, so I left her close to that area."

Hill smiled at her young assistant. "You might want to give Gabby a few days to acclimate to her new home before introducing Buster."

"Yeah, I was thinking that, too," Jess replied. "I need to be there so they don't play roughly."

"I'm pretty sure Gabby will keep him at bay, but supervision for a while isn't a bad thing. Will you add this lovely to the new cat section and bring one of the dogs?" Hill asked.

Jess picked up the cat. "Let's get you home," she said as she left the clinic.

Alice smiled at Hill. "She's going to make a great vet one day."

"Yeah, she is, and she's a great young woman, too." Hill sighed. "I'm trying to encourage her to have fun this summer between semesters. She needs to be a kid for a while yet."

"Hmmpph, good luck with that," Alice joked. "She is in heaven here."

"I kind of like it here, too, and it's great to know she's here after hours."

"Things are really falling into place, aren't they?"

Hill nodded. "Even better than I had ever dreamed."

†

After examining the dogs, Hill turned to Jess. "The only one I'm concerned about is the pug. His respiratory issues aren't uncommon for the breed, but his age works against him. He doesn't appear to be in pain, but we need to keep an eye on him."

"I'll keep a close check on him," Jess replied. "Jax, right?"

"Yes, that's his name. He's well past ten years old."

†

Alice saw the look in Hill's eyes as she talked to Jess and feared the dog wouldn't last long. That made her consider what they would do when the first animal passed away. She and Hill hadn't discussed that yet.

Hill smiled at her. "That luncheon was good, but the food wasn't all that filling. Can we go to dinner soon?"

"Of course," Alice answered. "Let's wash up, and we can head out."

Jess was playing with Buster when they walked out. "We are going to head out for today. We'll see you tomorrow morning."

"Sounds good, boss," Jess said. "Other than checking on Jax, anything else you need me to do?"

"Yes, have some fun with Gabby. Do you have something good to eat tonight?"

"I thought I'd cook breakfast. Simple and filling."

"Nothing like breakfast for dinner. I might be tempted if we didn't have a big breakfast this morning. I think there will be pasta in my near future."

"Enjoy then, and I'll see you tomorrow."

"Goodnight, Jess," Alice called to her.

"Oh, congrats on retirement," Jess called back.

"Thank you!"

On their way to the truck, they passed Betsy and Lou walking back from the lake. Lou smiled at them.

"Hey, Doc. I noticed there are still a lot of trees blown down on the way to the lake. Would you mind if I cut them into some wood for the pit? I know we'll be using a bunch before we leave."

"I've got a chainsaw in the toolshed, so you can knock yourself out tomorrow if that's really how you want to spend your time here."

"You just made her day mentioning power tools," Betsy teased.

"If you cut it into sections, I can bring the tractor out with a trailer so we can bring the wood back here," Alice suggested.

Hill looked at Betsy. "Your lady with power tools and mine with a tractor addiction. What more could we ask for?"

"Nothing at all," Betsy answered. "I wouldn't trade either of them for anything."

"We'll see you in the morning," Hill said and opened the door for Alice.

"Have a great night," Lou called out.

†

"Pasta, huh?" Alice asked when Hill climbed behind the wheel.

"That just flew out. This is your night, so you choose where we go," Hill answered.

"Pasta sounds perfect."

†

Jess said goodnight to Buster and checked on Jax and Rex before returning to her apartment. Jax was curled up, sleeping on a bed, snoring loudly. Rex took a tentative step toward her as she added food to his dish.

"How are you today, my friend? It's been a bit hectic, but I'll be back later to check on you. Maybe another treat? Has to be our secret, though."

Jess picked up Gabby and sat on her couch. "How are you feeling, pretty girl?" Jess was rewarded with a loud purr as she stroked down her back. "We will have you all better and out of this cast soon," she promised. "I'm hungry. Are you hungry?"

Gabby answered with a soft meow.

"Let's see what we can do about that." Jess placed a handful of crunchy food in her bowl, then scrambled eggs and made toast for herself. Gabby ate some of the dry food and sat staring at Jess while she ate. "Do you like scrambled eggs?" Jess dropped a small portion in her bowl and watched Gabby gobble it down. "I'll take that as a yes. Were you a homeless kitty? It seems you like people's food better than cat food. Is that what you are used to?"

Gabby hobbled over to Jess and rubbed against her leg. Jess bent down to pick her up and placed her in her lap. "We need to work on that. Kitty food is much better for you, but you can have a special treat occasionally."

Jess cleaned the kitchen and turned on the television before stretching out on the couch. Gabby was stretched across Jess' stomach, and they were soon napping. A loud noise on the television startled Jess awake, and she looked at the clock to see she had slept for an hour. Gabby's purring vibrated against her stomach.

"I can see that it's going to be dangerous snuggling with you," she teased. "I've got to check on the boys, but I'll be back."

Jess walked into the kitchen and picked up the bag of pretzel treats. Jax was still sleeping peacefully, so she walked down to Rex's run. Jess sat down in front of the gate and rubbed her eyes. "Sorry, I seem to have fallen asleep," she told him as she took a treat out and popped it in her mouth. She smiled when Rex licked his lips. "You want one?" She carefully eased her hand through the gate and dropped the treat a few feet into the run. "I think I aced my test this morning. I feel like I did pretty well, so all those hours of studying have paid off." Rex listened to her, and his eyes never left hers as he slowly crept forward to eat the treat. "That's a good boy, Rex. Do you want another?"

Jess would love to be able to reach through and pet Rex, but she knew contact had to be on his terms, and she felt like there was a lot of trust to be built before that happened. She patiently removed another treat and placed it closer this time. Rex sat and watched her, entirely in tune with her attempts to draw him closer. "I can't fool you, can I, clever boy? We will have some new visitors tomorrow. Some girls from a local group home will volunteer to work with us this summer starting tomorrow. They don't have real families and need love and friendship like us."

Rex surprised her by taking another step forward and bending down to eat the treat before retreating. "That wasn't so hard, now was it?" Jess placed another treat on the ground. "Last one for tonight." She was pleased when Rex didn't hesitate and walked to the treat right away. "That's good." She closed the bag and looked at him. "More tomorrow night. I might see if Doc has some other treats you can have. Goodnight, Rex." Jess stood, and he shied away. "I will see you tomorrow."

When Jess returned to her apartment, she placed Gabby in the carrier for the evening and walked into her bedroom. She was tired and knew tomorrow would be a busy day, so she decided to retire for the evening. She chuckled when she looked at the clock. "Eleven o'clock. That's the earliest so far this week."

†

"Thank you for a lovely evening," Alice said as she climbed into bed beside Hill.

"It was my pleasure. I'm excited you will begin a new chapter in your life," Hill answered.

Alice snuggled beneath the covers. "I am so ready for it. My turn to cook in the morning. What would you like?"

"I think it's time to break in that waffle maker you got today," Hill answered. "We will both need the carbs tomorrow."

"I can't wait to get on that tractor." Alice grinned.

"I can't believe Lou wants to cut firewood on her vacation."

Alice scooted closer to Hill. "We all have different things we enjoy."

"That's true." Hill kissed her sweetly and turned out the lights.

Rylie (Chey Springer)

CHAPTER FOUR

Chaos (Lisa Stafford)

Hill was delighted to see that Jess had made a pot of coffee in the office when she entered carrying Alice's laptop bag. She placed the bag on her desk and took a cup from Jess. "Do you want me to run one out to Alice?"

"No, let's give her time to cut without disruption." Hill smiled.

"What's on tap for today?"

"I need your help with something before making rounds," Hill said.

"Sure. What's up?"

"I need you to go online to the office supply store to help me select a small desk and office chair for Alice. She's decided to work out here with us."

"That's great news. Something about the size I have?"

"That should be perfect. Do you remember where we got it?"

"Leave it to me," Jess said, turning on the desktop.

"Start searching while I sneak out to check on Alice. She was excited to use the tractor today, but I know it's been years since she operated one."

"If we find what you want, I can pick it up if you loan me your truck. I can get everything assembled between projects. Don't forget the girls will be here at ten."

"I'm not sure there will be time to assemble a desk, so look to see if they have some already assembled. The chair will be a piece of cake."

"On it," Jess said as Hill left the office.

She could hear the tractor running in the distance when she stepped out of the compound. She was about to peek around the corner when Lou walked into view.

"Morning, Doc. She's doing just fine." Lou grinned. "I was coming to check out your chainsaw. Betsy will join me and help carry logs to the trail."

"Are you sure you really want to do this?"

"Yes, no doubt. I promise I can run the saw safely," Lou answered.

"Knock yourself out then. Let's go, and I'll show you where the saw and supplies are. You can put everything in a wheelbarrow to make it easier. Do you want some bottled water or a thermos of coffee?"

"Betsy's bringing a pitcher of lemonade."

"Let me at least treat you to lunch. We have a decent pizza company in town."

"I'll never turn down pizza," Lou said.

"Deal. Let me know if you need anything."

"Will do, Doc."

Hill walked back to the office and found Anita's number. She called her and asked for the girls to skip sack lunches today. Anita was delighted to hear they would be treated to pizza.

"I've got another job for you today," Hill told Jess. "I need you to order a bunch of pizza to be delivered for lunch for everybody."

"Our usual?" Jess asked.

"Yes, and lots of it. Betsy and Lou are cutting firewood for the campground, and the girls will be here. I already called to tell Anita not to bring sack lunches."

"That will probably be a big treat for them," Jess said. "Speaking of treats, do we have Rex-size treats?"

"There's a wide variety in the clinic storeroom. Do you think Rex would enjoy a treat?"

Jess looked at Hill, her cheeks flushed. "I have a confession to make. I've been sharing some peanut butter-filled pretzels with him at night. Not a lot, though, but I think he's beginning to trust me. He comes much closer now."

"If memory serves me correctly, some bison rings have peanut butter inside. The pretzels weren't too bad for Rex, so relax."

"Cool. Look what I found."

Hill joined Jess and agreed on a desk and chair for Alice. "I can order them for curbside pickup at nine when they open. We can unload after the girls leave. I'll order our pizza for delivery at twelve if that's good."

"Perfect," Hill said and handed Jess a credit card. "I'm going to start with Jax. Join me when you can."

"I won't be long, Doc," Jess said, tapping away on the keyboard.

†

Hill placed Jax on the exam table and listened to his breathing. She frowned as she heard the rattling in his lungs. She opened a drawer, pulled out a bottle of liquid steroids, and poured up a dose. "This may help some," she said and administered the drug. She weighed Jax, took his temperature, and was adding notes to his chart when Jess entered.

"How's he doing?" Jess asked.

"His breathing is still pretty congested, so I gave him a dose of liquid steroids. That may help him breathe easier and have an appetite. He's lost a few ounces this week."

"Do I need to dose him during the night?" Jess asked.

Hill smiled at Jess' eagerness to learn and help out. "I'll show you how later today when he's due for another dose."

"Thanks, Doc. Do you want me to take him back to his run?"

"Yes. How did Gabby do last night?"

"She did well. She ate well, used the litter box, and snuggled with me on the couch for a while. We were both so comfy we dozed for an hour after dinner."

"I bet it didn't hurt either of you. Bring her in so I can check Gabby quickly before you need to head into town."

Jess nodded, picked Jax up, and cradled him in her arms before leaving the clinic.

Hill searched the treat boxes until she found the one she wanted. She placed it on the counter and waited for Jess to return.

"Hey, pretty girl," Hill said as she took Gabby from Jess and gave her a quick check-up. Hill noticed Jess watching her anxiously as she examined Gabby. Hill watched Gabby take a few steps, and she didn't appear to be in pain and managed to walk well in the cast. "Relax, she's doing good." Hill picked up Gabby and stroked her head before handing her to Jess. "You can take her back and here," Hill said, giving Jess the treat for Rex. "For later tonight." She winked.

"Thanks, Doc."

"I'll finish rounds while you're in town," Hill said. She handed her the truck keys.

"I put your credit card in the middle desk drawer," Jess said. "I'll be back."

†

51

Hill poured two cups of coffee and carried them outside. When she caught Alice's attention, she waved her over for a break. "How's it going?" Hill asked, handing Alice a coffee.

"Good," Alice said and took a sip of coffee. "This is so relaxing." She looked up when she heard the sound of the chainsaw. "Is Lou cutting wood already?"

"Yeah, she started not long after you did." She smiled. "Betsy is supervising."

"Where's the truck?"

"I sent Jess to town on an errand. We are having a pizza party today since everyone will be working and playing hard."

"That's a great idea. How much can I cut today?"

"As much as you can from the gate to the compound. You can do more cutting next week."

Alice's face beamed with a smile. "Do you need my help when the girls arrive?"

Hill shook her head. "I think Jess and I can handle the orientation. You can meet them when we break for lunch, and then hook up the trailer to gather the wood Lou is cutting."

"Perfect." Alice drained the cup and handed it back to Hill. "Thanks for the coffee. I'll bring some water out later, but please call me if you need anything."

"I will." Alice reached down to start the tractor as Hill stepped away.

†

Jess returned just minutes before the van arrived from the group home. Hill smiled as four girls climbed out, and waited for Anita before approaching them. Anita introduced the girls, and Hill introduced herself and Jess. "Jess is a vet student going to college, and she lives onsite and helps me with the animals when she's not in school. She will be working with us this summer, too."

Jess looked at Hill. "I'll take the dogs if you want to show the twins the cat compound," she offered.

"What time should I return?" Anita asked.

Hill cocked her head. "Is four too late?"

"That will be great. Good for you, girls?" Anita asked.

"Definitely," one of the twins answered.

"Let's get to it then," Hill said. As she and the girls walked to the compound, she asked, "Okay, how do I keep you two separate?"

Lisa giggled. "I have pierced ears, and Lara doesn't. She's been too chicken to have them done."

"I'm with you, Lara," Hill said, pointing to her ears. "Okay, so you must always wear earrings," Hill teased.

Hill opened the run where Buster lived, and the girls followed her inside. They sat down, and it didn't take long for the girls to be surrounded by cats. Buster climbed up in Hill's lap and began purring. "This is Buster. Jess will be adopting him soon. Do you know what we do at Fairytail Farm?"

Both girls shook their heads. "We know you care for dogs and cats," Lisa said.

"It's much more than that," Hill said. "Fairytail Farm is home to dogs and cats that, for many different reasons, haven't been adopted. They may have medical issues or be old. Most people who go to shelters are looking for puppies or kittens, not older animals. So, typically, they stay in shelters until it becomes too crowded, and most shelters will put an animal asleep to make room for others with a higher chance of adoption."

"When you say 'put asleep,' do you mean they kill them?" Lara asked with tears in her eyes.

Hill nodded. "The proper term is to euthanize, which means they are given an injection that puts them to sleep so deeply their hearts stop beating."

"That's terrible," Lisa said. "They haven't done anything wrong but get old."

"It is terrible, but the animal doesn't feel anything after the needle prick, so it's painless for them. As a vet, I use that option only as a last resort when an animal is too sick or injured, and removing their pain is best for them. That's the only time it will happen here. We are committed to caring for and loving the animals here until they are adopted by special people or it's their time to pass."

Hill paused for a minute to let her words sink in with the girls. "Every animal here gets medical care from Jess and me. What we are hoping you will help with is the love part. As you can see, the cats are very affectionate and love attention. Do you think you can help with that?"

Both girls smiled and nodded. "Yes, we can," Lara answered. "You called him Buster. Do the others have names?"

"If they come to us with names, we keep them. I'm sure everyone will eventually have a name. Maybe you can help with that. Listen carefully as you play with them to see if they tell you a name they would like. Can you do that?"

"Oh yes," Lisa said. "Can we come to visit every day?"

"We will work out a schedule with Anita. We are closed on Sunday to give everyone a break, but we are open the other six days."

"I hope we can come as often as possible," Lara said.

"We would welcome your help. As you get used to handling the cats, we will add other chores, such as feeding and keeping the environment clean and healthy. How does that sound?"

"Perfect," Lisa said.

"Nope. That should be purrfect," Lara teased her sister.

Hill laughed. "That's right." Hill stood. "I'm going to check on the others. Are you okay here?"

"Yes, we are fine," Lisa said, calling Buster.

"I'll be back soon. I'm just next door if you need me."

"Okay, Doc Hill. Thanks for not giving up on them."

"I never will." Hill left the cat compound with a lump in her throat. *Do the girls think the world has given up on them?* "I sure hope not," Hill said as she walked to the dog compound. Alice had mowed halfway up the drive and wore a massive smile. A thought hit her like a punch to the gut. *These girls need love and care, just like the animals. Hopefully, we can provide that for them.*

When she stepped inside, she heard laughter from the run and looked out to watch Maggie toss a ball for Toby to fetch. Several dogs chased after it and fought to be the ones to take it back to Maggie. Maggie wore a smile almost as big as Alice's. She looked down the walkway, and Haley and Jess sprayed off the concrete runs into the drain. Hill walked over to them. "Looks great," she told them.

"Thanks, Doc. I'm waiting to see if Rex will leave his run so we can wash it down."

"Let me grab a couple more balls to help Maggie, and I'll see if I can coax him out. Shut the gate behind him if he comes out."

"Will do. I think we're good here," Jess told Haley. "You did well."

"Thanks," Haley said with a blush.

"If you coil our hoses onto the holders, I'll see if I can close Rex's gate."

Hill returned with a bag of balls of different sizes and walked out to Maggie. "You need some help?"

"I need at least two more arms." Maggie grinned.

Hill pulled out a small ball and tossed it for the pack. "I'll be right back." Hill took a rubber playground ball and walked to the end of Rex's run. She hoped he was curious enough to walk out far enough to allow Jess to close his gate long enough to wash his run. It seemed to work until one of the dogs rushed to her with a ball to throw. Rex paused to watch as Hill threw the small ball and then launched the playground ball. Several dogs tried to catch it, causing it to bounce more wildly. She saw Rex walking out of the corner of her eye to see what was happening. *Now Jess.* The sudden movement of the gate startled him, but he didn't bolt back inside. "Good boy, Rex," she called to him. She walked back to Maggie and sat beside her.

†

Haley worked to quickly wash down Rex's run. "He's angry, isn't he?" she asked Jess.

"Yes, but we don't know why. Rex had to be muzzled to keep him from attacking other animals or the shelter staff. We don't know anything about him other than his name. He's scared, angry, and lacks trust, but he's healthy and young, about four, and Doc Hill won't give up on him."

"He's sad too," Haley said. "I don't think he was physically harmed, but he's emotionally scarred."

Jess was shocked by Haley's assessment. "You are pretty spot on, and we are working hard to gain his trust."

"Do you think Doc Hill will let me work with him to build trust?"

"Only if you do it outside his run. He's too dangerous for you to be inside with him. Doc Hill can't afford to have him bite you. It would force her to put him down, and nobody wants that."

Haley shook her head. "I would never jeopardize that. I do think we have a connection."

"I don't think she'd have a problem if you promised to be safe. We can ask her if you want."

"I'd like that," Haley said. "I felt pulled toward him as soon as we arrived this morning."

"Be sure to share that with Doc Hill. She's a firm believer in connections. If you'll come out and tend the hose, I'll open his gate if he wants to return."

"All done," Haley said, and Jess opened the gate.

They could see Rex standing in the run, looking back toward them. He slowly began to walk inside. "I'm going to check in with Doc Hill. You okay here?"

"Yes, I'd like to talk to him when he comes back inside."

Jess nodded and walked out to the run.

†

Rex watched Jess leave and continued walking back inside. Haley sat in front of his gate, watching him. Haley had a special gift that came to life after the accident; no one else knew about it. While she was in a coma, something awakened in her. Haley learned she could see auras and read emotions from others, including animals. She researched the ability at school and discovered her new skill was empathy. Different colors surrounding the person or animal gave her clues to their moods or emotions. As Rex approached her, she could see his energy field surrounding him as deep red.

"Stubborn and strong-willed would certainly pertain to you," she told him as he drew nearer. "I know great hurt, too, and if you let me, we can be friends." His coffee-colored eyes were locked with hers. She felt tears pooling in her eyes as great sadness hit her in a wave. "My name is Haley, and all of my family were killed in a car accident. I was hurt badly and stayed in the hospital for months, and when I was well enough to be released, I had no one left to care for me or love me. I was taken into a home and given care, but it's not the same as having a loving family. You had a loving family once, too, didn't you?"

Haley heard a low whine come from Rex. She felt he was listening and understanding what she was saying. "I promise I will never hurt you, and I want to be your friend. Everyone here wants to love and care for you, but you must be strong enough to trust them. I know how hard that is, but I have faith you can show happiness and love to the right person or people. Jess and Doc Hill care for you deeply and only want to help you."

Rex lifted his head and cocked it to one side. Haley followed his movement. "You can trust me, but we will work on your terms. I can be patient and stubborn, too."

†

Hill had played fetch for a few minutes before returning to check on the twins in the cat compound. When she returned, she heard loud giggles coming from the area. Lara was covered in cats, begging for attention, while Lisa, Buster, and another cat played with a long stick with strings tied to the end. Buster jumped, trying to catch the strings, while the older cat pretended not to be interested. Hill saw her swat at the strings as Lisa moved them in front of her.

"Are you girls having as much fun as the cats are?"

"Yes, we are," Lara said between giggles.

"All right. I'll come and get you for lunch in a bit. I hope you like pizza."

"We love pizza," Lara said. "It's a real treat for us."

Hill imagined that the group home worked on a limited budget and could see how freshly made pizza could be seen as a treat to the girls. Hill walked into the clinic and returned with cold water bottles for all the girls and Alice. She handed each of them a bottle and walked out to find Alice.

†

Alice was finishing up a section surrounding the campground when she saw Hill walking toward her. The dust and grass she had kicked up mowing left her throat feeling parched, and she eagerly accepted the drink. "Man, that hits the spot," she said after a long gulp.

"You've made significant progress this morning. Lunch will be here soon. What do you think about swapping the mower for the trailer so we can use it for a lunch table?"

"That's one thing we didn't think of in our planning," Alice said. "It wouldn't hurt to have a couple at the campground either."

"I'll see what I can get ordered," Hill said. "Come get washed up after you switch the trailer and mower, and rest a few minutes. After lunch, we can all pitch in and load the wood onto the trailer."

"Do you have gloves for everyone?" Alice asked.

"I've got several bundles of brand new work gloves. They may be a bit big for the twins, but they will still work."

"How are the girls doing with the animals?"

"Everyone seems to be having a blast, and the little ones are full of giggles."

Alice handed Hill the empty bottle. "I'll go swap out the mower and come in to get cleaned up."

"Do you need help?"

"Naw, I've got this," Alice said. "I love you."

"I love you too, my sexy tractor girl," Hill replied, then returned to her office.

†

Hill sat at her desk, searched for picnic tables, and found six that could be delivered on Monday. She also contacted a local water company to order two coolers and containers of water. That way, the staff and visitors had no excuses for not staying hydrated. Hill washed her hands and walked out to find Jess.

"Pizza will be here soon. Will you round up the girls and show them where to wash up in the clinic?"

"Sure thing, Doc," Jess answered. "This has been a great morning."

"Yes, it has," Hill agreed. She walked to the tool shed for a pack of gloves and found Alice attaching the trailer.

"Will you pull that around front?" Hill tossed the gloves into the back of the trailer.

"Sure will, and then I'll come get cleaned up."

"You better use my bathroom in the office. Jess and the girls are using the clinic. I ordered the picnic tables and two water coolers so everyone could have cold water during breaks. Everything will be delivered on Monday."

"You've been busy too," Alice said as she climbed onto the tractor.

Jess and Haley met her in the dog compound. "What do you need us to do?" Jess asked.

"You can get Lou and Betsy and tell them it's time for lunch," Hill replied.

"Sure thing, Doc. I think Haley has something she wants to ask you. I'll be back soon."

Hill smiled at Haley. "What's up? Everything okay?"

"Yes, ma'am. I wanted to know if I could spend more time with Rex? I felt drawn to him the moment I got here, and I think we have a connection. I'd like to teach him to trust and love again."

Hill felt a smile growing on her face. "He's an extraordinary dog, but he can also be dangerous. Would you guarantee that you wouldn't endanger yourself or Rex? If he bit you, I would have to put him down, and I don't want that to happen."

"I don't either. I would take things at Rex's pace and not try to rush him. I feel a great sadness from him that I would like to take away if I can."

"Everything from outside his run for now," Hill stated.

Haley's eyes lit up. "Yes, ma'am."

"Go for it then. Jess and I are also working on gaining his trust, so another person showing him love certainly can't hurt."

"Thank you, Doc Hill."

"No, thank you for caring so much about Rex. I know he's a good dog."

A car with the pizza delivery pulled up in front of the compound. "Come help me set up our lunch, please."

As they walked past Rex, Hill noticed he had walked several steps beside Haley. *Maybe there is something between them.*

Haley took the four large pizza boxes while Hill tipped the driver and carried a bag of plates, napkins, and condiments to the trailer. The delivery girl returned to the car and brought a cold twelve-pack of soda.

"I almost forgot these," she said, handing the drinks to Hill.

"Thanks." Hill took the drinks and sat them on the trailer.

"Enjoy," the young woman said, returning to her car.

"I didn't think about picnic tables, but we will have some next week. So, today, we improvise."

"This will work just fine," Haley said as she spread the boxes across the end of the trailer and took out plates and napkins while Hill separated the drinks.

"That sure smells good," Alice said as she walked up with the rest of the kids.

"Jess went to get Lou and Betsy, but y'all can go ahead and get started," Hill said. "Next week, we'll have picnic tables to eat on, but today, we have to make do."

"I don't think the pizza will taste any differently," Alice said as she handed out plates. "Dig in."

†

After feasting on pizza, Jess and Haley disposed of the trash, and Hill handed everyone a pair of gloves. "To work off some of this pizza, we are going down the trail to pick up the wood Lou and Betsy have cut for the fire pit. Everyone ready?"

The kids all nodded. "Hop in for a ride," Alice said.

They were halfway done loading the logs when Hill's watch alerted that someone had driven through the gate. She frowned, not expecting anyone to visit today, and turned to Alice. "We have an unplanned visitor. Keep everything moving, and I'll find out who it is."

"Hello," Hill heard as she entered the dog compound.

"Hello," she answered. "I'm Hill. What can I help you with?"

"Good afternoon. My name is Terry, and I'm passing through the area from Texas, car camping. Your farm was recommended as a safe site to stay. I know I don't have a reservation, but I would like to stay if you have space."

Hill looked around her at the small SUV loaded with gear. "Are you alone?"

"Yes, just me. Out on the road for some adventures."

"How long would you like to stay?"

"Just a few days to recharge from the driving."

"Pick out a spot, and I will have Alice, my wife, get with you on the paperwork. She runs the campground while I deal with the animals. You caught us gathering firewood for the fire pit."

"May I offer to help? I've been cooped up behind the wheel for hours and could use some exercise."

Hill picked out a pair of work gloves from the bundle. "We never pass up help."

"Awesome. Is it okay to leave my car where it's at?"

"Sure, you can pick a spot later when we return."

†

The group was nearly finished loading the logs when Hill and Terry arrived. She introduced her to everyone, and they went back to work.

"Would you mind if I cut a few more while the trailer is unloaded?" Lou asked.

"I can stay and help Betsy carry the logs out to the trail," Maggie offered.

"Cut away then. We'll go unload and stack this and be back soon," Hill stated. "Hop on, everyone."

"Where do we want to put this?" Alice asked before starting the tractor.

"I think we will take some of the dried wood out of the shed and stack it near the fire pit for Lou, Betsy, and Terry to use. We can fill the shed up and stack the rest beside it. This should keep us in wood for a while."

"Sounds like a plan, boss," Alice said with a wink and drove them to the campground, parking close to the woodshed.

"Alright. Alice, let's form a chain. You can hand the dryer wood down the line, and Haley and I will stack it by the fire pit."

Terry and the girls formed a line passing the logs until they had a substantial pile by the pit.

"That should last for a while," Hill said. "Now, let's use our chain to refill the woodshed." She climbed onto the trailer and handed Haley the first log. Hill called for a water break once the trailer was unloaded and the wood stacked. "Jess, will you and Haley grab us some water?"

"Sure, boss," Jess said.

Hill looked at Alice. "Terry wants to stay with us for a few days. Do you want to register her while we collect the rest of the wood?"

"Would you mind if we waited until we're done?" Terry asked. "I'm enjoying the project."

"Fine with me," Alice said and climbed onto the tractor. "You traveling all by yourself?"

"Yes, I've decided to take a few months and go where the breeze takes me," Terry said. "I stopped to gas up in town, and a gentleman named Dan recommended I check this place out. I'm so glad he did. This place is beautiful."

Hill nodded toward Terry's car. "I see a kayak on your roof. There's a nice lake at the trail's end with kayaks or canoes for use unless you prefer to use your own."

"I will definitely check that out tomorrow." Terry smiled.

"Ready to roll?" Alice asked.

"Drive down to the lake to turn around so Terry and the kids can see the lake, please," Hill requested.

"Will do," Alice said and drove toward the trail.

†

"Thanks for all your hard work today," Hill told the girls when Anita arrived to pick them up.

"Thanks for an awesome day," Maggie said.

"See you on Monday?" Hill asked.

"Heck yeah," Lisa answered.

"Not tomorrow?" Lara frowned.

"Sunday is a day of rest for everybody," Hill answered.

"Thanks for the pizza," Haley said. "That was a great treat."

"Why don't we have a special meal on Saturdays then?" Hill suggested. "It won't always be pizza, but it will be different."

"I'm butting in here," Lou said. "But if you extend our reservation until next Sunday, I'll volunteer to grill hamburgers. We can have chips and some sides."

"That would be fantastic," Maggie said. "We can bring some baked beans and maybe something for dessert. We have cooking lessons at the group home."

"Sounds like we have a cookout planned for next Saturday then," Alice said. "We can coordinate dishes next week, and I can shop for whatever we need."

"We will definitely make baked beans and maybe a cake and some brownies," Anita said.

"You are welcome to join us, too," Hill said.

"I'd like that. How about I bring the buns and paper goods?"

"Perfect. My mouth is watering already," Hill teased.

Hill waved as they drove down the drive. "That was one of our best decisions yet," she told Alice. "The girls were in heaven today."

"They were a big help, too," Alice agreed. She looked at Terry. "Let's get you registered."

†

"Not to be nosy, but I assume the girls were from some sort of group home," Terry said.

"Yes, an eight-bed home, not too far from here. They started volunteering today and will be with us this summer while school is out."

"That's sad. They all seem to be great kids. It's obvious they enjoyed being here today," Terry said as she followed Alice to the office.

"They have much in common with our animals, so it's a good pairing. They both need love and someone who cares."

"Do you adopt your animals?"

"We do if we feel it's a good fit."

"I lost my cat last year from old age, and maybe it's time to think about getting another one."

"All of ours are older cats because they are hard to get adopted. Most people want puppies and kittens."

"I would actually prefer an older cat."

"Take a look at the ones we have then. Only one is spoken for. Jess lives on site, and I'm sure she will give you the rundown on all the cats tomorrow or Monday."

"I'll wait until Monday so she can enjoy her time off."

"Thanks. I'll give Jess a heads up so she will be prepared."

Alice had her sign off on the paperwork. "Is there anything else you need?"

Terry smiled. "Do you prefer cash or credit card?"

"Credit card, if you don't mind. How many days?"

"Let's start with three, but I may extend if you have availability."

"That shouldn't be a problem," Alice said. "We've just opened, so the schedule is open for now."

"I do have one more question. Do you have a business card or flyer I can share with people I meet?"

"Not yet, but I will have some before you leave. That's a great idea. Thank you."

"I'll also leave a review on your website. You should also encourage guests to do that to help with visibility."

"I will definitely do that. Thanks again."

Terry smiled. "No problem. Have a great night. I'm sure I'll see you Monday."

†

Hill had finished observing Jess giving Jax the steroids, and they walked into the office searching for Alice. They found her working away on the computer. "What are you working on?" Hill asked.

"Terry had a great idea to share business cards or flyers with guests to share with other campers they meet, so I'm creating business cards and some postcards. I can order from our local office supply store and pick them up Monday morning. Come tell me what you think of the design."

Jess and Hill walked around the desk. "Oh, I like it," Hill said.

"May I make a suggestion for the postcards?" Jess asked.

Alice looked up. "Of course."

"You can do an internet search and find borders to use. Maybe one with dogs and cats?"

Alice gasped. "You are a genius."

"Nope, just creative."

Alice looked up at them. "Terry is interested in adopting a cat as a travel companion, so expect her to come to you on Monday for recommendations. We need to determine if we will be charging an adoption fee and, if so, how much."

"You keep working on your postcards while Jess and I unload your desk and chair. We can discuss our thoughts while we are getting you set up."

"Crap, I forgot about that," Jess said. "Do you want me to pull the truck around to this end of the building?"

"That would save us a few steps," Hill replied. "Go ahead and move the truck. I'll meet you in a minute." Hill walked around the desk and kissed Alice. "Not bad for a first day of working together, huh?"

"Not at all. I feel like I'm wearing a few pounds of dust and grass, but it was fun."

"Yes, it was. I'll be right back."

†

When Hill arrived, Jess already had the box with the chair on the ground. "What did you think of today?"

"We got a lot done, and I think the girls made excellent volunteers. They demonstrated genuine care for the animals and didn't hesitate to help out with anything. I'm intrigued by the connection between Haley and Rex. I really think there is something there."

"There certainly seems to be. I guess time will tell. Haley seems patient and willing to move at Rex's pace. I think that will be critical," Hill added. "Ready to get this monster out?"

"It's not heavy, just awkward," Jess said. "Let me turn it sideways so we can be on the ground together."

Working together, they carried the desk into the office. Hill had already cleared a space for Alice. "Is this spot good for you?" she asked, pointing to the vacant spot.

"That will be perfect," Alice said. "Will you two come proof the final product?"

Jess and Hill looked at the screen. "Yeah, that's more like it," Jess said, giving Alice a high five.

Hill nodded. "They both look good. Finalize your order while we get your chair assembled. We can talk while we work."

Jess used a pocketknife to open the box after they carried it inside. "I'll take the box to the dumpster if you start reading the instructions."

"It should be fairly simple," Hill said.

"Famous last words," Jess teased and handed her the instruction booklet.

Alice waited until Jess left. "She knows you pretty well," she teased.

"We hit the jackpot with that young lady," Hill said.

When Jess returned, she looked at Hill. "You don't have it together yet?"

"Here, smart ass," Hill said, handing her the hex wrench. "One tool only."

"Have a seat. I've got this." Jess grinned at Hill, who sat on the corner of the desk.

"So, do we set up an adoption fee or not?" Hill asked Jess.

Jess looked surprised. "Are you asking me?"

"Well, yes. You are a big part of this project, so I'd like your opinion."

Jess grinned at her inclusion in decision-making. It made her feel special. "My vote would be yes. If a person gets something for free, it doesn't seem to mean as much, but if they pay a fee, they may be less likely to dump the animal after the newness wears off."

"That's one way of looking at it," Hill said.

Alice nodded her head in agreement. "You've got to consider that the animal they are getting has already been altered, examined, and is up to date on vaccinations, too. Those costs aren't free."

"Also true, so what do we charge?" Hill asked.

"I think seventy-five is reasonable and is less than what the shelter charges," Jess said.

"What if someone comes looking for an animal but cannot afford the fee?" Hill asked.

"I would think that would need to be determined case-by-case. I don't mean to judge, but if they can't afford the fee, can they afford the animal?"

"That's a valid question. Medical care and food aren't cheap." Hill looked at Jess. "What if an older person from our community were to come in looking for a companion?"

"That may be a different circumstance. Are we willing to provide the healthcare for free if they can't afford vet bills?"

Hill chuckled as Jess turned the assembled chair upright and sat down. "That is the bigger question."

Alice grinned at Hill. "You know you would say yes. You're a big old softy."

"For the right person, I probably would." She looked at Alice and then at Jess. "So, are we in agreement on seventy-five dollars?"

Jess nodded.

"I think that's fair," Alice said. "I have one more difficult question we need to start considering."

"We're in trouble now," Hill joked.

"What do we do when one of our animals passes? Do we pay to have them cremated, or do we create a pet cemetery on the grounds?"

"Whoa, you were kidding about a difficult question," Jess said.

"No, but it is something to consider. I'll do some research and see if we can get a deal on cremation since we have a non-profit status. Part of me says to bury them at their home, but another part says cremate and scatter. Let's circle back around to that one," Hill suggested.

Alice was about to speak when her phone rang. She answered and smiled. "Hang on, let me ask." She looked at Hill and Jess. "Do you two have dinner plans?"

"Not really," Jess answered.

"Why?" Hill asked.

"Betsy wants to know if we will join them and Terry for dinner at the fire pit?"

Hill nodded. "Sure. We need to feed up and scrounge some buckets for chairs."

"Betsy says to tell Hill we only need one bucket. We have a few chairs."

"I know we can find one," Jess said. "I'll gladly sit on a bucket for a home-cooked meal."

"Come down when you finish work. We have dinner prepped and will start cooking when you arrive. Oh, Lou wants to know if we can have adult beverages on site?"

Hill nodded to Alice.

"That's not a problem," Alice answered. "We'll see you soon." She ended the call. "That was nice."

"Yes, it was. Do you have some work you need to do while we make rounds?"

"I need to check emails and see if we have any reservation requests. It shouldn't take long," Alice said as she pulled out a planner. "I think we need a few whiteboards for scheduling." She grinned.

"Pick out what you want before you go on Monday to get your cards. We might as well set up an account there for supplies while you're at it," Hill suggested.

"I can handle that." Alice beamed.

"We'll be back soon," Hill said before she and Jess left.

†

Lou cooked a great meal of chicken, fried rice, and vegetables on her Blackstone grill. They all enjoyed cold beers while waiting for dinner and chatting around the firepit. Jess questioned Terry on what she was looking for in a cat to give her an idea of who to suggest.

"Someone mellow, like me, who would travel well in a car."

"Would they stay in the car while you're out?" Jess asked.

"Heaven's no. I used to carry Sammi in a backpack or on a leash. I swear she enjoyed hiking as much as me."

"Male or female?"

"Doesn't really matter. Sammi was a beautiful Russian Blue I got from a shelter in Texas."

Jess' head popped up, and she looked at Hill. Hill smiled and nodded.

"How would you feel about a Sasha? She's a Russian Blue, about four years old?"

"I would love to meet her," Terry said.

"Tonight or tomorrow?" Jess asked.

"I can wait until tomorrow, and if I like her, can I go to town for some supplies and try her in the car tomorrow?"

"That would be a good idea," Hill agreed. "We will provide a small bag of food, but you'll need other supplies."

"No problem," Terry said, rubbing her hands with excitement.

"So, we can adopt from you?" Betsy asked.

"Yes, we are always looking for good homes," Hill answered.

Lou smiled. "Betsy has fallen in love with Toby since the first time he howled at her."

"Toby is a sweetheart," Jess said. "He loves to play fetch."

"Lou has a great throwing arm," Betsy bragged.

"Please tell me you have an adoption or re-homing fee," Lou said.

"We've decided on seventy-five dollars since all our animals are altered and up to date on shots," Hill explained.

"That is way too cheap," Terry said, "but I'll take it."

"It's more important to us that the animal goes to a caring home, but the money will be used on other animals that come to us," Hill stated.

"So, do we plan two overnight visits tomorrow night?" Jess asked.

Betsy looked at Lou. "Yes, please."

Jess looked at Terry and Lou. "I can take you both to town for supplies tomorrow after the introductions if you'd like."

"Isn't tomorrow a semi-off day for you?" Terry asked.

"I don't have anything planned, but I know the best places to shop."

"Count me in then," Betsy said.

"Me too," Terry said. "We can shop til we drop."

†

"Thanks for a fantastic meal," Hill said. "It's getting late, and my old bones are groaning." She looked at Jess. "Call me if you need me."

"I will, boss. Be careful going home, and thanks for a great day."

"We will. You okay with Jax's schedule?"

"I've got it, and I'll document it in his chart, too."

"We'll see you all Monday then," Hill said.

†

Jess accepted another beer from Lou as they watched Hill and Alice drive away. "I bet we see her tomorrow."

"She seems extremely dedicated to this place," Betsy said.

"The farm has been her dream for years. We have one dog, Jax, who's not in the best shape, so I wouldn't be surprised if she comes out to check him."

"You seem to love it here just as much," Terry pointed out.

"Meeting Doc Hill and Alice was the best thing ever. I was working two jobs trying to pay for tuition, and once we started talking, Doc Hill and I had the same love for animals. She pays for my tuition, gives me free room and board, and a stipend for expenses to live here."

"You work very hard here," Lou said.

"I don't look at it as work. I love learning from Doc Hill, and Alice is the sweetest woman you'll ever meet. There's no way I could ever repay them."

"Sure there is. You become a vet to make Doc Hill proud," Lou replied. "That would be payment enough for Hill."

"That's probably true." Jess smiled.

When the fire started dying, Jess offered to add more wood.

Lou shook her head. "I don't know about y'all, but I think it's time to call it a night. Today was a long but fun day."

"Yes, it was," Jess said, then stood and stretched. "A hot shower and a comfy bed are going to feel great. I'll see y'all in the morning."

"Go ahead, and I'll dowse the fire," Terry offered. "Thanks for a great dinner."

"Goodnight, everyone," Betsy said.

†

Jess made her final rounds, and after treating Jax, she made notes in his chart. Alice's question about what happens when one of the animals dies weighed heavily on her as she carefully noted his vital signs and the dosage of medication. Jax would probably be their first if the steroids didn't clear up his congestion. She wiped a tear from her cheek and closed his chart. After locking the compounds, she walked to her apartment. Gabby hobbled to the door to meet her, and Jess picked her up gently.

"How's my baby girl doing?" She sat on the couch with her for a while until Gabby started to nod off. "I need a shower and some sleep. We'll have some time together tomorrow," she promised as she placed Gabby in her carrier. "Goodnight, baby girl."

Archie (Mary McNeely)

CHAPTER FIVE

Cora (Valerie Dunne)

Jess wasn't surprised when she returned to the farm to find Doc Hill's truck parked in her spot. She was actually relieved. She hoped to talk to the Doc about something weighing on her mind. After helping to deliver the supplies to Terry and Betsy, she walked into the dog compound. As she expected, Doc was giving Jax an examination.

"Fancy meeting you here," Jess teased.

Hill shrugged. "I've been pacing all morning, worried about Jax. Alice threatened me with bodily harm if I didn't come to check him."

"How's he doing?"

"It's too soon to hope for a full recovery, but I see his lungs improving. Jax is fighting hard, so the least we can do is fight with him."

"He actually played a bit this morning," Jess reported.

"That's an excellent sign."

Jess shuffled her feet. "Do you have a few minutes to chat?"

Hill looked at her with curiosity. "Sure, why don't you take Jax and put him up while I make notes on his chart."

Jess picked Jax up and took him back to his run. She took a deep breath and returned to the clinic. Hill was sitting at her desk, making notes.

"Take a seat. I'm almost done."

Jess took a seat in Alice's chair and started fidgeting.

Hill finished typing and looked at Jess. "What's got you nervous as a house cat?"

"Is it obvious?"

"Yeah, but that's okay. What's up?"

"I need some personal advice."

"Advice is free." Hill smiled.

"I was up late texting with someone from school who wants to take me on a date." Jess blurted it out in one breath.

"Well, that's not terrible. You are a great person. What's the dilemma?"

"I have several. First, the someone is a woman from one of my classes."

"And what?"

"I've never really dated anyone. I don't want to end up a forty-year-old virgin."

Hill broke out laughing. She held her hand up to apologize. "I'm sorry, Jess, I didn't mean to laugh, but you're twenty-three, and I guarantee you will sleep with one or more people in the next seventeen years."

Jess' face glowed with embarrassment.

"Tell me about her."

"Her name is Blakely Summer. She's a grad student studying to be a nurse practitioner. We had anatomy together, and I'll be honest, it was hard to keep my eyes off her in class. It was probably a good thing I recorded my class lectures."

"So, it's safe to say you are attracted to Blakely?"

Jess nodded. "I've never felt like this about anybody before. I've had a few crushes, but nothing ever went beyond that."

"What's holding you back from saying yes?"

"Doc, I've never dated anyone. How do you do it?"

Hill's eyes grew wide. "Jess, I'm probably the last person in the world you should be asking for dating advice. I come from the generation of lesbians that included a U-haul on the third date and toaster ovens."

"Seriously, Doc?"

"Not Alice and I, but it was widespread for our generation of young queers. We had known each other for some time before we both became single at the same time. We ran within the same circles in college, and when we both realized we had a mutual attraction, it was at least five dates before we moved in together. We lived in the same apartment complex, so we didn't need a U-haul," Hill teased.

Jess chuckled and relaxed a bit.

"I'll be honest, I don't have a clue about how your generation dates. All the Snapchat, texting, and Tiky-tok stuff is way beyond me."

Jess laughed. "It's TikTok, Doc."

"See what I mean?" Hill looked into Jess' eyes. "My advice. She likes you, and you are attracted to Blakely, so say yes and see what happens. A date is not a lifelong commitment. That comes much further down the road."

"What about sex?" Jess asked.

"Ah, sex with the right woman is fantastic. But you need to make sure she feels right to you. Is it an expectation to have sex on the first date?"

Jess shrugged. "I hope not. I'm not ready for that yet."

"Then don't let Blakely or anyone else make you rush into something you're not ready for. Go on a date and get to know each other before you tumble into bed together. If Blakely is right for you, you will discover that soon enough; if she's serious about you, she will wait until you're ready. If she pressures you, that should be a red flag she's only interested in a hookup. Pump your brakes if that happens. You deserve better."

"Thanks, Doc."

"I am sincere about that. You don't deserve to have your heart broken for someone else's good time."

Jess let Hill's advice sink in.

"What type of date is she asking for?"

"Dinner and a movie, Friday night," Jess said.

"That sounds pretty safe," Hill said. "Pick her up so you have control over when the night ends. When you take her home, you have to decide if you want to go inside with her if she offers. Some might take that as a commitment to continue the night. Don't rush. Ask for another date and see what happens from there. Beyond everything else, communication is critical. Don't tell her something unless you really feel it."

Jess nodded.

"When and what movie?"

"We didn't make it that far yet."

"Alice and I could go out and chaperone from a distance," Hill said. "She'd never know we were there."

Jess smiled. "Doc, you aren't right, but I appreciate that you care."

"If I haven't told you lately, I'm very proud of you, and you have been a vital part of the farm's success."

"Don't make me cry," Jess teased.

"I mean every word of it," Hill said with a serious tone.

"Thank you."

"So, what's the next step?"

"Text to accept her offer?"

"You might want to call her to finalize plans," Hill suggested. "Would probably be faster than texting back and forth."

"Got it. Thanks for talking with me."

"Anytime. How'd it go with Toby and Sasha today?"

"It's hard to tell who is happier, the animal or human."

"I hope tonight goes well for all of them. And you," Hill said.

Jess smiled. "You need to get some rest. Tomorrow is going to be busy."

"I can take a hint," Hill teased and stood to leave. She was surprised when Jess reached for her and hugged her close. Hill draped her arm over Jess' shoulder as they left the clinic. "Hell, if I was forty years younger and single, I'd be tripping over myself for a date with you."

"Don't push it, Doc."

"Okay, but it's the truth. Just don't tell Alice I said that."

"My lips are sealed. Have a good night. I'll lock up and see you tomorrow."

"Have a good night, Jess."

"You too. Drive safe."

†

Jess walked into her apartment, and Gabby rushed over to her. Jess picked her up and cuddled her as she walked to the kitchen. She saw the bison treat Hill had given her for Rex. She placed food in the bowl for Gabby.

"I forgot something. I'll be right back." Jess picked up the treat and headed to the dog compound.

Heat lightning lit up the sky as she returned to the dog compound. "We could use some rain," Jess said aloud. She opened the door, and several happy faces greeted her as Jess walked by their runs. Jess was pleased to see one of the happy faces belonged to Jax. His rear wiggled wildly as she bent down to speak to him. "You look like you are feeling better." Jax licked the fingers of her hand. She looked at the bison ring in her other hand. "I think everybody should get treats tonight. I'll be right back." Jess walked into the clinic and grabbed a handful of soft treats before returning to the run. When she reached Rex, she smiled and held out the bison ring. "I've got something special for you, my friend." She reached through the opening to present her offering. Jess saw that Rex was interested in the treat and held her ground. "Come on, big boy, I know you want it." She remained still as he crept close. "That's it, Rex. I won't hurt you." Jess wasn't prepared for his sudden movement as he lunged forward to take the treat, but she was proud she didn't recoil. "Good boy," she told him as he returned to his bed with the prize. "Enjoy your treat, and I'll see you in the morning."

When Jess exited, she could see the campers around the fire pit. She was briefly tempted to join them, but the phone in her pocket vibrated, reminding her she had a call to make. Gabby waited for her on the couch, and Jess removed her cell phone to call Blakely. Ten minutes later, she ended the call with a fist pump.

"I have a date," she told Gabby.

†

Hill entered the house and found Alice sipping wine in front of the television. She sat beside her and smiled. "I think our young friend is falling in love."

"Jess?" Alice asked. "It's about time. She's sweet and too adorable to be single. Who is it?"

"A young woman named Blakely in one of her classes. She's studying to be a nurse practitioner."

"Another smart cookie. That's a good start."

"You want to hear something funny?"

"I'm all ears."

"Jess asked me for dating advice. I haven't been on a date in a gazillion years."

"That's not surprising. Jess thinks the world of you, and you are quite the romantic," Alice said.

Hill leaned over and kissed Alice. "I don't know if that's true, but I have the one right for me. She's never dated anyone before, which I found incredible. She is cute and a real sweetheart."

"One thing about late bloomers is they typically know what they are looking for and find it's worth the wait."

"I sure hope so. I know it's bound to happen, but I'd hate to see Jess heartbroken."

"Maybe she will be one of the lucky ones to find the right person off the bat. Lord knows you and I worked through several lovers before we found each other."

"You were so worth the wait," Hill said. "We've got a busy day planned for tomorrow, so I'm going to shower and call it a night."

"I won't be long. I want to watch the end of this show, and I'll join you."

Hill stood and leaned down to kiss Alice. "I'll keep the bed warm."

"Thanks, love. I plan to cook breakfast and then go to the office supply place to pick up our order before heading to the farm."

"Sounds great," Hill replied and left the room.

Ali Spooner

Zoey (Robin Haspiel)

CHAPTER SIX

BELLE (DAWN MEYERS WARD)

Alice sent Hill off with a belly full of waffles and walked her out to the truck. "I think I'll pick up some deli meat, bread, and condiments to store in the refrigerator for lunches this week. Any special requests?"

"Some pastrami if they have it. Honey ham and some cheeses if they don't."

"I think I can handle that," Alice said. She kissed Hill and returned inside.

†

Hill opened the gate with the remote and drove to the parking lot. Lou waved at her from the fire pit. There was a slight chill in the air when she stepped out of her truck, but she knew the sun would be out quickly to warm things up.

Jess was holding a black cat in her arms when Hill arrived inside. "Who is this?"

Jess shrugged. "I guess word has gotten out about us, and someone dropped her sometime last night. She was curled up in front of the door this morning. She's about to become a mama, too."

"Let's give her an exam, and then you can introduce her to her new home. We have plenty of room to separate her from the others until the kittens arrive." She followed Jess into the exam room. "Yep, definitely pregnant. The kittens are active, so she may not be far from giving birth. She is young and healthy, so I don't foresee any problems. This is probably her first litter. Once she gives birth, I will spay her to prevent other pregnancies. Have you thought of a name yet?"

"No. Any suggestions?" Jess asked.

"She's black as coal. Let's call her Coal Kitty."

"That sounds good to me." Jess grinned and picked up Coal. "Let's get you some food and settled into your new home, Coal Kitty."

Hill entered her office and looked at the list of things to do today. The picnic tables and water coolers would be delivered today, and she expected Dan to bring more animals from the shelter. The girls would be here to volunteer, and she needed to plan the cookout on Saturday. "Yep, it's going to be a busy day." Hill left the office to check on Jax. She was surprised to find Lara holding him as he covered her in kisses. She checked her watch. It was barely eight.

Anita looked up and smiled as Hill approached. "I hope you don't mind the girls coming early. They have been pacing the house since seven."

Hill chuckled. "They are welcome anytime. Girls, put your lunches in the refrigerator, and we can get to work."

"They have plans for each of them to bring a side or dessert for Saturday. Are you sure that's all they need to bring?" Anita asked.

"That should be more than plenty," Hill answered.

"I'll see you at four then," Anita said.

"Have a great day." Hill turned around to find that Haley had stopped to visit with Rex. She was shocked that he was licking her fingers through the chain link fencing. The super-aggressive dog that had arrived last week was starting to show signs of progress. Rex shied away when one of the twins rushed past.

One of the twins, Lara, she thought, approached her. "I have someone new for you to meet. We had a beautiful black cat we named Coal find her way here this morning. She's pregnant and will have her kittens soon. I'm sure she would enjoy some loving after everyone else is fed."

"That's right up my alley." Lara smiled.

Maggie walked over to Hill. "Where's Toby?" she asked, frowning.

Hill hadn't thought about how attached the girls would get to the animals. She smiled to comfort her. "Toby has a new home. Lou and Betsy have adopted him as a travel companion. I'm sure they won't mind if you visit with him and play ball."

Maggie nodded, but Hill could see that she was disappointed. "Toby will have a great life with them and be treated like a prince. That's a win for Toby and the farm, to find a happy ever after for an animal."

Maggie wiped at her eyes. "I know, but I will miss him."

"I will, too, but many more animals need your love and care. We have new animals coming out today that would love to play with you. Terry is also adopting a cat, Sasha, who looks like a cat she had for many years."

"Do you think that will happen often? That campers will adopt?" Maggie asked.

"It's nothing we plan for, but if a camper and an animal are a good match, we will make the adoption happen," Hill explained. She placed her hand on Maggie's shoulder. "We need to be happy for them."

"I am," Maggie said, but Hill could hear the sadness in her voice.

"Go see what Jess has planned for you this morning. I'm going to need some of your muscle later this morning."

"For what?" Maggie asked.

"We have six picnic tables being delivered today. I will need some muscle to get them placed."

"Why so many?"

"Three for the campground, two for here, and one for the lake. It may be nice to have lunch by the water some days. I know a black lab who loves playing in the lake."

"Really?" Maggie said.

"He will retrieve a ball that you throw into the lake. Be warned, though, you will get wet," Hill teased.

"Could I take him out later?"

"After lunch, when we have the tables set up. I'll go with you," Hill promised.

"Thanks, Doc," Maggie said and searched for Jess.

†

Hill walked over to Haley. "Rex is responding well to you."

"He wants to be a good boy," Haley said. "He's feeling more at home here."

"That's good to hear. Keep up the excellent work." Hill handed Haley several treats and left the compound. She walked over to the campground to talk with Lou and Betsy.

"Good morning," Lou said. "It looks like the crew showed up early today."

"They were excited," Hill said, reaching down to pet Toby.

Betsy emerged from the camper. "Morning, Doc. Would you like some coffee?"

"I'm good, thanks, Betsy. I wanted to ask you and Lou something," she said, sitting beside Lou.

"What's up?" Lou asked.

"I didn't think about the girls getting attached to the animals so quickly. Maggie was sad when she couldn't find

Toby this morning. I explained to her how happy he was to be adopted, which is one of our goals at the farm."

"What can we do to help?" Betsy asked. "He's such a sweet boy. I can see why she would miss him."

"Would you mind if she came down and played fetch with him for a while this week so she can see how happy he is?"

Betsy smiled at Hill. "I can do you one better. I can take pictures of them together that you can give her."

"You know what else, honey?" Lou asked. Betsy and Hill waited for her to continue. "We can take pictures of our adventures and send them to Hill to share with Maggie. Would it be okay to mail them here?"

Hill smiled. "I love that idea. Of course, you can send them here. Maggie would be tickled. I'll keep it a secret until the first mail arrives."

"We'll be at the beach next week, so that will be our first stop," Betsy said.

"Perfect," Hill said. "Thanks. I'll let her know it's okay to come down later."

"Anytime, Doc."

Hill heard a vehicle approach. "Our water coolers have arrived. Alice is right behind them. She went to pick up business cards and the postcards to share with y'all and Terry."

"Awesome," Betsy said.

"We also have a load of picnic tables being delivered. Three will be placed around here, so think of where you would like one," Hill said.

"I can help you move them," Lou offered.

"Are you kidding? I have plenty of young muscle for that." Hill smiled.

†

Hill showed the deliveryman where to set up the two water coolers while Alice took her purchases to the office. "This place is a buzz of activity this morning," Alice said when Hill entered.

"The girls almost beat me here this morning."

"A bit excited are they?"

"Yeah, but our first disappointment."

"What do you mean?"

"I thought Maggie would cry when she couldn't find Toby. I explained that Lou and Betsy had adopted him, and that he would have a great new home with them. I talked with them afterward, and Lou had a great idea to send Maggie pictures of Toby's adventures with them."

"That is a great idea. Do you want some coffee?"

"Yes, please. I haven't made it to the coffee pot yet."

†

Hill hadn't finished her coffee when Jess and Maggie entered carrying two large bags of tennis balls. She cocked her head in confusion. "Where did those come from?"

"Susan, from the local tennis club, just dropped these off. She heard about the farm and had a bunch of tennis balls she donated to us that were too flat for competition." Jess grinned and held out a business card. "I thought you might want this to send a thank you."

Hill took the card and handed it to Alice. "Would you mind sending them a note of thanks?"

"I'll take care of it this morning. It's good to hear that word of the farm is spreading in our community, and they are stepping in to help out. Why don't you place the balls in the feed room?" Hill looked at Maggie. "We will try some of them out with Hank at the lake later this afternoon."

"Great." Maggie smiled and followed Jess from the room.

"We also had our first drop off this morning," Hill told Alice. "A very pregnant black cat met Jess this morning. We will be having kittens soon."

"Oh wow," Alice said.

"The best news of the morning comes from Rex and Haley."

"Really?"

"I watched him lick her fingers as she talked to him this morning. She seems to be getting through to him."

"That's an amazing start," Alice said. "I know he has a lot of issues to work through."

Jess poked her head back into the office. "Doc, the tables are here."

"No rest for the wicked," Hill said, kissing Alice before leaving the office.

†

For the next hour, Hill gave directions for where she wanted the tables placed. Three went to the campground, and two were set outside the dog compound. "Where does the last one go?" Alice asked.

"I thought we might load it on your trailer and take it to the lake before you mow again. Would you mind helping Maggie and me with it?"

94

"Not at all. Let me go hook up the trailer and pull it around."

Hill looked at Maggie. "Go get some tennis balls and put Hank on a leash."

Maggie's face beamed as she rushed toward the feed storeroom.

Jess looked at Hill. "She was disappointed Toby was adopted, so I told her she could work with Hank at the lake."

"Got it," Jess said. "We'll wash down the runs while you're at the lake."

"Keep an eye on Coal and the twins, too."

Maggie walked out with Hank on a leash, carrying two tennis balls. Hank's mouth dripped with saliva as he saw the balls in her hand. It was hard to tell who was more excited.

Jess helped Hill load the picnic table onto the trailer. "You sure you don't need help?"

"Naw, we got this. Alice can hold onto Hank while Maggie and I unload the table."

Jess smiled and nodded toward the campground. "Already getting broken in."

Hill turned to look, finding Lou, Betsy, and Terry drinking coffee at one of the tables.

"Great addition," Hill said. Hill, Maggie, and Hank climbed onto the trailer. She nodded to Alice, who started the tractor down the path to the lake.

†

Once the table was in place, Hill sat and unclipped the leash from Hank. She looked at Maggie. "Knock your socks off."

Maggie turned to the lake and hurled the ball, and Hank raced toward the water and jumped in, swimming furiously toward the ball bobbing in the water.

"I'll see y'all for lunch. I'm going to get some grass cut."

"Thanks, Alice," Hill said, watching Maggie and Hank playing.

Hill stretched her legs out and watched Hank reach the shore. "Get ready for... a shower." She laughed as Hank shook the water from his coat, surprising Maggie. Hill hadn't gotten her warning out in time, and Maggie squealed in shock.

"I guess I should have anticipated that," Maggie said. Hank danced in front of her, waiting for her to pick up the ball he had returned to her.

"It's part of the package deal with a Lab around water," Hill agreed.

Maggie moved a few yards down from the table and let the ball fly. She had a strong arm, hurling the ball near the center of the lake.

"I hear you are a softball player," Hill stated.

"Third base and leadoff hitter," Maggie answered nonchalantly.

"You'll have to tell me when your games are next year. I'd love to come watch you play."

"You would do that?" Maggie asked.

"Yes. I love softball, and I have a feeling you're good at it. You've certainly got the arm for it."

"The coach from the university has watched several of our games, and she seemed impressed. I hope it will lead to a scholarship offer when I graduate. I'm saving my money for some new equipment. My spikes are about shot, and my glove came from a thrift shop. The school provides bats, but I think they came from the thrift store, too." Maggie chuckled as she threw the ball.

Hill remained quiet as she watched Maggie and Hank play. Her mind was whirling with an idea. She wasn't big on giving kids stuff without their effort to earn the item, and she considered a bargain with Maggie.

Hank was breathing hard when he climbed from the bank. "Why don't you give him a break for a few minutes? I've got a proposition for you."

Maggie sat across the table from Hill and wore a curious look on her face.

"I have an idea. Jess lives on site, which you know, and she works here daily. Between school and working here, she doesn't have much free time. If you're interested, I'd like to talk to Anita about you working weekends once school starts. Jess could have weekends off, and you could earn money to buy your equipment."

"Hell yeah," Maggie said, clapping her hand over her mouth. "I'm sorry. I would love that. Would you do something else for me?"

"Like what?"

"Save the money for me, so I'll have it when it's time? Sometimes, things go missing from the home." Maggie dropped her eyes from Hill's.

"Why don't we open a savings account for you?" Hill suggested. "I'll write a check for you, and you can ask Anita to take you to the bank after school to deposit your earnings."

"That would be great," Maggie said.

"Deal." Hill offered her hand to Maggie for a handshake. "I think Hank can retrieve a few more balls. You will need to give him a bath to make sure he's clean after swimming in the lake. Then we can break for lunch. I'm getting hungry."

"I am too." Maggie smiled and called for Hank.

As they walked back, Hill looked at Hank. "You wore him out, but he sure had fun."

"I did too. I'll give Hank a good bath, then it should be lunchtime."

"Do you know where all the supplies are?"

"Yes, Jess showed us where everything is."

"Good."

†

Alice and Jess made sandwiches and joined the girls around the new picnic tables for lunch. "That was a great pastrami sandwich," Hill told Alice.

"The addition of picnic tables was perfect."

"Sure beats sitting on buckets," Jess teased.

Alice looked at the girls and then Hill. "Do we have time for dessert, boss?"

"There's always time for dessert," Hill answered.

"I'll be right back." Alice left the table.

Hill looked at Jess, who shrugged. "No clue."

Alice returned carrying a platter of brownies. "I forgot to bring milk."

"I got this," Jess replied. "Haley, will you get us some cups from the water machine?" Jess returned with a gallon of milk from her apartment. "Now we're set."

†

Hill smiled when she saw the progress Haley was making with Rex. By Friday, he was trotting beside the fence of his outdoor run. Jess walked up beside Hill as she watched them together. "That doesn't look like the same dog brought to us in a muzzle, does it?"

"No, it doesn't. Rex actually looks happy for the first time."

Hill smiled at her young assistant. "I need to put some thought into what the next steps will be. Rex's making great progress, but I'm not sure we can trust him yet."

"I think we should work with Haley to see if he will respond to commands from her," Jess suggested. "I'd bet my last dollar; he's been trained before. Rex is very intelligent."

"That's a good idea. Are you all set for tonight?" Hill asked.

Jess nodded. "I think so. I pick her up at six for dinner."

"Nervous?"

"Petrified," Jess answered.

"Just relax and be your fabulous true self. Don't change your behavior to something you think Blakely would appreciate. She knows the real you already, and that's what she's attracted to."

They were interrupted by Lara, who came running to find Hill. "Doc Hill, Coal is having her babies," she hollered.

"Well, let's see if she needs help," Hill said.

Lara raced ahead as Hill and Jess followed. "Grab some gloves and a few towels in case we need them," Hill said to Jess.

Lisa was sitting next to Coal, talking to her in a soothing voice. They had set up a cardboard box for her to have her kittens, and Coal was stretched out inside. One kitten had already breached, and Hill watched as Coal's muscles contracted to push the kitten the rest of the way.

Hill slipped gloves over her hands and entered the enclosure with Jess and Lara. She knelt to pick up the kitten and placed it next to Coal for her to bathe it. Hill looked at Lisa and Lara. "Coal will clean each of them to stimulate them and bond with them. When she's finished, we can help them find a nipple to start eating."

"How many will she have?" Lara asked.

"Four, I think," Hill said as another kitten breached. "They are ready for the world." She sat next to Lisa and Lara. "I think we can handle this if you want to finish so you can prepare for tonight," Hill told Jess.

"Thanks, Doc. Holler if you need me." Jess stepped from the enclosure and resumed her tasks.

"Their eyes are closed. Does that mean they are blind?" Lisa asked with concern.

"Not at all. Kittens won't open their eyes until one to two weeks. If these babies have short hair like Coal, then probably a week. If Dad was long-haired, it may take two weeks. I don't know why, but that's how it is. To protect their sensitive ears, they will not hear either until they are about three months old."

"Will they recognize us if they can see us?" Lara asked.

"Yes, once they are big enough to be handled, they will begin to recognize your scent in a few days."

When all four kittens were born, it was getting close for the girls to go home. When the kittens were all suckling, Hill looked at the girls. "We need to add a bowl of food and water for Coal and then give her time to rest tonight."

The girls raced to get food and water for Coal and placed it in her box.

"That's perfect," Hill praised. "Let's go see what the others are up to."

"We've got kittens," Lisa told Maggie when they entered the dog compound.

"How many and what color?"

"Four, all black like Coal," Lisa answered.

"That's cool," Maggie said, smiling.

"What's all the excitement?" Alice asked as she and Lou walked up.

"Coal had her kittens," Lara said. "Four mini-me's." She grinned.

"That's fantastic. Are we all set for the cookout tomorrow?" Alice asked.

Maggie nodded. "We are baking desserts tonight. Haley will make the baked beans, too. Will we be able to heat them up tomorrow?"

"Yes, in Jess' kitchen," Alice answered.

"I'm all set for the burgers," Lou said, rubbing her hands together.

†

The twins rushed to Anita when she arrived to tell her about the kittens, and Maggie was playing fetch with Toby. Haley was sitting in front of Rex's run.

"He looked happy today with you," Hill said.

"We're getting there," Haley said.

"Tomorrow, I'd like to work with you two to see if Rex knows some simple commands," Hill said. "I have a feeling he already knows some."

"I do too. Rex is a smart boy," Haley said as Rex licked her fingers.

"Have you treated him yet today?"

"No."

"Run, get him a couple while the twins have Anita distracted," Hill teased.

Haley rushed to the feed room for snacks as Hill walked toward the group forming at the front of the compound.

When the girls left for home, Hill turned to Alice. "I'd like to keep an eye on Coal for a little while if that's okay."

"That's perfectly fine with me," Alice replied. "I haven't checked emails today."

"Would you two join us for some fried chicken then?" Betsy asked. "Terry and I are going to town in a few minutes."

"Only if we can pitch in to buy it," Alice said, handing her a twenty.

"That sounds like a plan. Any special requests?" Betsy asked.

"A gallon of sweet tea," Alice said.

"Go finish your work, and I'll get you when we return."

"I'll see you in a few minutes," Hill said. "I'm going to check on the kittens."

Alice nodded and walked toward the office.

Hill checked the kittens and then stopped at Rex's enclosure. "You did well today. You love Haley, don't you?"

Rex wagged his tail and stepped forward to take the treat Hill offered.

†

Jess was exiting her apartment when Hill passed by. "You look nice and smell good, too," Hill said.

"Thanks, Doc. Why are you here so late?"

"Checking on the newborns, and then Alice and I are having dinner with the campers. Have fun tonight. Invite Blakely out for burgers tomorrow night if you want. The more the merrier."

"I will." Jess smiled. "See ya, Doc."

"Drive careful."

"You too."

Jess felt her hands trembling as she programmed Blakely's address into her phone. She drove to Blakely's apartment and breathed deeply before walking to the door. She knocked and waited for the door to be answered. Her eyes grew wide when the door swung open. Blakely wore dark jeans with a low-cut sweater.

"Hey, hang on and let me grab my bag," Blakely said.

Jess appreciated the moment to calm her heartbeat. She had never seen Blakely look so beautiful.

"All set?" she asked when Blakely returned.

"Yes, ma'am," she answered.

Jess walked ahead and opened the car door for Blakely. Jess' nose filled with the sensual perfume Blakely wore, and her heart rate increased again.

"Breathe," Jess said as she walked to the driver's door.

220

Ali Spooner

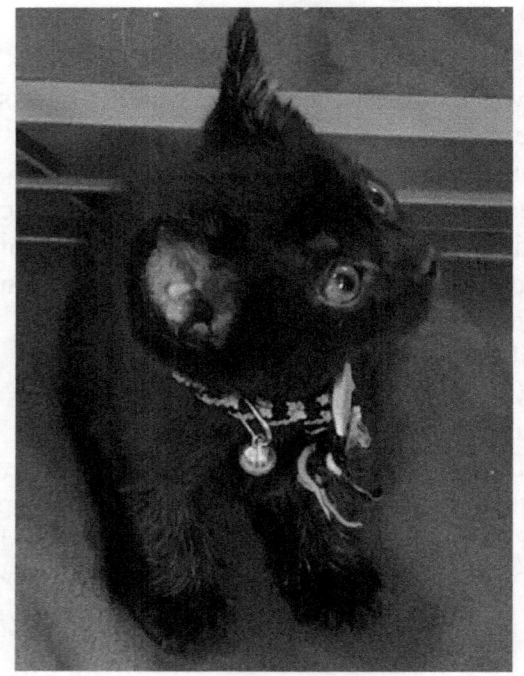

PINKY (SHYLA ALLISON)

CHAPTER SEVEN

CHRIS (SEFTON DOF)

Hill and Alice arrived early the following day. Hill was eager to find out how Jess' date went, and Alice had several reservations to book. Hill was checking on the kittens when Jess arrived.

"Good morning, Doc. How are the babies?"

"Looking good. Busy nursing already today," Hill said as she filled Coal's food bowl. "How did it go last night?"

"Pretty well. Blakely is going to come out this afternoon for the cookout. We had a great time."

"Good." Hill smiled.

"We shared nice kisses at her front door, but I didn't go inside her apartment."

"No need to rush. I look forward to meeting Blakely," Hill replied.

"She's excited, too. We talked a lot about this place last night. We may have another volunteer this summer." Jess grinned.

"That's good. We can use another set of hands for the next project I'm dreaming up."

"What next?" Jess asked.

"I'd like to fence in a large open dog park with a small pool for the dogs to enjoy this summer."

"I don't want to brag, but I'm pretty good with an auger if we can borrow one."

Hill shook her head. "Tom and his crew are donating the fence, but I need help digging out a pool, adding drains, and burying a hard plastic pool form. Digging water lines, too."

"Hard work, but it sounds like fun. The dirt we move can be mounded for the dogs to climb and play on."

"That's a good idea. I think I'll rent a Ditch Witch for the water lines. It will be faster and easier."

"When do we start?"

"Tom and his crew will knock out the fencing on Monday. The pool insert will be here on Tuesday, so we can dig the water and drain lines. Then, digging the pool begins. It won't be huge or deep, so we can knock it out in a day, two at most."

"That sounds like a plan to me."

Hill smiled at the eagerness in Jess' voice. "I'll call this morning and get a rental reserved for the Ditch Witch."

†

Hill rummaged through the tool shed for a long tape measure and four survey flags before tracking down Alice. "I need your help before you start mowing."

"I've still got to add the reservations to the whiteboard, but that won't take long. What do you need?"

"I need someone to help me measure the dog park dimensions. It shouldn't take long."

"I'm right behind you then," Alice replied. "Have you decided on a spot?"

"Not far from the current runs, so we will have easy access to water and can link the runs in the future if we want."

"That makes sense."

They finished marking the plot as the girls arrived. "I'll make a pot of coffee if you want to get the girls started," Alice said, walking back to the office.

Hill looked at Haley. "After you store your lunch, grab a bunch of treats and meet me at Rex's enclosure."

"I'll be right there, Doc," Haley replied.

Maggie and the twins carried desserts and a dish of baked beans. "Jess, can we store these in your apartment?" Hill asked.

"Sure, no problem," Jess said, leading the girls inside.

"I delivered the buns and condiments to Lou," Anita said. "Can you think of anything else we need?"

"Not right off my head. I'll call if I think of something," Hill replied.

"I'll see you this afternoon then," Anita said, walking to the van.

†

Hill flipped a five-gallon bucket and sat in front of Rex's enclosure. "Let's see what this smart boy knows. Let's start with sitting," she told Haley, and she gave her a visual command as well.

Haley used the combination, and Rex took a seat. "Good boy."

"Now lay and point to the ground." Hill wasn't surprised when Rex lay on the ground. "Say 'Come' next and offer him a treat."

"Come, Rex," Haley said, and when he approached, she said sit. "Good boy," she said, offering him a treat.

"Down, then roll over," Hill said.

Rex performed each task to perfection. "Now 'Stay,' and I want you to walk out to the fence of his run and call him."

Haley held her hand up in a stop sign and said, "Stay," as she walked out to his run through another enclosure. Remarkably, Rex sat watching Hill, and when Hill nodded to

Haley, she called for him. "Come, Rex." Rex took off, running directly to Haley.

"Amazing." Hill waited for Haley to treat Rex and then called him. "Come, Rex."

Rex looked at Haley and waited for her to point to his enclosure and say, "Go," before he moved an inch. "A one-person dog." Hill smiled. "Good boy, Rex," she said, offering him a treat. He was still cautious but stepped forward to accept the treat.

Haley jogged back to Hill. "What do you think?"

"I think he's a very disciplined and intelligent dog and responds best to one trainer. You've done really well with him. I want you to practice having him heel by walking beside you as you walk the fenceline. Don't forget to offer him treats randomly."

"I think I know a little more about him," Haley said.

"Like what?"

"I think Rex lost his person and doesn't know why she never returned, and whoever had him afterward couldn't bear his grief and anger, leading them to abandon him."

"What makes you think it was a she?" Hill asked.

"Just intuition. Rex responds better to females than males."

"That's true. Go practice with Rex, and maybe we can come up with some new things for him to learn." Hill had an idea. It was a long shot, but maybe she would hit on something. She walked into the office and sat in front of her computer. She pressed keys and pulled up obituaries of the last three months within a hundred miles.

Hill was scrolling through the screens of reports when Alice brought her a cup of coffee. "I'm going to start mowing.

I brought clean clothes if I get too dirty." She chuckled and looked at Hill's screen. "Obits?"

"Haley thinks Rex lost his person, and that's why he's so angry and sad. I know it's worth a long shot, but it's worth a try to help us figure him out. He's been very well trained by someone. We just need to figure out who."

"Good luck with your search. Call me if you need anything."

"I will. Love you," Hill said, taking a sip of coffee.

"I love you too."

Hill continued her search, and she was about to call it quits when her attention was caught by an obit for a young woman that popped up on the screen. Hill read aloud. "Kelly Foster, twenty-three, died in a traffic accident on April tenth. She was survived by her parents, Robert and Mary, and her companion, Rex." Hill sat staring at the screen. "Incredible," she said as she scrolled through photos from the file. A beautiful woman knelt beside Rex, wearing a law enforcement uniform. "Could he have been her K-9 partner?" Hill scribbled some notes and bookmarked the obit. Next, she googled Kelly Foster, which pulled up an article on her death. Hill's eyes filled with tears as she read the news regarding the young woman's death.

Hill searched the internet and found an address and phone number for the Fosters in a town twenty miles away. "Nothing to lose," Hill said as she picked up her phone and dialed the number.

"Hello," a woman answered.

"Is this Mrs. Foster?"

"Yes, this is Mary Foster. Who is this?"

"My name is Dr. Hillary McCall. I'm a vet, and I have a question for you."

Hill could hear the woman begin to cry. "You have Rex, don't you?"

"Yes, ma'am. I do. He was given to me by our local shelter, and I'm trying to help him. Can you tell me what happened?"

"Our daughter Kelly raised him from a pup, and they adored each other. When she wasn't working, Rex was constantly at her side. They were inseparable."

"I read she was in law enforcement. Was Rex her K-9 partner?"

"No, she was working toward a position in the K-9 division, but Rex was her personal companion. When she was killed, I didn't know what to do for him. I tried to explain that she wouldn't return, and somehow, he understood. He would howl for hours and went days without eating or sleeping. His grief was so intense. Robert tried to take him for walks, but Rex became aggressive. We couldn't stand the thought of having him put down, so Robert took him to the shelter. We hoped someone could help Rex and he would find a loving home."

"He has with me," Hill said. "Was Rex ever taken to her grave?"

"No. Robert thought that was ridiculous," Mary said. "Do you think it would help?"

"It might. May I take Rex to visit?"

"Yes, please. It's worth a try." Mrs. Foster gave Hill the address and general location of her daughter's gravesite.

"Thank you, Mrs. Foster."

"Thank you for what you're doing with Rex. Kelly loved him so much."

"I'm sorry for your loss. I promise to do what I can for Rex."

†

Hill burst into tears when she ended the call. She was drying her eyes when Jess came into the office.

"Doc, are you okay?"

Hill nodded. "Haley gave me a clue about Rex's owner. I was able to track down his story. Rex is grieving the loss of his person." Hill pulled up the photo of the two of them from her obit.

"Was he a K-9 dog?"

"No, just her companion. She raised him from a puppy and trained him very well. He's so smart but doesn't understand why she left him." Hill looked at Jess. "Will you copy this photo onto my iPad? I'd like to see if he recognizes her."

"If he does? What then?"

"Then we go for a ride. Rex has never been to her grave. I think he deserves to know Kelly didn't abandon him. The cemetery isn't far from here."

"I think you need to fill Haley in on what's going on," Jess said. "You know she'll want to go."

"I'll do that if you call Anita and make sure it's okay for Haley to ride with me."

"Do you think Rex will be safe?" Jess asked.

"I'll muzzle him until I feel it's safe."

"May I go to help?"

"Yes. I'll get Alice to work with the girls while we're gone. Will you send Haley in while I call Alice?"

"Sure, Doc, and then I'll call Anita to explain what's happening."

"Thank you," Hill said, calling Alice and asking her to come to the office.

†

When Haley and Alice arrived, Hill explained what she had found. "When you told me Rex lost his person, and it was a woman this morning, I started searching. I contacted the young woman's mother and got permission for Rex to visit the gravesite. I want to show him this picture and see if he recognizes her." Hill turned the iPad around to show them the picture.

"She kind of looks like Jess," Haley said.

"I thought so too."

"We're good," Jess said, entering the office.

"Alice, will you work with the rest of the girls while we're gone?"

"Of course I will."

"Haley, I assume you want to go, and Anita has given you permission. I will need to muzzle Rex to ensure he is safe."

"Will you let me do it?" Haley asked.

"We can't allow him to bite you," Hill said.

"He won't," Haley said.

"We'll do it together then," Hill said. "Let's go see if he recognizes Kelly.

†

"Call Rex to us," Hill told Haley as she knelt near the gate.

"Come, Rex," Haley said. Rex strolled confidently to Haley's command.

Hill took a deep breath. "Ready?"

"Yes," Haley answered.

Hill turned the iPad toward him so he could see the photo. "Kelly," she said.

Rex whined as his eyes landed on the picture. "Is this your Kelly?" Haley asked.

Rex wagged his tail and whined again.

"Do you want to go see Kelly?" Hill asked, picking up a leash. "We have to muzzle you for the ride," Hill said, showing him the leash and muzzle, repeating Kelly's name as she walked into the enclosure.

"Sit," Haley said, and Rex sat on his haunches.

Hill handed Haley the muzzle and clipped the leash onto his collar. "Be careful," Hill said.

"Here we go, Rex," Haley said.

Hill was astonished that Rex didn't twitch when Haley slipped the muzzle onto him. "Do you want to lead him out to my truck?" Hill offered her the leash.

"Let's go. Heel, Rex." Haley led Rex out of the enclosure to Hill's truck.

"You two can take the back seat," Hill said, confident that Haley would be safe with Rex.

Jess opened the back door.

"Load up," Haley said and climbed in behind Rex.

†

Hill entered the cemetery and followed Mrs. Foster's directions to locate the gravesite. She parked the truck and turned to look at Haley. Rex had his head in her lap, and she was stroking down his back. "What do you think about taking the muzzle off?"

"I think it's safe," Haley said.

"Go ahead," Hill said.

Haley removed the muzzle and opened the door. "Stay," she said until she climbed down. "Come, Rex."

Hill pointed out the headstone, and her heart ached when she saw the photo of Rex and Kelly framed in the headstone. Rex walked over to the stone, licked the picture, and lay on the grave.

Haley sat beside him and placed her hand on his back while Hill and Jess sat across from them. "Rex," Hill said, "Kelly couldn't come home to you. She would have if she could, but I know Kelly loved you very much. You were her best friend."

Rex's tail thumped on the ground whenever Hill spoke Kelly's name. He placed his head in Haley's lap and looked up at her. "I will love you and be your best friend if you let me," Haley said. Rex licked her hand and then stood to lick her cheek. Rex turned and walked to Jess and Hill to repeat his show of affection. "I think he understands we love him and will be good to him," Haley said. "He's happy to know Kelly didn't want to leave him."

†

Haley looked closely at him and saw that the red aura surrounding him had disappeared and been replaced with yellow. "His anger is gone, and he's becoming happy again," Haley told them. She looked at Hill. "I have a favor to ask."

"Go ahead."

"When I age out of the home next year, can I adopt Rex? I don't know what will happen to me, but when I can, I'd like to take him home with me."

"I have a solution if you hear me out," Hill said. "I want to add another apartment at the farm and offer to pay your college tuition if you continue working there. You have exceptional talent that benefits the animals. Then, when you graduate and choose to move on, Rex can go anywhere with you."

Haley cocked her head at Hill and smiled. "That would be perfect, Doc. I would love that. Would you like to be my boy?" Haley asked Rex.

Rex stood and covered her face with kisses. Then he walked to the headstone and licked the picture as if saying goodbye to Kelly.

"We can come back for visits," Hill told Haley and Rex.

"Let's go home," Haley said, and Rex jumped back into the truck. "Muzzle?"

"No, I don't think he needs it anymore. We do need to keep him on a leash until we see how he reacts around other animals and humans." Hill smiled at Haley. "I believe Rex will be fine, thanks to you."

†

When they returned to the farm, Haley and Rex went back to his run, and they played fetch for nearly an hour until it was time for lunch. Rex was indeed a different dog, and Hill couldn't have been happier.

"Wow. What a transformation," Lou said as she joined Hill to watch them play.

"Incredible," Hill said and turned her head when she heard an approaching vehicle. Dan from the shelter was pulling to a stop. "No rest for the wicked," Hill said and walked to meet Dan.

"That cannot be the same dog I brought in with a muzzle a few weeks ago," Dan said as he watched Haley and Rex.

Hill nodded. "Yes, it is. Isn't it amazing?"

"You have got to tell me your secret," Dan said. "He nearly tore my arm off, and now he's covering her with kisses."

Hill told him about Haley's ability to sense Rex's emotions and how they pieced together his history.

"That's incredible. I wouldn't have believed it if I hadn't seen it myself," Dan said.

"Who do you have for us today?" Hill asked.

"Two feral kitties trapped by a homeowner and one super energetic Jack Russell."

"That will be a perfect substitute for Toby. One of our campers has adopted him, which saddened Maggie, one of our volunteers. She loved playing fetch with Toby."

"This little guy will be a great substitute and keep her busy," Dan said. "Congrats on finding a great home for Toby."

"He will have great adventures with Lou and Betsy. They will send us pictures of where he's traveled with them."

"That's a great idea," Dan said.

"And keep us in mind if someone is looking for a black kitten in a couple months. We had a pregnant cat dropped off who just had a litter of four."

"I certainly will. I'll grab the cat crate if you want to lead the Jack Russell out."

"Any named?" Hill asked when she clipped a leash on the small dog.

"Nope, we've just been calling him JR."

"Creative," Hill teased. "Let's go."

"How's the cat with the broken leg?" Dan asked.

"She's doing great. She should be ready to come out of the cast soon. Jess has taken excellent care of her."

"Jess will make a great vet one day," Dan said.

"Yes, she will," Hill answered as Jess and Maggie approached.

"Who do we have here?" Jess asked.

"JR and two feral cats," Hill answered. She handed the leash to Maggie. "Will you take him for a run and bring him into the clinic after he has done his business?"

"Absolutely," Maggie said as she and JR jogged away.

"The ferals are notched, so they've been altered, and both are negative for Fe-Luke," Dan said as he handed Jess the crate.

"Place them in a separate enclosure so we can quarantine them for a few days to be safe," Hill said.

"Sure thing, Doc," Jess said. She took the cats inside and returned with the crate for Dan.

He was still watching Rex. "I still can't believe that's the same dog."

"The power of love works wonders." Jess smirked.

"Yes, it does. Have a great day, and I'm sure I'll be seeing you next week."

"Thanks, Dan," Hill said and walked with Jess inside. "Do we have time for a quick exam on JR before Alice has our lunch ready?"

"I'm sure we do," Jess answered with a grin. "If we can get him back from Maggie."

†

The group was finishing a late lunch when a small car arrived. Hill saw the smile grow on Jess' face and knew it must be Blakely. "Bring her around to introduce her, and then you can give her the grand tour," Hill stated.

After introducing Blakely, Jess took her into the compound to start the tour. Alice leaned into Hill. "She's a cutie," she whispered.

"Yes, she is," Hill agreed.

"Can I play with JR some more?" Maggie asked.

"Good luck trying to wear him out," Hill replied.

"Would it be okay if I took Rex on a walk to the lake?" Haley asked.

"I think he would enjoy seeing more of his new home," Hill answered.

"The twins are already back inside playing with the cats, so I've lost all my assistants," Hill told Alice. "Would you help me with another quick measuring project? I'd like to start envisioning where the dog pool will go."

"Sure. I'll pick up here while you collect more flags and your measuring tape," Alice replied.

†

Alice helped Hill mark off space for the ten-by-twelve dog pool and then smiled when she looked at Hill. "I've got another idea," Alice said. "Since we are running water lines, why don't we include a drinking fountain for the dogs? I saw some small fountains at the builder supply store that would be perfect. I may be able to get one donated for us."

"I love that idea. That way, the dogs could have fresh running water while they play. Good suggestion, my love," Hill answered. "I was thinking of adding a bench, too, so if our campers need a dog park, they can sit and watch them play."

"Another great idea. I will see what I can get," Alice replied.

Lou walked over to them. "Looks like you two are coming up with another project."

Hill chuckled. "We are going to make this spot into a dog park, and it will have a small pool and a water fountain. When you return, the farm's dogs will have access to it, and Toby will have a bigger spot to play with his friends."

"I wish we didn't have to leave," Lou said. "We love it here. Would you consider a long-term rental if we decide to spend the winters in a warmer climate?"

"Absolutely. We would welcome you anytime, for however long you wanted," Alice replied.

"I love working on projects, but having to blow snow every day to leave the house is getting old," Lou admitted.

"We would welcome your extra hands anytime," Hill said. "Is there anything we can help with for the cookout?"

"Nope. I was coming to ask if you wanted me to start cooking around four?"

"That should be great. Anita will be here by then. We can get the tables set up, the beans warm, and a cooler full of drinks carried out," Alice said.

†

Hill took Jax to the clinic. "We haven't checked on you lately," she said as she carried him into the clinic. She passed Jess and Blakely on the way, and Jess shot her a concerned look.

"Is Jax okay?"

"Yes. The steroids have worked well, but I haven't examined Jax in a few days," Hill replied. "He could also use a good nail trimming," she said as he wiggled in her arms.

"I can do that while you set up for his exam," Jess said, reaching for Jax.

"Have you finished your tour already?"

"This place is fantastic," Blakely said. "I couldn't keep from crying when Jess told me Rex's story. So amazing."

"I can't get over what a different dog he has become today," Hill replied. "Lou will start cooking at four, so we can set up the tables and coolers at about three-thirty."

"That should give us time to walk down to the lake," Jess said while she trimmed Jax's nails.

"Haley and Rex are down there, so bring them back with you," Hill said. "Will you weigh Jax for me?"

"He's gained back those two ounces," Jess said. "Plus one."

Hill listened to his lungs and then handed the stethoscope to Jess. Jess listened to his heart and lungs. "Everything sounds clear and strong," she reported.

Hill handed Jax to Jess. "We must still closely watch the old man, especially when fall and winter arrive. I'll get some sweaters ordered for him to help keep him warm."

"Could I get some for him?" Blakely asked. "I'd also like to volunteer if you want more help."

"We always welcome another pair of hands. I'm sure Jess can help you pick out sweaters suitable for Jax. Thank you, Blakely," Hill said.

"I love what you are doing here and wish more places would open like this. I can't stand the thought of an animal being euthanized because an owner is tired of it."

"It happens all too often, unfortunately," Hill said. "Will you take Jax home on your way to the lake?"

"Sure, Doc. Thanks," Jess stated. "This has been a great day all around."

"Yes, it has," Hill said. "Thank you for all your help. Now get out of here and show Blakely our beautiful lake."

Hill entered her notes on Jax and walked to the office for a cup of coffee. Alice was typing away on her laptop as Hill took her seat. She looked up at the whiteboard. "Wow. The campground is filling up quickly."

Alice looked up at the sound of Hill's voice. "Yes, it is, and I have two more reservations to add."

"Did you ever think this dream would come true?" Hill asked.

Alice turned to her. "Of course, with you every day, it only gets better."

"Were you surprised about Lou's long-term request?"

"Not particularly. Lou and Betsy have been dropping some hints. I think it would be a great idea."

"The best part is, if we grow beyond our original plan, we have ample room to expand," Hill said.

"That's true. With some extra muscle, we could clear space for another campground near the lake."

"That might be a winter project for us," Hill said.

†

It was impossible to tell who had the most fun at the cookout. Lou was in her element, cooking for everyone, and Betsy and Terry were perfect hostesses. The girls played with the animals after eating while Anita sang the praises of the farm.

"It's incredible to witness the change in the girls since they started here," Anita said. "They are excited to participate in this project and can't wait to get here. Sundays are tough because they can't come to visit."

"They have all been a vital part of our success so far and have been a joy to work with," Hill said. "Their hard work allows me to devote more time to the physical care of the animals, and the love those girls demonstrate for them is heartwarming."

"We couldn't have asked for better campers to teach us the ropes of campground life. We have learned so much from the three of you," Alice said to Terry, Betsy, and Lou.

"We believe in you and what you are accomplishing here," Lou said. "You can bet you will be seeing us often."

123

"Same here," Terry said. "I've never felt as at home at a campground as I do here, and we both got new companions out of the deal."

"I know Toby and Sasha are going to loving homes. Something they both deserve," Hill replied. "We hope you will keep in touch and stay with us when you travel through our area."

"I've already got you programmed in our phones." Betsy grinned.

Hill looked at Alice with a grin. "After you asked about a long-term rental, Alice came up with a great idea. What do you think about us clearing a campground site closer to the lake for longer rentals?"

"I think it would be a huge asset. Just one thing. Wait until I get back to help," Lou teased.

"It wouldn't even start until this winter." Hill laughed.

"Perfect," Lou said.

†

Betsy surprised the girls when she brought a tray of ingredients for S'mores, and they laughed as they created the sweet treats around the fire pit. When everyone was stuffed with the treats, Anita nodded to the girls. They each gave everyone a hug and thanks for the cookout. Maggie played with Toby and hugged him briefly before rushing to the van.

Lou looked at Anita. "Don't worry. She will be fine," Anita assured Lou.

"We have plans to keep her involved in Toby's life," Lou said. "Thank you for caring so much for these girls. They are a wonderful bunch."

"This place means so much to them, and your kindness is appreciated. We all had a lovely time tonight."

Hill walked to the van with them. "Thanks for a great week. Start thinking about what we can do next Saturday, and I'll see you on Monday." She waved as the van pulled away and returned to place an arm around Alice. "We aren't the only ones that will miss the three of y'all."

"We will be back," Terry said.

"Will we see you before you pull out Monday?" Alice asked.

"That's a good possibility as early as you two show up," Lou said.

"Yes. I'm in no hurry to leave either," Terry said.

"Great. I think we will head home for tonight. Thank you for making this a fun night for all of us," Hill said. She looked at Jess. "Will you lock up after making a final round?"

"Will do, boss," she said, reaching for Blakely's hand.

†

"That was so much fun," Alice said when they pulled into the garage. "I don't know about you, but I'm whipped."

"Let's rinse off and hit the sack. We can sleep in tomorrow and enjoy a lazy day," Hill said.

"We'll see how long that lasts," Alice said.

"True, but at least we have the opportunity. What we do with it is up to us."

"Blakely and Jess make a cute couple, don't they?" Alice asked.

"Yes, they do. I hope things work out well for them."

"Me too. They seem to be perfect for each other."

†

Jess led Blakely through the compounds as she did a final food and water check on everyone before locking up. She pulled out a special treat for Rex and knelt to talk to him. "You did great today." She offered him the treat, and he licked her fingers. "I'll see you tomorrow."

Jess asked when they entered the apartment. "Would you like a beer?"

"I'd love one," Blakely replied and sat on the sofa.

Gabby looked up at Jess as she placed food in her bowl. "I didn't forget you, baby girl." She stroked down the cat's back and walked to the fridge to remove two beers. She handed one to Blakely and sat next to her.

"I see why you love this place so much," Blakely said. "If there is a heaven on earth for animals, this place is it. Not just the animals but the people here, too. I can feel the love you and the girls have for the animals."

"Having them volunteer has been a great experience. They are such great kids. I wish I could adopt all of them," Jess grinned.

"Maybe in a few years." Blakely chuckled. "What are your plans once you graduate?"

"I'll probably work at one of the clinics in town or open my own practice. I hope to take over here when Hill decides to retire and travel. I don't see that happening for a while yet." Jess took a sip of beer. "What about you? What are your plans after graduation?"

"I've already had a few offers I'll need to consider to remain local. I don't want to move to a big city and get lost in the crowd." Blakely smiled at Jess. "You will still have a few more years after I graduate."

"You can teach me all about adulting then." Jess grinned.

"I'd love to, but I think you are way ahead of me," Blakely said.

"How so?" Jess asked.

"Most people our age are only thinking about the right now. Partying and having fun are the priorities, but you are dedicated to your passion for animals and committed to seeing your goals through."

"That's true, I guess. I've never been into the party scene."

"I've never seen you out anywhere before, not that I go out all the time, but class was the first time I noticed you. I would have noticed you if you were out clubbing," Blakely said. Her hand reached out to stroke Jess' face. "You are a beautiful and genuinely kind person."

"Thanks," Jess said, blushing.

Blakely took a drink and set her beer on the table. "I'm very attracted to you in more ways than just sexual. I love your intelligence and your kindness to others. I realize this is somewhat new for you, but I want you to know we will go at your pace. I want us to be a long-term couple, not a one-and-done."

Jess leaned in to kiss Blakely. "Thank you. I'm very attracted to you, but I'm not ready to take the next step. Close, but not quite there yet."

"I can work with that, and I know you are worth the wait. It doesn't make waiting to be with you easier, but it will make our first time more special if we're both ready."

Gabby hobbled over to the sofa and meowed for Jess to pick her up. Jess leaned down and cuddled her. "I hope you don't mind cats."

"I love them, but who else?" Blakely asked.

"When Gabby gets her cast off, I'm also adopting Buster. I was prepping for him when Gabby arrived, and I needed to postpone that plan for a couple of weeks."

"One for each of us," Blakely said, taking Gabby from her arms. Gabby started purring as Blakely started scratching under her chin.

"Perfect," Jess said and moved close to cuddle with them.

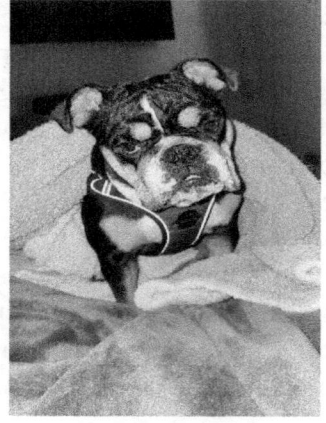

MONROW (PAIGE KINNEY)

CHAPTER EIGHT

THE TWINS (JULIE MEACHEN)

Hill and Alice were sad to see Terry, Lou, and Betsy leave on Monday morning but knew they would return in the future. When they were ready to go, Lou and Terry approached them and handed Alice an envelope holding four hundred-dollar bills.

"What's this?" Alice said.

"We want you to continue our Saturday nights with the girls," Terry said. "It's the least we can do for them."

Alice nodded. "It's not necessary, but thank you. We will continue the tradition and think of y'all every time."

Lou smiled. "I'll call as soon as I know when we are heading back this way."

"Me too," Terry said. "I'll definitely stop back on my way home."

"We'll be ready for you," Alice said. "Safe travels, and stay in touch."

Jess joined them as they watched Terry and Lou drive away. Toby sat in Betsy's lap as he left for his new life and adventures.

"I'm going to miss them," Jess sighed.

"Our first campers will always be special. We have three more arriving this week to prepare for," Alice said. "The bar is set high, but I bet we enjoy them also as much."

"I could use a coffee before the fencing crew gets here," Hill said, walking toward the office. "Our Ditch Witch is being dropped off today, too," Hill said.

Alice's eyes lit up. "Do I get to run it?"

"That was the plan," Hill said. "Jess and I can run the lines and have them ready to install once you have them dug."

"Do I have time to run into town to check on a fountain?"

"You have all the time you need," Hill said, handing her the truck keys.

Alice stretched up to kiss Hill. "I'll see you later then."

"Coffee before we start work?" Hill asked Jess.

"Sure," Jess said, following her inside.

†

Hill enjoyed her coffee and poured another cup. When the girls arrived, she walked out to help Jess feed the animals. "Good morning, ladies. You know the routine."

"Morning, Doc," Haley said, carrying their lunches to store in the refrigerator.

"Feed up and let everyone out to play while it's nice out," Hill said. Jax was dancing around the food bowl. "Yes, you too," Hill chuckled. Her watch alerted her to someone arriving, and she saw Tom and the fence crew coming to install the fence. She walked out to greet them and go through her plans with Tom.

"Alright, we'll get right on it. I hope you don't mind I upgraded the fencing from hog wire to chainlink. My supplier donated the chainlink when I told him about the farm and today's project."

"Please give me his name and address so we can send him a thank you," Hill requested. "I'm tickled we are receiving such good support from the community."

"What's the smaller section marked?" Tom asked.

"I'm having a small liner delivered for a dog pool," Hill said. "We'll use the soil to make mounds for the dogs to play on and a small fountain for fresh water for them to drink."

"That sounds pretty cool. How do you plan to dig it out?" Tom asked.

Hill showed him her hands. "The old-fashioned way with sweat and a good shovel."

"I have a small excavator at the shop that can knock that out in fifteen minutes. Will you allow me to dig it for you?" Tom requested. "I can get the crew started and go back for it and be back in thirty minutes."

Hill nodded. "I never turn down help. Thank you for doing so much."

"I believe in what you are doing here," Tom said.

"Thank you."

"My pleasure," Tom said and began barking out orders. "I'll be back shortly," he said as he climbed back into his truck.

†

Jess walked up. "What was that all about?"

"Tom is going back to his shop for an excavator to dig our pool," Hill explained. "His fence supplier also upgraded us to chainlink for the park."

"That's a great way to start the week," Jess said. "Save our backs for other work."

Hill grinned at Jess. "We still have water lines to assemble when you're ready."

"No time like the present," Jess said.

Hill poured out the last of the coffee. "Let me get rid of this coffee, and I'll meet you out back. Get Maggie to help you carry the PVC pipes to where we will run the lines."

"Yo, Maggie," Jess called out and motioned for Maggie to come over.

Hill smiled when she saw Rex and Haley playing in his run. "What a change," she said as she returned to her office.

†

Hill and Jess were gluing the last section of the pipe when Alice returned. "Looks like she had a successful trip," Hill said.

"Did you have any doubt? Who can say 'no' to Alice?"

"Good point. I know I can't," Hill said. "Let's see what she got and bring her up to speed." Tom had returned with the excavator and was almost finished digging the pond. He had made three large mounds of soil for the dogs to play on, and the crew had half of the fence installed.

Alice stepped out of the truck and smiled. "Wow, maybe I should go back out and come back later," she teased. "Come look what I got donated."

Hill and Jess walked to the back of the truck. "Now that's a water fountain," Hill said. Inside was a three-tiered water fountain. "That should fit everyone, even Jax."

"That was the plan. The owner donated three benches, too. We just need to assemble them," Alice reported.

"Go get the drill and bit set," Hill said to Jess. "We can knock these out in no time. That fountain looks heavy. Maybe I can borrow a few of Tom's guys for a minute. Pull the truck next to the pool, and we can unload." Hill smiled at Alice. "You did well."

Tom and two of his men unloaded the fountain and placed it where Hill wanted. "That's perfect. Thanks, guys." Hill

133

looked at Tom. "Can I buy your guys pizza for lunch for all their hard work?"

"It's not necessary, but we could stay on the job if you did," Tom agreed.

"I'll take care of it," Hill said. She turned to walk away and stopped. "Could you do me one more thing?"

"Sure, what's up?"

"Make a sign to hang on the fence with your name, the builder's supply store name, and your fence supplier to name everyone who donated to the project."

"That's easy," Tom said. "Thank you."

Hill turned her head at the sound of a large rig approaching. She smiled at Alice. "I do believe you have a new arrival to check in."

"Look again. I have two." Alice smiled.

Hill turned and saw a second smaller camper behind the first. "I'll order pizza for lunch and help Jess with the benches, but holler if you need me." She looked at Jess. "Get everything unpacked, and I'll be back in a few minutes. Is pizza good with you?"

"Pizza is always good for me. Thanks, Doc."

Hill walked inside and called the girls together. "Will your sack lunches be good until tomorrow?"

"Yeah, there are sandwiches and fruit," Haley said. "Why?"

"Could you eat pizza instead?" Hill asked.

"Heck, yeah," Maggie said.

"Pizza it is, then. Now get to work," Hill teased, and the kids scattered.

Hill entered the office to order pizza and two twelve-packs of soda for lunch and then returned to Jess. "I thought you would have one put together by now?" Hill said when she saw Jess reading the instructions.

"I'm just making sure I've got everything laid out right. Are you ready? They look pretty simple," Jess said.

"Famous last words." Hill chuckled.

†

Alice walked over to greet the new campers. "Welcome to Fairytail Farm," she said as four women emerged from the two rigs. "I'm Alice, and I'll be getting you checked in this morning. If you want to select your spots, I'll get your paperwork from the office and be right back."

Hill was exiting the office when Alice arrived. She stopped to kiss her. "Two couples," Alice said as Hill smiled and walked out to assist Jess.

Alice grabbed her folders and returned to the campground as both rigs were settled into campsites. She sat at one of the picnic tables as two women approached.

"Good morning. I'm Karen, and my wife, Joy, is leveling our unit. This is my baby sister, Sue, and her wife, Tina is setting them up. This place is buzzing with activity," Karen said.

"We are putting in a dog park with a pool and fountain," Alice explained. "The tall woman is my wife, Hill. She's the vet and owner of the farm with me. The cutie working with her is Jess. She's a vet student who lives on-site and will be your after-hours contact if you need anything. I'll introduce you when they finish putting the benches together."

"Sounds like you have some plumbing to do," Karen said.

"Yes, we have a Ditch Witch rented for the water lines."

"I'd love to help if I can. I'm a licensed plumber," Karen said.

"We never turn down help," Alice said. "Where are you from?"

"Kentucky, headed to south Florida for a few weeks," Sue said.

"You have reservations for four nights. Is that still correct?" Alice said.

"At least four," Karen said. "Do you have availability if we want to stay more?"

"We have a couple of arrivals mid-week, but I don't think an extension would be a problem."

"Good. We did some research online, but can we get a tour? This place looks awesome," Joy said.

"Sure. We have some young volunteers working with us. Would you mind if they gave you a tour?"

"That sounds good. Let's go," Karen said.

The women followed Alice to the dog compound, and Alice called Haley. "Haley, would you give these ladies a tour?"

"Sure thing, Ms. Alice."

"I'll get up with you for the paperwork after your tour," Alice said. "I'll catch up with you in a minute."

†

Jess and Hill had finished the first bench when Alice arrived. "Is it safe to sit on?" she asked.

"You can be our guinea pig," Jess said.

Alice sat on the bench. "Very comfy. Our day just keeps getting better. One of our new campers is a licensed plumber and wants to help with the water lines."

"That's a relief," Hill said. "I'm not a plumber and could probably muddle through it, but I'd be more comfortable with a professional. We can start on it after lunch if that's good with everyone."

"We already assembled the pipes and laid them next to the ditch you dug," Jess said.

"The pool liner doesn't arrive until tomorrow. We should be able to have all the lines ready when it comes and have the fountain hooked up." Hill smiled. "This is going to be great."

"Get back to work and finish the benches. I'll tell Karen you will start on the lines after lunch."

"Invite them to join us if you want. I ordered plenty," Hill said.

"I will," Alice said.

"You heard the lady. Let's get back to it," Hill teased.

†

Alice caught up to the group in the cat compound and listened to Haley talk about the cats. She smiled, hearing the excitement in Haley's voice, and Alice was proud of her for touring the guests. "Thank you for giving the tour, Haley. Will you round up the girls and get cleaned up for lunch? Pizza will be here in a few minutes."

"Yes, ma'am," Haley replied and talked to the twins before searching for Maggie.

"A trail behind the compound also leads to a small lake. We've got canoes and kayaks there for guests to use if you're interested." She led them to the picnic table at the campground.

"Haley said she and the three other girls live in a group home. I think it's wonderful you are giving them this experience," Joy said. "I was a social worker in my former life."

Alice smiled. "The girls have been a part of making this project a success. I don't know what we'll do when school starts back in the fall."

"I bet they are here when they leave school," Joy said.

"We have pizza ordered, and you are welcome to join us if you would."

"Thanks, but we stopped for an early lunch to allow you to get moving before we arrived. We were a bit ahead of schedule," Karen said.

"Someone couldn't wait to get here," Joy teased.

"We are glad to have you. Our first campers rolled out this morning, and we were sad to see them go. They left with a new dog and cat," Alice said.

"You adopt?" Tina asked.

"We do if it's a good fit for the animal and human," Alice said.

Tina looked at Sue. "Can we consider a cat?"

Sue smiled. "No way I can say no to you," Sue said.

"I'll let the twins introduce you to the cats after lunch. They are our feline professionals," Alice said.

"Thank you." Tina grinned.

Alice reviewed the paperwork with them and had them sign the contracts. "Do you want our credit cards?" Karen asked.

"Not until you've decided to extend your stay," Alice said.

"I think your lunch is here," Joy said, pointing at the car coming down the drive.

"I'll bring Hill down after lunch, and she can explain her vision for the fountain and pool," Alice told Karen.

"Excellent," Karen replied.

†

Hill placed the last bench on the ground. "Lunch is here if you want to bring your guys to the picnic tables," Hill told Tom.

"We'll be right behind you," Tom said.

Alice and Hill set up the tables, and everyone except one young man filled a plate. "Are you not hungry?" Alice asked.

"I'm allergic to tomato products, ma'am, but I'll take a soda."

"I've got this," Haley said. She rushed inside the compound, returned with two of their sack lunches, and handed them to the young man. "Nothing special, but you're welcome to them."

"Thank you, miss," he said with a smile and opened the first bag.

Hill smiled. She was proud of Haley's quick thinking and compassion for the young man.

†

With Karen's expertise, the water lines were finished by late afternoon. They were finishing the drain line when Karen frowned. "I just realized we are missing something," she said. "We need the connections for the drain line from the pool."

"I knew something was missing," Hill said.

"No biggie." Karen pulled out her phone and pulled up a product at the local hardware store. "This is what you need," Karen said, showing Hill the picture.

"Will you send that to me, and I'll go get one?" Hill asked.

"I'll ride with you if you want," Karen replied. "We're all set up at the campground."

"Sure. Thanks," Hill said. "Give me five to wash, and I'll pick you up."

Tom and the crew were packing up after finishing the fence. "We're all done here. I'll work on that sign and bring it out next week," Tom said.

Hill pulled him into a hug. "Thank you for everything. The dogs are going to love the new park."

"My pleasure. Let me know if you have any other projects I can help with," Tom replied.

"I will," Hill said, and walked inside to wash her hands.

"All set?" Alice asked.

"I'm missing a part for the drain, so Karen and I are going to town. Do you need anything?"

"Not that I can think of," Alice said. "We do need a team meeting in the morning, though."

"Oh? What's up?"

"We need to plan for a Grand Opening event and a Fourth of July party," Alice replied.

Hill nodded. "Yes, we do. I was also going to invite Mrs. Thompson out for a visit so she could see our progress."

"Why don't I arrange to pick her up on Wednesday after the dog park is complete?" Alice suggested.

"That works for me," Hill replied. She kissed Alice. "I won't be gone long."

"Take your time, I've got emails to answer," Alice said.

"Will you send Jess to town for some fried chicken? I'm so tired I don't feel like cooking," Hill said. "It's a good tired, though," she added.

"That does sound good," Alice replied.

"Thanks, love."

†

"Thanks for all your help today," Hill said when Karen climbed into the truck.

"No problem. I miss working with my hands sometimes, and you are working hard to make this place successful. It's the least I could do to help."

Hill's phone rang, and she answered Dan's call on the truck's audio system.

"Hey, Dan, what's up?"

"Would it be okay to bring out some more animals tomorrow? We got slammed over the weekend."

"Sure, that's not a problem. I'll be out there. Any medical issues I'll need to take care of right away?"

"One young dog that was torn up badly. We've done our best to stitch him up, but he will need close monitoring so he doesn't rip the wounds open again. We just don't have the space and personnel to handle that."

"Jess and I will take good care of him," Hill replied.

"That's why you are always my first call. I'll see you in the morning."

"Bring him out tonight if you need to. I'm in town for an errand, but I'll be at the farm for a while yet."

"Are you sure?"

"Yes, you can bring the others out in the morning," Hill said.

"I'll see you in about an hour. Thanks, Hill."

"No problem, Dan."

†

"Do you often get calls like that?" Karen asked.

"An emergency call once a month or so. Dan brings out animals, usually once a week, to stabilize the numbers at the shelter."

Hill dialed Jess to update her on the new arrival and arrange a small containment area to limit the injured dog's movement.

"I can finish the pool if you need to attend to an injured dog," Karen offered.

"No rush. The pool liner won't be delivered until the morning, so we're good. Thank you."

Karen selected the part they needed. "Will you at least let me pay for this?"

Hill smiled. "If you insist."

Hill dropped Karen off at the campground. "We'll have all hands on deck tomorrow to install the pool liner and finish the drain. Thanks again for all your help."

"My pleasure," Karen replied.

Hill carried the bag into the office and placed it on the counter.

"Jess said we've got an emergency, so I'm going for the chicken. She's a much better assistant than I am." Alice smiled.

"You do quite well," Hill said and kissed her. "I need to check to ensure we have everything set up."

"I'll be back with the chicken in a bit. Love you."

"Love you, too," Hill replied.

†

Hill found Jess working to install a divider in one of the dog runs. She had placed food and water bowls and a large bed in the back of the run. "This should work," Hill said.

"What do you know about the dog?" Jess asked.

"Not much other than he was pretty torn up and needed a bunch of sutures. We will need to monitor him closely for infection and make sure he doesn't tear open the wounds."

"Will you sedate him tonight?"

"If he isn't already sedated, yes," Hill replied. "No need for him to be in pain." Hill saw the small cot in the front of the run. "Are you planning to sleep in here?"

"Yeah, I thought I would for at least tonight."

"Gabby might get jealous," Hill teased. "You could bring her in here."

"I'll check on her when I wake to monitor the pup. Temperature checks and pain meds?"

"At least temp checks," Hill answered. "I'll need to see if they started him on antibiotics, too."

Dan pulled up, and Jess and Hill went to greet him.

"What do you know about him?" Hill asked as Dan opened the sliding door.

"Not much. One of the state police brought him in after they cut him out of some barbed wire. He's got some pretty deep lacerations we sutured."

"Any name?" Jess asked as Dan lifted the small dog in his arms.

"None yet. I hear you're good at coming up with names." Dan smiled at Jess.

"Let's take him to the clinic so I can give him an exam," Hill instructed.

Dan placed him gently on the exam table.

"Has he been started on antibiotics and pain meds?" Hill asked.

"I'll run back out for his chart," Dan said.

Hill began her examination and found over a dozen lacerations across the dog's body. He shivered in Jess' arms.

"In pain or scared?" Jess asked.

"Probably both. He doesn't look more than a year old."

Dan returned with a folder and a bag of medications. "He had pain meds and antibiotics three hours ago. I brought some in case you need them."

"Thanks. We'll give him another dose and get him settled in a run. The sutures are intact and not weeping. That's a good sign. No temperature either." She looked through the chart. "No other tests were run yet?"

"No, we haven't run anything yet. No worms according to his fecal test, but that's all."

"We'll let him settle in before we start testing," Hill said. "Isolation procedures until then," she told Jess.

"Got it," Jess replied. "If you'll dose him, I'll carry him to his new home."

"Anything I can do?" Dan asked.

"I think we've got him from here. I'll see you in the morning."

"Thanks, Doc. He appears to be a sweet boy," Dan said.

"We'll give him the best of care," Hill replied.

"I know you will. See you tomorrow."

Hill administered the medication and looked at Jess. The dog was still shivering. "A warming blanket might help."

"I'll get him settled in," Jess said.

"I'll enter him into the computer. Any idea for a name?"

"Walter," Jess said.

"Walter it is then." Hill chuckled.

†

It was late when Hill and Alice rose to leave. "Are you sure you don't want me to stay with him tonight?" Hill asked Jess.

"No offense, but I would be more comfortable on that cot than you." Jess grinned.

Hill looked at Alice with a shocked look. "I think she's inferring I have old bones."

"Well, if the shoe fits… wear it." Alice chuckled.

"Ouch. We'll see you in the morning then." Hill hugged Jess. "Call if you need anything."

"I will. Good night."

"Good night," Hill said and opened the door for Alice. Hill climbed in behind the wheel. "I'm so glad she volunteered. My bones are too old for a cot."

"I'm ready for our nice soft bed," Alice said.

"Me too." Hill smiled as she closed the gate behind them.

HUSKY (DEVON ENGLERTH)

CHAPTER NINE

BELLE (KATE RIPLEY)

After checking on Walter, Hill smiled at Jess.

"Jess, call the crew to the picnic table. We need to have a meeting this morning," Hill said. "Bring us a fresh cup of coffee and your schedule book," she told Alice.

Hill looked around at their small group when they sat around a picnic table. "We need to make some plans and wanted your input."

"Is everything okay?" Haley asked.

"Things couldn't be going any better. Thanks in large part to your help," Hill said. "We've decided to host two events. A Grand Opening for the community to visit and tour the program and then a Fourth of July celebration," Hill stated.

"When are you thinking of a Grand Opening?" Jess asked.

"Soon. The dog park is the last big project we had planned. At least for now." Hill grinned.

"A Saturday morning?" Alice asked. "The seventh is in two weeks and the fourteenth in three."

"That would allow more people to attend and give us time to get flyers around town," Hill said.

"Don't forget the internet," Jess said.

"Can we be ready by the fourteenth?" Alice asked.

"If Jess will drive us, we can deliver the flyers," Haley said.

"We can also bake some cookies and brownies," Maggie said.

"Lara and I can make tea and lemonade," Lisa said.

"Alice, can you and Haley create our flyer, send them to the printer, and post one on our website?" Hill asked.

"We can do that this morning," Alice said.

"Jess, will you, Maggie, and the twins create a menu and shopping list of items we'll need?"

148

"On it, boss," Jess answered with a smile.

"Now, what do we want to eat on the Fourth?" Hill asked.

"The Knights are cooking butts as a fundraiser," Alice said. "Why don't we get a few and have pulled pork sandwiches?"

"That works for me. Maggie, will you make more baked beans?" Hill asked.

"Yes, Doc. Just let me know how many pans."

"Two pans, I think. I want to invite Anita and the other girls to join us. We can have chips and macaroni salad with the sandwiches," Hill said.

"Blakely and I will make the macaroni salad," Jess offered.

Hill looked at the girls. "Desserts?"

"How about rice crispy treats and brownies?" Lara asked.

"We could pull out the ice cream maker from the pantry and have ice cream to go with the brownies," Alice suggested.

"Sounds like we need to make another shopping list. Jess, you're in charge. Alice, will you order two butts from the Knights?" Hill asked.

"How about a cake for the Grand Opening?" Alice asked.

"That's good. I recommend we stick to finger foods and snacks since we have no idea if anyone will show up. Maybe a few bags of chips and pretzels, too."

"We can pull the picnic tables from the campground for the morning," Jess said.

"Haley, will you give the tours like you did with Karen?"

"Sure," Haley answered.

"Okay, anything we haven't talked about?" Hill asked.

"Will you need help when the pool liner is delivered?" Jess asked.

"Yes, I'll need young muscle to move it into place," Hill said. "We are close with our dimensions, so it should fit snuggly. Once it arrives, Karen and I will add the drain fixture, and we can move it into place."

"We can try it out this afternoon," Maggie said.

"Yes, if everything goes as planned," Hill said. "One last thing. Tomorrow, we will have a unique visitor. Mrs. Thompson has donated a large sum of money to the project, and Alice will bring her out tomorrow to show off our progress. Haley, I want you to lead the tour."

"Yes, Doc." Haley swelled with pride.

"So, tomorrow morning, everything needs to shine," Jess said.

"We can wash down the runs as soon as we arrive in the morning. Maybe we can come early?" Maggie said.

"That works," Jess said.

"Okay, let's get at it," Hill said as she walked into the office to note Walter's chart. Jess reported Walter had a calm night, sleeping through most of the night after she gave him additional doses.

Hill had a second cup of coffee, and when the truck arrived with the pool liner, she walked to the dog park. Karen met them, and together with the kids, they placed the liner in the hole Tom had dug for them. "Almost perfect," Hill said. "Jess, will you bring a shovel and the reciprocating saw from the shed?"

†

An hour later, Hill nodded for the water to be turned on and squirted Jess with the hose. "Oops." Hill chuckled.

150

"It actually felt pretty good." Jess grinned as she backed away.

Hill smiled as the fountain started pumping water. "It will take an hour or so to fill the pond." She looked at Karen. "Thanks for all your help."

"Piece of cake," Karen said.

Hill looked at Haley. "Do you want to give Rex a bigger area to play and watch the pool for us?"

"Sure. Do you think it's too early for Rex to play with someone else?" Haley asked.

Hill looked at Jess. "Hank could hold his own with Rex. Good luck keeping him out of the water."

"That might be a good test for both of them. Grab a few balls and bring Rex in first." Hill looked at Jess. "Will you bring Hank in to introduce them?"

"Sure, Doc. I'll stay with them until we're sure they will interact well," Jess stated.

"I won't be far away either," Hill answered. "I'll try out one of the new benches."

†

Hill was relieved when Rex and Hank enjoyed playing together. She was surprised when Rex charged her with a ball in his mouth for her to throw. Hill took the ball. "Sit." She waited for him to sit before throwing the ball. Rex raced after it, returned, and dropped the ball at her feet. "Good boy," Hill said and tossed the ball again. Hill smiled as Haley approached.

"Are you stealing my job?" Haley teased.

"Heaven's no. I'm still impressed with the change in Rex since you two met."

"He's happy now," Haley said.

Rex returned and dropped the ball between them. "Sit and shake," Haley said.

Rex followed her instruction and then licked her face.

"Alright, kissy face," Haley said and tossed the ball.

Hank was frantically chasing a giant plastic ball in the pool. He was barking and having the time of his life.

"I think Hank is pretty happy, too."

Haley looked at Hill. "You've given us all a new home."

Hill could only smile at Haley. Her heart was lodged in her throat, and she was unable to answer. Alice rescued her, walking to the fence and calling them out.

"Lunch is ready. Let's eat.

†

After lunch, Maggie asked if she could speak with Hill. Hill led her into the office, and they sat together. "What's up?"

"I've been invited to a softball camp next month for a week at the university. "Could I work some weekends to make up for being away for a week?"

"Do you think you could drive a tractor?" Hill asked. "Alice will be busy with the campground and planning the events. I wouldn't want the grass to get too long. Could you stay for an extra two hours each day to mow and then on Sundays? I can drop you home, and Jess can take you home on Sunday."

"I'm sure I can learn." Maggie smiled.

"Let me clear it with Alice first. She's overprotective of her tractor," Hill teased. "Is there a fee for the camp?"

"I've already paid it from the money I've saved."

"I guess we need to go equipment shopping this weekend, then," Hill said.

Maggie shook her head. "I haven't done the work yet. I can manage with my current gear."

"I have no doubt you will earn every cent, but I want you to go to the camp with the best. It's an excellent opportunity for you to make a good impression."

"I promise I will work hard at the camp and here as much as possible," Maggie said.

"Does this look like a worried face?" Hill asked, pointing at her smile.

"Thanks, Doc," Maggie said and hugged her neck.

"Clear it with Anita so I can take you shopping on Sunday morning. You can cut the grass when we get done if she's good with the schedule."

"I will," Maggie said. "I'll get back to work now."

"Will you please find Alice and ask her to come see me?"

"Yes, ma'am," Maggie said, and rushed from the office.

†

Hill poured two fresh cups of coffee when Alice entered.

"Maggie seemed excited about something. What's up?"

"She's been invited to a summer softball camp for a week. She wanted to work extra hours to make up for the week she's gone."

"I hope you told her that wasn't necessary," Alice said.

"Quite the opposite. I want Maggie to earn every opportunity she gets."

"Okay, so what do we need to do?"

"I suggested Maggie learn to mow from you so you can concentrate on the campground and planning the events," Hill replied. "Will you allow her to mow two hours a day after the others leave, and on Sundays?"

"You pretty sure she can do it safely?"

"That young woman can do anything she puts her mind to," Hill answered.

"Let's do it then. I can teach Maggie to mow tomorrow after I take Mrs. Thompson home."

"Thank you. I will also take Maggie shopping Sunday morning for new equipment."

"Might as well send her off with the best," Alice said.

"Exactly," Hill said and leaned over to kiss Alice.

"I can teach her how to weed eat, too, so we can look tailored," Alice grinned.

"She can push mow or weed eat areas she can't get to with the tractor," Hill said.

"Works for me. We can do some trimming this afternoon," Alice said. Alice stood to leave. "I forgot to tell you, the kittens have opened their eyes. Lara was so excited to see them up and exploring after lunch."

"That's great news. How are the plans coming along?"

"I think we have the events planned out. We'll just need to do some shopping and baking, which should be fun."

†

With Maggie's help with trimming, the compounds and dog park looked great. Hill was excited for Mrs. Thompson to see their progress in such a short time. When Anita arrived to take them home, Hill walked out with them. "Y'all did a lot of work today. I think we're all set for our visit tomorrow. Thanks for all your hard work."

"See you tomorrow," Haley said as she closed the door and climbed into the passenger seat.

Alice walked up to them. "We're looking good, huh?"

"Lunch is on us tomorrow," Hill said. "I think we all deserve it."

"Pizza?" Maggie asked.

"Sure. We can always do pizza," Hill said. "Rest up, and we'll see you in the morning."

"We'll be here early to wash out the runs," Haley said.

"See you in the morning then," Alice said.

They watched the van leave and heard Karen approaching with a six-pack of beer. "I think you three have earned a cold beer after today. Where's Jess?"

"She's checking on Walter," Hill said.

"How's he doing? He's the one that got cut up in the barbed wire, right?"

"He's healing well. I think he'll make a full recovery," Hill said.

Karen passed out the beer and handed one to Jess when she arrived. "Are you all set for your VIP visit tomorrow?"

"I think we are as ready as possible. These old chicken houses have really changed in the last few months." Hill draped an arm around Alice.

"This place is incredible, and you all are angels for doing what you're doing," Karen said.

"It's been our dream for years," Alice said. "With all the help we've gotten, we are way ahead of where we thought we would be."

Karen smiled. "People believe in what you're doing for these animals. I wish more communities would follow your lead."

"Maybe one day." Hill sighed.

"Has Tina picked out a cat yet?" Jess asked.

"She's trying to decide between two," Karen said. "I have a feeling she might ask for both."

"They do better in pairs." Jess smiled.

"That's what Sue keeps telling her, too. Joy wants to know if you will join us for dinner. She grilled chicken breasts, and Sue tossed a salad while Tina fried rice. We have plenty, and I know y'all have worked hard today. Will you allow us to treat you for a change?"

"Beats the turkey pot pie I was planning to bake." Jess grinned.

"We'd love to. Thank you," Hill replied.

"Let's go then," Karen said. "So, who's the VIP you have visiting tomorrow?"

"Mrs. Thompson is a mature lady who has created a foundation to keep the farm going for years. She's been a client for years, and her dog Boscoe will come to live with us when she passes. We wouldn't be this far ahead of schedule if it weren't for her generous support."

"She sounds like an incredible woman," Karen said. "Another beer?"

"I'm driving, so I need to change to something safer," Hill said.

"Sweet tea?"

"Sweet tea is perfect."
"For me too," Alice and Jess added.

FINLAY (NICOLE MORRIS CLARK)

CHAPTER TEN

UMIKO (HEATHER ANDERSON)

"Do you want a quick breakfast?" Alice asked when Hill poured a cup of coffee.

"Maybe some toast," Hill replied.

"Nervous?" Alice asked.

"A bit."

"Mrs. Thompson will be very impressed with what we have accomplished. Relax and enjoy the visit."

"Will you explain about the girls when you pick her up? I don't want to mention anything that might make them uncomfortable."

Alice smiled. "I sure will. It might give her another charity to support after she meets the girls."

"I hadn't thought of that," Hill replied. "Will you make my toast to go?"

"Yes, I will. I'll pick up Mrs. Thompson and see you by nine. Is it okay to bring Boscoe?"

"Absolutely," Hill replied. She leaned in to kiss Alice and take the toast she offered. "I'll see you soon."

†

The girls were already hard at work when Hill arrived. She sought out Jess.

"They've been here sprucing up since seven. I barely had time to brush my teeth," Jess teased. "Gabby removed her cast last night. Do you think she needs another?"

"Probably not if she removed it on her own. How is she moving?"

"Like nothing ever happened," Jess said.

"Let's give her an exam after Mrs. Thompson leaves, but I think she's telling us she's all healed."

"That's what I thought, too. Walter is moving around well this morning. His eating has picked up, too."

"We still have a few days before we can start removing sutures. Eating better is a good sign that Walter's perking up. Showing any signs of pain?"

"None that I can pick up on," Jess said.

"Good. Have you had coffee yet?"

"Nope, but I did start the pot," Jess said.

"Great. Let's get a cup and check on the girls," Hill suggested.

†

Haley had her hair pulled back in a ponytail, and her outfit was pressed and starched. "Wow, you look very professional, Miss Tour Guide," Hill said.

"We all picked out our best and got everything ironed last night. We know how important today is for you."

"Thanks, Haley." Hill smiled. "Will you share Rex's story with Mrs. Thompson?"

Haley nodded. "If you'd like me to."

"He's definitely a success story, mostly because of you," Hill told her. "He's also like the poster child for the farm. He would have surely been euthanized if he had been left at the shelter because of his aggression. If not for you, we wouldn't know the sweet, loving dog we see today."

Haley blushed. "He is a sweet boy."

†

When Alice arrived with Mrs. Thompson, Hill took a deep breath. She didn't know why she felt it necessary to impress the older woman, but she was nervous about the visit. She and the girls were as ready as possible for their visitors. Mrs. Thompson and Boscoe climbed out of Alice's car, wearing a big smile.

"Good morning. This place looks much different than it did six months ago," Mrs. Thompson said.

"Thanks, and welcome to Fairytail Farm. Hey, Boscoe," Hill said, giving the dog a scratch under his chin. Hill introduced Jess and the girls. "Haley will give you a tour of the facilities, but I'll be with you if you have any questions."

"Thank you, Haley," Mrs. Thompson said. "Maggie, would you mind keeping Boscoe company? I hear you have the best throwing arm of the group."

"Sure. We can play in the new dog park while you tour. Come on, Boscoe," Maggie said, taking Boscoe in her arms.

"Where do we start?" Mrs. Thompson asked Haley.

"Let's start in the cat compound," Haley said.

"Kittens?" Mrs. Thompson said that when she saw the four black bundles of fur, the twins were playing with them.

"We had a very pregnant mama dropped off here a couple of weeks ago," Haley said. "The twins, Lara and Lisa, are our cat specialists," Haley bragged. "They provide the care and love for all the feline residents."

"They are adorable. The kittens, too," Mrs. Thompson said.

"I love the idea of the campground. Has that proven successful?"

"It has, and I hope to add another campground by the lake for long-term campers. We've had several requests for long-term rental spots," Hill said.

"We've also adopted out several animals to campers who visit," Haley said.

"That's excellent news. I know you house many animals that haven't been looked at for adoption at the shelter."

"Many of our campers so far have been older women looking for older animals that can travel well with them," Hill added. "It's been positive so far."

"Are you getting most of your animals from the shelter?"

"Yes. Several others have been brought to us with injuries or medical issues that require treatment. So far, so good."

"I know they will get excellent care from you. Jess is a vet student, right?"

"Yes, she's our live-in staff and helps me with the medical care to get hands-on experience."

"That sounds like a win-win situation," Mrs. Thompson said.

Hill pointed out Jess' apartment. "We plan to add another apartment next year for Haley. She graduates next year, and we want to keep her local. As you will see in a few minutes, she's magical with animals."

"What do you plan on studying?" Mrs. Thompson asked.

"Psychology, I think," Haley said. "I want to help kids and animals that have suffered trauma."

"Very admirable," Mrs. Thompson said.

"Thanks. The clinic for exams and a small sterile surgical area," Haley said as she opened a door.

"This is all very impressive, Hill. I can't believe how you have transformed this old chicken farm."

"It's taken a lot of hard work, but Jess and the girls have been critical for getting us this far. We are starting to get some support from the community, too. The dog park was created with mostly donated materials and labor."

As they moved onto the dog compound, Haley introduced her to Walter. "A State Law Enforcement Officer found him tangled up in barbed wire. The shelter staff did an excellent job of stitching him up, and he has been recuperating well with us."

"He looks like a sweet boy," Mrs. Thompson said.

"He is, and we hope to move him out of isolation soon once we are confident he is completely healed."

Hill smiled at Haley. She was proud of the tour and the information she provided Mrs. Thompson.

Hank and the other dogs danced excitedly as they passed each run. "I want to take them all home, but I know they have a great home here," Mrs. Thompson said. When they reached the final run, she stopped and looked at Rex. "Who is this handsome boy?"

"This is Rex." Haley smiled at Mrs. Thompson. "Rex has a unique story. We can go to the office for coffee if you'd like, and I'll tell you his story."

"That sounds intriguing," Mrs. Thompson said. "Lead the way."

Hill poured them coffee as Haley and Mrs. Thompson sat at the small table in the office.

"Rex was the first animal brought to the farm. As you can see, he is beautiful and in excellent health, but he required sedation and a muzzle to be brought here from the shelter." Haley paused to sip her coffee. "Rex was the first animal I met when I began volunteering here at the farm, and I immediately felt a connection to him. He was extremely angry and aggressive toward other animals and humans, to the point the shelter almost euthanized him."

"Oh, my goodness. So what happened?"

"My family and I were in a fatal car accident, and I was the only survivor. I was hospitalized for months as my injuries healed, but I had no family, so I was given a home with Maggie and the other girls. My accident unlocked a particular talent within me, and I found I could communicate with Rex and others. My trauma caused my empathic ability, and I want to use it to help others."

"I'm sorry you lost your family," Mrs. Thompson said.

"Thank you. I've found a new home here," Haley answered. "With Doc Hill's help, we discovered the root of Rex's anger. His person was killed in an accident, and he thought she had abandoned him. Rex was so aggressive with her family that they dropped him at the shelter without any information. Doc was able to help me put the pieces together, and we located the family and learned his person was killed, and Rex never understood why she never came for him." Haley took a breath. "Doc Hill found a picture of them together, and Rex responded to the photo. We took him to the cemetery where she was buried, and the same image is on her headstone." Haley sighed. "It may sound crazy, but we talked to Rex about what happened with his person, and he understood she didn't abandon him. He lay on her grave for a while, then stood and licked her picture before turning toward us. From that moment on, Rex has been a different dog. He understands we love him and want to be his new family. I plan to adopt him once I finish college. Until then, we will live here with Doc Hill."

Mrs. Thompson fished a tissue from her purse. "That is such a heartwarming story. Rex is lucky to have the two of you in his life."

"He's a good boy, and I feel fortunate to have met him. We have so much in common. His love and trust have helped me, too." Haley wiped at a tear on her cheek.

Mrs. Thompson looked up at Hill. "Did you ever dream anything like this would happen here?"

Hill shook her head. "Not even in my wildest dreams. The experience is beyond anything I could have imagined on so many levels."

"I'm thankful that you have allowed me to be a part of this, but I have one more request," Mrs. Thompson said. "I know you will provide a living arrangement for Haley when she graduates, but please allow me the opportunity to pay for her education. I can start a scholarship that will provide Haley, Maggie, and the twins or other worthy students to attend college. You would administer the scholarship selections, and you know I have the means to do this, and I would love to help."

Haley's tears were flowing, and Mrs. Thompson offered her a tissue.

"All I need is a yes to make it happen," Mrs. Thompson said. She looked at Haley, who was unable to speak.

She nodded her head and squeaked out a "yes."

She turned to Hill. "What say you?"

"I would love that," Hill said.

"I'll make it happen then," Mrs. Thompson said. "Do you have other needs here?"

"Nothing that I can think of," Hill answered. "I hope you will join us for the grand opening and our Fourth of July cookout."

"Send me an invite," Mrs. Thompson said. "I'll get back to you next week. I'm sure there will be papers to sign at the University. Will Alice be a co-administrator?"

"I'm sure she would," Hill said.

"I'll ask her when she takes me home," Mrs. Thompson said. She turned to Haley. "Thank you for a great tour and everything you do here. When the time comes, I hope Boscoe will have someone who loves him like you love Rex."

"I can guarantee he will," Haley said. "When the time comes, but I hope it will be years from now."

Mrs. Thompson sighed. "I hope so, too. Can you spare Alice to take me home?"

"You bet," Hill said.

Mrs. Thompson stopped in front of Rex and reached through the gate. "You are one fortunate dog."

Rex licked her fingers and looked at her with warm brown eyes.

"I will see you again soon."

Alice met them at the front of the compound, and they walked out to the dog park where Boscoe and Maggie were playing. They could hear Maggie giggling as Boscoe licked her face.

"Boscoe, are you ready to go home?" Mrs. Thompson called out to him.

He looked at her and back to Maggie. "You can come back out to play soon," Mrs. Thompson said. Boscoe rushed over to her. "Thanks for watching over my boy, Maggie."

"We had fun," Maggie said as she patted Boscoe's head. "You can come play anytime."

Hill walked them to Alice's car. "Thank you for everything," she said and hugged Mrs. Thompson.

"Thank you for bringing these dreams to life. I'll talk to you soon."

†

Hill poured a cup of coffee and sank into her office chair. Haley knocked on her door and entered.

"Come on in," Hill said. "I'm very proud of how you did today. You were extremely informative and professional."

"Thank you. I learned by listening to you," Haley said. "Can you believe Mrs. Thompson's offer?"

"Yes, she's very generous and loves helping where she can. She saw the same thing in you today, which I have witnessed for weeks," Hill said. "You have such a bright future ahead."

"I won't let you down," Haley said.

"Don't worry about me. Don't let yourself down," Hill said.

"I'll do my best," Haley said.

"The pizza should be here soon. Will you find Jess and ask her to bring Gabby to the clinic?"

"Sure." Haley walked over to Hill and hugged her. "Thank you."

"You're welcome," Hill said. "Now scoot."

†

167

Jess brought Gabby in for an exam. "I think she's ready for some company. Are you ready for Buster?"

"I will be by tonight," Jess said. "Is it safe to let Gabby sleep with me now? Buster is not used to staying in a carrier, and I have plenty of room."

"I can't believe you haven't already snuck Gabby into your bed," Hill teased.

"I did exactly as you instructed," Jess replied.

"She's good to go. If you're ready for bed hogs, go for it," Hill said. "Let me know when the pizza gets here."

"I will. Thanks, Doc."

Alice walked in as Jess left. "Is Gabby all healed?"

"Yeah, she took her cast off this morning."

Alice handed Hill some folded money. "What's this?"

"Money for Maggie's softball gear," Alice said. "Mrs. Thompson said to let her know if that wasn't enough."

Hill flipped through the bills. "Wow, that should set her up nicely."

"Are you still going shopping on Sunday?"

"That was the plan," Hill said.

"You can go today if you want. Do you plan to let Maggie work extra since it's not coming out of your pocket?"

"That's up to her. I can pay her for the extra work, so she can have spending money. I like the idea of her establishing a bank account. That will be a good experience for her."

"Yes, it will. Do you want me to send Maggie in?"

"I'll talk to her after we eat. Pizza should be here by now."

Jess came to the door. "Lunch is here."

"Good. My toast is long gone." Hill stood and followed them from the office.

†

Hill looked at Jess. "Can you and the ladies handle things around here while Maggie and I go to town?"

"Sure, Doc. I think it's time we try out the new dog park," Jess said.

"Alright. Have fun and keep everyone safe," Hill replied. "If we're not back by four, tell Anita I'll bring Maggie home." She looked at Maggie. "Ready to do some shopping?"

"What?" Maggie said. "I thought we were doing that Sunday."

"Nope. Can't wait," Hill said. "Unless you really want to."

"Heck no. Let's go," Maggie replied.

On the way to town, Hill handed the envelope with cash that Mrs. Thompson had left with Alice. "Mrs. Thompson wanted to help you get equipped for camp. I'll pay the difference, and you can work that off."

When she opened the envelope, she found six one-hundred-dollar bills. Maggie's eyes were filled with tears. "I've never seen this much money."

"Mrs. Thompson was impressed with you today and wanted to help. It won't be enough to cover everything, but I'll kick in the rest."

"I can make this work," Maggie said.

Hill shook her head. "I want you to go with the best regardless of the price tags. Besides, good equipment will last a long time if you care for it."

Maggie nodded and turned to look out the window to hide the tears that slid down her cheek.

†

Determining who had the most fun at the sporting goods store was hard. Hill watched as Maggie tested out nearly every bat on the rack but kept returning to an Easton Firefly. "You keep coming back to that one. Does it feel the best to you?"

"Yes, but it will eat up half of my money," Maggie said.

"What did I say about price tags?"

"I know," Maggie replied.

"Gloves next?"

"That's an easy choice," Maggie replied. "I've had my eyes on a Mizuno forever."

"Show me," Hill requested.

Hill watched Maggie search through a selection of gloves until she found the one she wanted. "How's it feel?"

"Perfect. Now, batting gloves and cleats? Do you need some socks, too?"

Maggie nodded. She selected two batting gloves and pushed the cart to the shoe department. She picked out a six-pack of socks, and Hill took another and placed them in the cart. Hill took a seat while Maggie browsed the cleat selection. The smile on her face was priceless. Maggie examined each shoe and was beaming when she brought three boxes over to the bench.

"So Nike is the brand." Hill chuckled. "Try them all on."

Maggie was trying on the third pair when a tall woman approached. "Hill McCall, where have you been?"

Hill looked up to see Jerry Simpson approach. "Hey, Jerry. Been busy with a new project."

"The farm?" Jerry asked.

"Yes, how did you know?" Hill asked.

"Mrs. Thompson came in for some toys for Boscoe the other day and told me all about it. The farm sounds like a great project." Jerry looked at the cart and then at Maggie and cocked her head.

"I'm sorry, this is Maggie. She is one of our volunteers and was invited to the university's softball camp this summer. Maggie, this is Jerry Simpson. She was a heck of a ball player back in the day."

"Many years ago. You know when the dinosaurs roamed," Jerry said. "You must be pretty good to get an invite. What position?"

"Third base." Maggie smiled.

"She has quite the arm on her," Hill said. "The dogs are keeping her arm in shape." She laughed.

Jerry looked at the cart. "You've made some great choices, but don't leave yet. I'll be right back."

Hill looked at Maggie and shrugged. "Have you found a pair that feels good?"

Maggie nodded. "The blue with the orange swoosh."

"Nice looking shoes," Hill said. "Is there anything else we need to look for?"

"I think this will do," Maggie said.

"Hold that thought." Hill nodded as Jerry returned.

"The Easton bats come with a bat bag. I've also added some glove oil, a few Easton water bottles, and visors. Is there anything we've missed?" Jerry smiled.

"I've never had so much gear." Maggie grinned. "Thank you."

"Let me know how the camp goes, and make sure I get a copy of your game schedule," Jerry said. "If you're ready, I can get you checked out."

"I hope you'll join us for our Grand Opening soon," Hill said as they walked to checkout.

"I'd love to. Just let me know when," Jerry said.

"I'll drop by with an invite soon," Hill answered.

Maggie removed the items from the cart, including the bag.

"The bag and its contents are free of charge."

Maggie smiled and nodded before placing all the items on the counter and reaching for her envelope.

Hill could see her holding her breath as each item was rung up. She watched as Jerry hit the subtotal button and then reduced the total by twenty percent, bringing the total to six fifty and change. She took a hundred-dollar bill from her wallet and handed it to Maggie.

"Thanks, Doc," she said, and handed the bills to Jerry. "Thank you for the extra discount too, ma'am."

"Dang, I thought I was pretty slick sliding that in there," Jerry said. "Consider it an investment for future entertainment. I'm sure I'm going to enjoy watching you play."

Hill smiled. "Sharp kid. She doesn't miss much. Thanks, Jerry."

"My pleasure. I'll see you soon," Jerry said. "Good luck at camp if I don't see you before."

"I'll see you at the Grand Opening." Maggie surprised Hill by giving Jerry a hug.

As they left the store, Hill checked her watch. "I'll drop you at home since it's after four."

"Thanks, Doc," Maggie said as she loaded the bags into the truck.

†

172

Maggie gave Hill directions to the home. "Would you like to come in?"

"I think you need some help carrying everything inside. Would you mind giving me a tour?"

"Sure thing."

Hill and Maggie carried the bags into the home. Anita greeted them with a smile. Hill returned her smile. "Sorry it took so long. We were having fun."

"I can tell." Anita grinned. "Maggie, will you show Doc Hill around?"

"Yes, ma'am."

They dropped Maggie's bags into the bedroom she shared with Haley and then introduced her to the other girls in the home. Lisa and Lara heard Hill's voice and rushed inside to see her. "Can you stay for dinner, Doc?" Lisa asked.

"Not tonight, but thank you. May I get a rain check?"

"Tomorrow night, bring Ms. Alice and Jess too?" Lara asked. "Lisa and I are making spaghetti for dinner."

"I'll check with Alice and Jess to see, if you're sure it's alright," Hill said.

"They've been dying to ask you to dinner," Anita said. "We'd love to have you. Dinner is at six."

"Is there anything we can bring?" Hill asked.

"Just your appetites," Anita said.

"Deal," Hill said with a wink to the twins. "I'll see y'all in the morning."

Maggie walked Hill to the truck. "Thanks for everything, Doc." She stepped in and hugged Hill.

"You're very welcome. Alice could help you write a 'thank you' note to Mrs. Thompson."

Maggie nodded. "I'll do the mowing or whatever you need."

"Yes, but I still want you to open a bank account. It will be a good experience for you and allow you to spend money on camp and whatever else you need."

Maggie nodded and stepped back. "See you in the morning."

†

Hill walked into the office to find Alice and Jess sipping coffee. "We have a dinner invitation tomorrow night, so I hope neither of you has plans. The twins are cooking spaghetti for us."

"That sounds great," Jess said.

Karen knocked on the door. "We've got extra burgers and fries if you ladies will join us."

Hill looked at Alice, who nodded.

"I'm all over a burger right now," Jess said.

Goldi (Chris and McGee)

CHAPTER ELEVEN

RAYE THE BAG LADY (JM DRAGON)

Maggie rushed to Hill the following day when they arrived. "I'm going to start mowing this afternoon if that's okay. Will you give me a ride home when you come for dinner?"

Hill nodded. "I don't see a problem with that."

Maggie shuffled her feet for a second. "Um, can Ms. Alice help me with a 'thank you' note for Jerry? I was pretty surprised when I opened the bag, and there were other items inside than what she told us."

"I'm not surprised. What else?"

"Sticks of eye black, compression sleeves for my arms, and two pairs of sliding shorts."

"Damn, I wish we had those shorts back in my day. I had more than my fair share of raspberries until I finally caught on to the bump slide technique. There was no way I was going in head first, either." Hill cocked her head. "Speaking of heads. Do we need to get a helmet for you?"

"No, the school provides those, and I will get a customized one at the camp this summer. That alone was worth the camp fee."

"True. Get to work, and maybe you can start mowing earlier," Hill told a beaming Maggie.

"Could I make one last request? I noticed the firepit wood is getting low. If you could cut more downed trees into sections, I can load, quarter, and store them for you Sunday."

"I'll see what I can do," Hill replied.

†

Hill walked into the office to pour a fresh cup of coffee. Alice was working on her laptop. "Can you spare a few minutes this morning? Maggie wants your help to send Jerry a 'thank you' note for some extra gear she gave her."

"Yeah. That's no problem. I'll break when Maggie comes in."

"She also said if I cut more downed trees into sections, she would haul, split, and stack them on Sunday. She plans to mow today, so I told her she could start earlier if her duties were finished. What are you working on?"

Alice turned in her chair. "I'm making a list of people and businesses we need to send an invite to for the Grand Opening. I was thinking maybe the twins could help me deliver them this week. They came out nice." Alice opened a box of invitations and showed one to Hill.

"Those are nice. I think the twins would love that assignment."

"I'll ask them at lunch. What are your plans for the day?"

Hill shrugged. "Everyone is healthy, and no treatments are due, so I may cut some trees."

"With a spotter?"

"I'll take Maggie if Jess can spare her. That way, she'll know where the trees are on Sunday. I'll get the saw and tools ready, so send her to find me when you're done with her."

Hill leaned over to kiss Alice. "Love you. See you at lunch."

"Be careful."

"Always." Hill grinned and walked to the campground to check the firewood. The woodshed was still full, but the outdoor stack was running low.

"What's up, Doc?" Karen asked.

"Oh, hey. Maggie said we were running low on firewood, so I checked our stash. I will cut some downed trees for Maggie to haul on Sunday."

"Want some help? The others have gone to town for a grocery run."

"I never pass up help. Mostly just need a spotter to make sure I'm safe."

"We could haul some today if you want."

Hill shook her head. "Thanks, but this was Maggie's idea, so I will let her handle that part. We can drop a section by the trail to mark the areas where we've cut."

"That should be easy enough." Karen smiled. "Meet you out back in five?"

"Perfect," Hill answered.

Hill updated Alice on the change of plan so Maggie could mow instead of cutting wood with her. She removed bottled water from the fridge and walked to the tool shed. She was loading the saw and supplies when Karen arrived.

"All set?"

"I do believe we are."

†

Hill waved at Haley as she and Karen walked past the runs. "Do you need help?"

"Thanks, but we're just cutting up some downed trees. Keep working with Rex," Hill called back.

Haley and Jess had created a short obstacle course to use with Rex and potentially some other dogs. She and Rex were practicing jumping through mounted hoops of varying heights.

"They make an amazing pair, don't they?" Karen smiled.
   "A match made in heaven," Hill said. "They came together in a critical time in both their lives."

BARNEY (IRIS FAULKNER)

CHAPTER TWELVE

LUCIPURR (KELLY DURAN)

The days flew by as everyone worked on their assignments for the Grand Opening. Karen and her family had moved on, and several new campers had come and gone. Only two were left on the event day, leaving room for parking for their guests. Alice and the twins had done a remarkable job delivering invitations, and Hill was overwhelmed with the turnout. Haley and the twins gave tours to the guests, and several envelopes with donations for the farm were handed to her or Alice.

When Jerry arrived, she waved Maggie over to help her with a few boxes. "What's this?" Hill asked.

"Some toys and other items have been taking up space in my stockroom," Jerry replied. "I thought you might be able to use them."

"I'm sure we can find a use for them." Hill smiled. She turned to Maggie. "Will you store the boxes in the office and give Jerry a tour if she has time?"

"I'd love one." Jerry smiled.

†

Hill's gaze traveled to the dog park. Mrs. Thompson and Jess were seated on one of the benches, watching Boscoe play with several small dogs. They seem to be having a serious conversation. *No telling what that woman is cooking up now.*

"Can you believe the turnout we've had?" Alice asked as she brought Hill a cup of coffee.

"It's been great. Dan brought his girls, and he asked about the kittens. He wants to surprise them with kittens when they are ready to be weaned."

"They will be going to a great home then," Alice said. "Is there a fenced yard at the group home?"

"Yes, they've got a nice-sized backyard. Why?"

Alice nodded toward the dog park. "Anita and some other girls have been playing with JR for quite some time. I wonder if they can have a pet?"

"Why don't you find a way to ask Anita today? We can provide him with medical care. I also wanted to talk with you about something else regarding the home, but it can wait until later."

"I will." Alice smiled. "They would be good for JR and vice versa."

"It will also help them learn to be responsible pet owners," Hill added.

"Maybe we could propose visits to the local schools to talk with kids about that."

Hill chuckled. "That would be a great activity for you."

†

When the crowd started thinning out, Alice and the girls began cleaning up from the event as Hill walked Mrs. Thompson and Boscoe to her car. "Thank you for joining us today. This wouldn't be possible without your generosity."

"Maybe not as quickly, but you would make this dream come true without my help. The scholarship foundation is funded and ready to begin taking applications. I hope the first will be Haley's."

"She and Alice have already begun working on her application and financial aid programs."

"There's one more thing I'd like to do," Mrs. Thompson said. "I know you plan to add a second apartment for Haley. I'd like to cover the cost of that." She handed Hill a check for fifty thousand. "If that's not enough to build and furnish the apartment, please let me know."

Hill found it difficult to hold back her tears. She wiped at her eyes. "Thank you again."

"I can't put in the work you all do, so at least allow me to financially support any project you develop." Mrs. Thompson hugged Hill. "You are doing great work here on so many levels."

"The farm has grown beyond my dreams," Hill admitted. "The support from the community today is heartwarming."

"You have the drive and the means to do something most can only dream of. I won't live to see it, but maybe one day, there won't be a need for those gut-wrenching commercials about abused and abandoned animals on television."

"That would be a dream come true." Hill held Boscoe while Mrs. Thompson climbed into her car.

She reached for Boscoe and placed him on the seat tether. "Let's go home, Boscoe. I feel a nap coming on."

"Drive safe. You and Boscoe can visit any time, so don't be a stranger."

"We'll be back." Mrs. Thompson grinned.

†

Blakely was helping Jess and the girls feed everyone after the guests left. Alice had invited Anita into the office to discuss pet adoption. Anita had assured Alice she would check the regulations and get back to her. She had enjoyed playing with JR and thought he would be the perfect choice for her high-energy girls.

"Would you mind if Haley stays a bit longer? I'll drop her home in an hour or so," Hill asked Anita.

"Sure, that's fine." Anita rounded up the rest of the girls to drive home.

Hill watched them drive away and turned to find the four of them watching her. "Team meeting," she called out and pointed to one of the picnic tables.

"What's up, Doc?" Jess grinned.

"Our benefactor, Mrs. Thompson, has come through again. She wants to pay for the build-out and furnishing of the second apartment Haley will use while in school."

"That's cool," Jess said. "So, what do you need us to do?"

"I would like the three of you to study your apartment. Discuss what works and what would be an upgrade in the new apartment."

"We could share a kitchen," Jess suggested.

Hill shook her head. "You and Haley would be fine sharing, but we have to look beyond the two of you. Unless you plan to live here forever," Hill teased.

"I could," Jess said, "but maybe not in an apartment. I know it's down the road a bit, but would you consider allowing me to build a permanent home here?"

"I think that could be arranged." Hill smiled, forcing back tears. "So, today, I want you to look at the layout. Later, you can develop a furnishing list. Once we agree, I'll call Tom and get on his schedule next spring for a build." She smiled at them. "One more thing. Thanks for making today perfect. We received several other donations that will help keep us supplied."

"Maggie said one of the boxes Jerry brought had sweaters," Jess reported. "Do we need to look at getting more for this winter?"

"Inventory what she sent. It wouldn't be a bad idea for the smaller dogs. The heating system should keep things comfortable inside, but I know they will want to go outside daily."

Alice smiled. "I have another proposal we need to discuss. Today, one of our guests works in the vocational department of the women's prison. They have a workshop, and she asked me about them making collars and leashes for the program."

"We could use some of the donations from today to fund that," Hill said. "Will you follow up with her next week to see how much it would cost to fund the project?"

"I sure will." Alice smiled.

"Last item. Is anyone besides me starving?" Hill asked.

"My stomach has been growling for an hour," Jess answered.

"Hot subs, chips, and brownies good with everyone?"

"Sounds perfect," Alice replied. "Want me to make a run?"

"I thought we might go together. Will you make a list of orders while I hit the restroom?" Hill asked.

†

Hill left with Haley to take her home. Alice had already left, leaving Jess and Blakely at the farm.

"Are you in a rush to go home?" Jess asked.

"Not at all," Blakely replied.

They returned to the apartment, and Jess walked to the kitchen. "Beer?"

"Sounds great."

Jess removed the caps from two bottles and carried them into the living room, handing one to Blakely as she sat next to her. "Today turned out great. Thanks for being here."

"I had fun," Blakely said. "This place is amazing. Do you really think you'd like to live here permanently?"

"Right now, yes. I know that could change, but I want to take over for Doc Hill one day, and there is plenty of room to have a private residence on site."

"That would make a lot of sense to live here. Would you still need to work in town at a clinic?"

"Part-time, at least, at first," Jess said. "What about you? What plans do you have after you graduate?"

"I've already got offers from several clinics. I'm not positive about whether I want to specialize or not."

"That's great, to have options." Jess took a sip of her beer. "I'm happy you will stay here and not get lured into a big city."

Blakely smiled. "I'm not a big city girl. Besides, you will be here."

Jess could see the passion in Blakely's eyes, and her heart raced with excitement. *Should this be our first night together?* She knew she had fallen in love with Blakely, and how she was looking at her right now took Jess' breath from her lungs. Jess struggled to speak but finally asked, "Will you stay the night?" Jess felt the heat rising up her neck to her cheeks as she searched Blakely's face, waiting for her answer.

Blakely smiled. "I thought you'd never ask."

†

After sharing several heated kisses, Jess smiled at Blakely. "Why don't we move to the bedroom?" She stood and offered Blakely her hand.

Blakely nodded shyly and allowed Jess to lead her to the bedroom, their cold beers a distant memory. Jess dropped her hand and lit a candle beside the bed before turning to Blakely.

"This is new for me," she admitted.

Blakely stepped into her arms. "Just relax and let our desire take over."

Jess felt her body shiver when Blakely's hands pulled the shirt over her head, but she was far from cold. Her body was on fire at the touch of Blakely's hands on her skin. She removed her own shirt and placed Jess' hands on the fastener of her bra. Jess' fingers trembled as they brushed against bare skin as she released the clasp, and the bra fell open. Blakely dropped it to the floor and reached for Jess' hands to cover her breasts. Jess felt her knees weaken as her hands gently cupped the warm, smooth flesh. Blakely's nipples grew hard from her touch, grazing her palm as Blakely watched her reaction.

Blakely broke the connection long enough to remove Jess' sports bra; they were suddenly skin to skin as she kissed her deeply. Jess moaned deeply into Blakely's mouth as their bodies pressed together, and Jess' hands roamed across Blakely's bare back.

"Your skin is so warm and soft."

"I've been waiting for weeks to feel your hands on me," Blakely whispered, her lips brushing Jess' cheek.

"I'm sorry for making you wait," Jess said.

"I'm not. The wait will make tonight more special. You are definitely worth the wait." Blakely grinned up at Jess. Her hands released the belt and fastener on Jess' jeans. Jess kicked out of her shoes and allowed Blakely to slide her pants down her body. When Jess was left with nothing but her boi short underwear, she helped Blakely remove her pants and led her to the bed.

Blakely stretched out on the bed and reached for Jess to join her. She turned onto her side and let her eyes and hands roam across Jess' body.

Jess could feel her underwear dampen with desire as Blakely's fingers circled her nipples, causing them to grow painfully erect. She gasped when Blakely's mouth covered her breast, her warm tongue teasing her nipple. "Damn, that feels good," she groaned.

"It will feel even better soon," Blakely promised, her breath warm against Jess' skin, as her right hand drifted down between Jess' legs and cupped her mound, giving it a gentle squeeze.

Jess felt on the verge of erupting as her body experienced so many new sensations. She was eager to experience her first orgasm with Blakely and then to reciprocate the attention she was enjoying with her lover.

When Blakely moved on top of Jess, she looked into her eyes. "Am I rushing you?"

Jess shook her head. "No. Everything feels terrific."

Blakely nodded and lowered her hips onto Jess. Their bodies fit well together, and she pressed them together as they shared kisses, and her fingers teased Jess' body. Blakely was breathing hard when they broke a heated kiss. "I want to touch and taste you," she whispered with a husky voice filled with desire.

Jess looked into her eyes. "I trust you." She could hear the tremble in her voice from excitement.

Blakely nodded and rolled onto her side to guide Jess' underwear down her body. The fingers of her right hand trailed down Jess' body and tenderly teased the warmth of her opening. Jess gasped again with the rush of pleasure Blakely's actions were eliciting.

Jess felt Blakely's mouth cover her breast with tender kisses as she entered her body with a finger. Jess bit her lip to keep from crying out how good it felt in fear of scaring Blakely. Instead, she placed a hand on the back of Blakely's head. "This all feels so good."

Blakely had begun slowly stroking her finger inside Jess. "Can you handle another finger?"

"I think so." Jess gasped when a second finger entered her.

Blakely's head popped up, and her hand froze. "Too much?"

"No. Not at all. It feels great."

†

Blakely froze when Jess gasped after she inserted a second finger. The last thing she wanted to do was hurt Jess. Blakely was relieved when Jess confirmed it felt tremendous and resumed gently thrusting her fingers. Her fingers glided smoothly in the welcoming wetness, and she could feel Jess' muscles contract around her fingers. She knew that Jess had never been involved sexually with anyone before and vowed to make the experience memorable for her. Her mouth moved slowly down Jess' midsection as Jess' hips began rising to meet her fingers' strokes. She could feel the increase in her breathing through the rise and fall of her chest as her hand stroked softly across her skin. Jess' eyes were clamped shut until Blakely's hot breath brushed across her swollen clit. They shot open with a look of surprise and glowing with excitement. When Blakely covered the sensitive flesh with her mouth, Jess exploded with an intense orgasm, crying out in pleasure. Blakely slowly removed her fingers and held Jess as her body returned to normal.

†

"That was freaking incredible," Jess told a smiling Blakely.

"Yes, it was, and I'm happy you enjoyed it, but I'm not done with you yet." Blakely grinned and moved down between Jess' legs. "Now I get to really taste you." Blakely's tongue caressed the soft skin between Jess' thighs, planting tender kisses while watching her lover's face. When her fingertips slowly opened the folds of Jess' entrance, Blakely felt Jess shudder and her eyes closed. "Open your eyes so I can watch you come," Blakely whispered.

†

Jess had never experienced anything that felt this wonderful. When Blakely asked her to open her eyes, they locked into Blakely's, and she could see her passion mirrored in the eyes that sparkled back at her. Even though Jess knew what Blakely was about to do, she wasn't prepared for the sensation of Blakely's tongue exploring inside her entrance.

She felt her hands grip the bedspread and her teeth biting her lip in her effort to hold her body's response for just a little longer. Blakely's touch was fantastic, but her mouth and tongue felt incredible. Jess lasted what felt like an eternity, but it was mere minutes before her struggle was lost, and her hips bucked as the intense orgasm rushed through her body. "Oh, Blakely," she said before her world went dark.

†

Blakely fought panic when Jess fainted. She had never had this experience with any of her few lovers. Blakely scrambled up the bed and held Jess in her arms. "Jess," she whispered as her hand caressed Jess' face. "Wake up, sweety." She sighed with relief as Jess' eyes opened wide in surprise.

"What, what happened?" she cried out.

"Um, you fainted, sweety." Blakely smiled.

She saw the embarrassment on Jess' face. "It's okay. I know the first time can be pretty intense."

Jess wiped her hand across her face. Blakely watched as a tear stained Jess' cheek. The panic returned, and her heart lurched. "Are you okay?"

"I am more than okay," Jess replied. Before she could continue, Gabby jumped on the bed, purring loudly. Jess' hand reached out to stroke her soft fur. "I would purr too if I could," she said, smiling at Blakely.

Blakely relaxed and stretched out beside Jess, who was petting Gabby lying across her stomach. "Mama's just fine, little girl," she said with a chuckle.

They comforted Gabby for a few minutes, and then Jess stood, carried Gabby from her bed, and closed the bedroom door.

"What was that all about?" Blakely asked.

"We don't need an audience while making love, and I'm hoping we are not through for the night. I want to make you feel the way you made me feel."

"I'm more than happy to oblige." Blakely smiled and reached for Jess.

†

Jess suddenly remembered this was a new experience for her, and her apprehension must have been evident to Blakely. Blakely smiled at her. "This is your first time, so relax and listen to what my body wants. I will also give you some nudges. Don't rush and enjoy yourself."

Jess took a deep breath to relax and leaned into Blakely for a kiss. Blakely had confidence in her, and Jess learned quickly from how Blakely's body reacted to her actions. She was in awe the first time Blakely had an orgasm with her, and that relieved the pressure to perform. They spent several hours exploring each other and fell asleep, their bodies entwined.

Ali Spooner

ROKU (CHRIS VAN GRUNDY)

CHAPTER THIRTEEN

SADIE (DONNA ASHE)

Alice expected new campers to arrive in the morning, and Maggie would be out to mow grass, so Hill opened the door to the truck for Alice. "This is promising to be a beautiful day. Thanks for the great breakfast."

"You know I love cooking for you on the weekends," Alice said with a smile as she climbed into the truck.

Hill was happy to see community members active on such a fine morning. Several were out mowing their yards or trimming bushes. A young teenage boy that Alice recognized from school was washing his truck. He looked up and waved as they passed.

Hill activated the remote to open the gate at the farm and chuckled as they approached and saw that Blakely's car was parked beside Jess'. "I guess our young assistant had a sleepover last night."

"For goodness sake, don't tease her too badly today," Alice warned.

Hill feigned shock. "Would I do that?"

"You absolutely would, so take it easy on Jess today. This is her first, remember."

"I still find it hard that no one has captured her heart before this. Kids these days," Hill said with a chuckle. "I would have been all over that at her age."

"Hillary McCall! Listen to you. Don't forget you're an old married woman." Alice smiled as she teased her wife.

"Married, yes, but we're not old. Yet."

Alice reached for her hand. "I hope we have many more years before we feel old."

"I've no doubt we will. We have all these youngins running around to keep us busy."

†

When they entered the compound, Jess and Blakely were leaving the apartment. Hill noticed that both women wore bright smiles that changed to a look of surprise when they saw her.

"Good morning, ladies," Hill said and kept walking.

"Good morning, Doc," Jess said. She reached for Blakely's hand and walked her to her car. "I wish you didn't have to work today," Jess told Blakely when they reached her car. "This is usually a laid-back day."

"I'll be off at four. Would you like me to come back out?"

"I would love that. I'll cook something for dinner," Jess offered.

Blakely turned to Jess and kissed her softly. "Don't cook. Enjoy your day, and I'll bring something when I come."

"That works for me." Jess opened the car door. "Drive safe and have a good day."

"I'll be back as soon as I can."

Jess closed the door and watched her drive away.

She knew Hill and Alice would be in the office making coffee, so that's where she was headed. If she was going to get teased, she might as well get it over with.

†

Hill was pouring coffee when Jess entered. "You want a cup?"

"Sure," Jess answered.

"I hope we didn't run Blakely off this morning," Hill said.

"She has to work today but will be back later tonight."

"Good," Hill said and handed her the cup of coffee. "What plans do you have for today?"

"Just the usual. Get everyone fed and watered, and then out to play. Do you need something?"

"Just your opinion. Anita has agreed to let the home have a dog. What do you think about JR?"

"He would be perfect for all those girls. Maybe they could finally wear him out." Jess smiled at the thought.

"I will let the girls choose who they would like, but I think he'd be perfect for them, too."

Alice was sitting at her desk, going through the mail while drinking her coffee. She picked up a thick envelope and smiled when she saw the address. "Lou and Betsy have sent us a package."

Hill smiled. "Bring it over, open it up, and let's see what they sent."

Alice carried the envelope to the table and pulled out the contents. Hill was the first to laugh when she saw the photo of Toby in sunglasses and a T-shirt. Lou and Betsy, their first campers, had adopted the small beagle and he was living a fine life, according to the photographs.

"Lou says Toby is well and was the main attraction on the beach, but he hasn't met a stranger yet."

"He looks happy and so cool in his shades and bandanas." Jess flipped through a few more of the photos. "Oh, my goodness. Look." She picked up a picture of Toby wearing Mickey Mouse ears at the front of the Disney World theme park.

"I like this one, too," Alice said. She was holding a photo of Toby riding in Betsy's lap with the wind blowing his ears while sticking his head out the window.

"Maggie should be happy to see these," Hill said. "She even included a set for Maggie."

Alice smiled. "I'm sure she will, and I'm glad they are sending these as they agreed. Maggie will be out today to mow, right?"

Hill nodded. "I'm sure she'll be rolling in any minute now."

"Ask her to go over the campground this morning to freshen it up, please," Alice said as she separated the photos.

"Yes, boss," Hill teased.

†

Hill left the office to check on the dogs. It was such a beautiful day, and she didn't want to waste it being inside. Soon enough, the summer heat would arrive to roast them all. A cool breeze floated through the compound as she turned to see the van coming to drop Maggie off. Anita was driving and smiled when she saw Hill approach.

"Good morning, Maggie. Alice has a surprise for you in the office. Go check it out and then get to work."

"I will, Doc." Maggie took off at a jog.

"Good morning, Anita."

"Morning, Doc. How are you?"

"Great, thanks, and you?"

"It's such a beautiful day. The girls want to go to the park for a picnic."

"That's a great choice. Would you ask the girls which dog they want to care for at home? I have one in mind, but it should be their choice."

Anita chuckled. "I strongly suspect it will be JR, but they may surprise me. He's the one they talk about the most."

"He would be perfect for active kids." Hill nodded. "Let me know who they decide on."

"I will," Anita stated.

Hill closed the door to the van and walked back into the compound. Jess had finished feeding the dogs and was about to move to the cat compound. "I'm going to get Maggie started mowing, and then I'll let some of these guys run in the park."

"Want some company and an extra throwing arm?" Jess asked.

"Absolutely," Hill answered.

Hill walked out to the shed and checked the tractor's fluids while waiting for Maggie. She was topping off the fuel when Maggie rushed out. "You're all set," Hill said.

Maggie pulled Hill into a hug. "Thank you."

"For?"

"Everything you've done for me and everyone else."

"You've worked your tail off out here. I should be thanking you."

"You do when you take such good care of us. I've never had anyone who cared or supported me as much as you."

Hill saw the tears in her eyes. "That won't change. You are a talented young woman, and your hard work should be rewarded. Are you ready for softball camp?"

"I can't wait. I probably won't sleep tonight."

"Would it make you nervous if I came to watch some?"

"I would be proud to have you in the stands."

Hill saw the sparkle in Maggie's eyes. "I'll be there then. Probably Tuesday after you've settled in a bit."

"That sounds great. Ms. Alice said to mow the campground first."

"Please. We have new campers coming in this afternoon. Make it look sharp."

"I'll trim it too with the weed eater, and add to the firewood if it needs refilling."

"I checked it yesterday, and it's good for now, but thanks for offering it."

"All right. I'd better get going then."

"Don't forget to break for some water, and we'll make sandwiches for lunch," Hill said as she stepped away from the tractor.

†

Hill returned to the compound and began opening runs for the dogs. "Let's go play," she told them as they trotted beside her to the park. When she opened the gate, Rex and Hank made a beeline for the pool with the smaller dogs behind them. JR ran circles around them, and when he saw Hill sit on one of the benches, he picked up a tennis ball and rushed to her. Hill took the ball and heaved it as far as she could. JR wasted no time in chasing it down.

Hill alternated between throws for JR and Hank. Rex sat patiently beside her. "I'm glad to see you so happy with Haley. We all love you, but she loves you most." Hill smiled when his ears perked at the sound of Haley's name. She was so busy she hadn't heard Jess approach.

"Is Rex talking back with you yet?" she teased.

"Yes, in his own way. I'm glad to see you. They are wearing my arm out." She handed Jess two tennis balls. "I'm glad to see that smile on your face. I take it last night went well?"

201

"It was amazing," Jess said, her cheeks flushed.

"Good. You two make a cute couple."

"Thanks, Doc. I like her. A lot."

"Be good to each other and don't take life too seriously. Have fun while you can."

Jess nodded. "Would you still consider me being off for a long weekend later this summer? I thought we could go to the beach if we could coordinate schedules."

"You can take as much time as you need. I can cover things here. You will be missed, but I may see if Haley can help more when you're gone."

Jess grinned. "You know those kids will do anything for you. All you have to do is ask." She nodded toward Maggie on the tractor. "Perfect example."

Hill nodded. "I told her I would come watch her at camp Tuesday. She seemed genuinely excited."

"It's been a win-win situation for everyone, but you've given the girls more love and attention than they've probably had in a long time."

"They are a good bunch. I'm glad they have come into our lives."

†

Alice stepped outside and shielded her eyes from the sun. Maggie had finished mowing the campground and was busy trimming. She looked toward the dog park and saw Jess and Hill sitting on a bench, tossing balls for the dogs. She walked through the gate.

"Is this a private conversation?"

"Nope, sit with us. There's a project I would like to discuss that maybe Jess can help with," Hill said.

Alice sat next to Hill. "What's up?"

"I meant to bring this up earlier, but everyone has been so busy preparing for the Grand Opening it slipped my mind. You probably noticed the sparse items when we visited the group home. I'd like for you to order some things for them."

"Like what?" Alice asked.

"A larger television, maybe a laptop or two, some new linens, an air fryer, and anything you can think of that will make it more homelike."

"I can help pick out the electronics," Jess offered.

Alice rubbed her hands together. "You know how I love to shop. Do I have a budget?"

"I'm thinking two thousand, but more if you need it," Hill answered.

"Are we doing this?" Alice asked.

"Yes, are you okay with that?"

"We could shop from Amazon and deliver it to the group home. I don't think they will take long to realize where it came from." Alice smiled. "Your call."

"I don't have a problem with them knowing where the items come from. It might be wise to ask Anita if there are items they need that we haven't accounted for."

"I can do that. When do you want me to start?" Alice asked.

"Whenever you're ready."

Alice looked at Jess. "This afternoon?"

"That's good with me. How big of a television are we talking about?" Jess asked.

Hill shrugged her shoulders. "Sixty inches and a wall mount?"

"That's a good-sized television. That should be perfect for eight to watch," Alice said.

"Laptops for schoolwork and research or gaming?" Jess asked.

"No gaming. I think that's just a waste of time," Hill said.

"I agree. It's a huge time suck and can be addictive," Jess replied.

Hill looked at Anita. "We'll get the dogs settled if you want to call Anita. What time do you expect your guests?"

"Right after lunch. That will give us time to shop. I think we should make a list before we start to keep up with orders," Alice suggested.

"I'll be right behind you," Jess said. "What are you going to do, Doc?"

"I'm going to walk down to the lake for a bit. I'm no good for shopping."

†

Hill assisted Jess in getting the dogs back into their runs and kissed Alice on her way out of the compound. Walking to the lake, she could smell the sweetness of laurel and other blooming flowers. The hum of the tractor faded the farther she walked. The scurrying of small animals as they foraged brought a smile to her face. If she had remembered to get a fishing rod, she could have done some fake fishing. Maggie had chuckled when she saw Hill's fishing rod with a jellyworm that was so old and dried out that it had cracked as it hung on the shop wall. She had teased Hill about never catching a fish on something that damaged. Hill remembered looking at Maggie and telling her that fishing wasn't always about catching. Sometimes, it was more about relaxation and serenity than hooking the "big one."

Maggie had smiled with comprehension. "That sounds pretty cool, actually."

Hill sat at one of the picnic tables and enjoyed the feel of the sun on her skin. A small flock of ducks floated on the lake, and Hill watched a rabbit take a drink before disappearing into the brush. The deep blue sky was crisscrossed with lines from jets heading to unknown destinations. Hill released a deep sigh. Semi-retirement with Alice was more spectacular than she ever dreamed. They were possibly busier than when they had both been employed full-time, but it was at tasks they had dreamed of together. The farm had quickly developed with Mrs. Thompson's and others' donations. Hill felt like they were years ahead of the original plan and she smiled, thinking of all the projects completed in the last few months.

Her eyes drifted across the lake to the spot they had planned for long-term campers. She wasn't sure she could wait until fall or winter to start development. Maybe with Jess and Maggie's help, they could start clearing the trees that needed to be removed. Hill chuckled. "I guess I can't be satisfied without a project," she spoke aloud. She envisioned the small campground with a combination bath house and laundry facility. That would be a special perk for long-term residents. Hill was excited that Lou and Betsy had shown such interest in the project and were eager to help with development. Hill was lost in her thoughts when Alice sat beside her.

"You look deep in thought."

Hill looked at Alice. "Just planning the long-term campground in my head. We should talk with Jess soon to see where she would eventually like to build her home. I'm excited that she wants to be the next generation to keep the farm going."

"Jess loves it here and loves working with you."

"She's going to make a great vet," Hill said with a smile.

"Yes, she is and shares the same vision for the farm. We couldn't ask for a better replacement for you and me."

"Many years down the road," Hill added.

"Yes. Many years from now." Alice leaned in to kiss her. "Jess and Maggie were making sandwiches and sent me after you."

"You could have called."

"I would miss walking back with you if I did." Alice stood and reached for Hill's hand. "Come on. I'm hungry."

SHILOH (EMILY CUBBAGE)

CHAPTER FOURTEEN

MERCURY (AC MILLER)

Maggie smiled and waved when she saw Hill sitting in the stands among a small group of people. Hill waved back and gave her a thumbs-up sign. Maggie and the other campers were stretching for warm-ups before breaking into their groups for the day, so Hill looked around at the other spectators. Several were equipped with iPads, video cameras, and a radar gun to measure speed. She determined they were local college and university staff scouting future prospects. Trying not to be too obvious, Hill moved closer on the bleachers to see if she could pick up on some of the conversation.

Multiple players for each position and coaches were on the field as they took infield practice. Maggie was second in line for the third base position, and Hill was impressed that she had fielded each ball hit to her cleanly and without a bobble. Her throws to the first baseman were on target and had some pop. At first, one of the players actually responded to the pop in her glove by shaking her hand.

"That kid has a strong arm and good range," one of the scouts said to another. "What's her name?"

"Maggie Simpson, the other scout replied. "She definitely checks off some boxes. She's fast on the bases, also."

"How has she been batting?"

"She put two over the fence yesterday on a decent pitcher. I think one of the college players will be pitching today before they scrimmage. That should be telling."

Hill's chest swelled with pride hearing the praise from the scouts. She knew how important softball was to Maggie and the potential scholarship she could earn from playing. Maggie wouldn't have to worry about college if a scholarship didn't work out. Hill would guarantee that Maggie would have every opportunity she could. Maggie held a special place in her heart and would put in the work to successfully fulfill her dreams. All she needed was an opportunity, and Hill would ensure she got one.

After a grueling thirty minutes of infield drills, the coach called for a water break. Maggie jogged over to the dugout and took a long drink as a pitcher and catcher got warmed up. The loud pop of the ball in the catcher's mitt had some girls looking worried, but Hill noticed that Maggie studied the pitcher, timing her release on her pitches. After drinking, she picked up her bat and began stretching and swinging in time with the pitches.

Hill saw the coach smile and walk over to her. After a short conversation, Maggie retrieved her helmet and approached the plate.

"Let's ring her up," the catcher called out to the pitcher.

"Bring it," Hill whispered.

Maggie confidently tapped the clay from her cleats and stepped into the batter's box. The first pitch was wide of the plate, and Maggie let it pass for a called ball. The second pitch came in hot, but Maggie had the timing down and swung, driving the ball back up the middle above the pitcher's head. The shortstop on the field never had a chance to reach the solidly hit ball. The next ball, she fouled off deep outside of the left field.

Hill enjoyed watching the smug look on the pitcher's face disappear when she saw how far the ball carried. It would have cleared any outfield fence if Maggie could have kept it in the field of play.

"Take this one to the right field," the coach instructed.

Maggie nodded and reset her feet in the batter's box. The pitch was inside, and Maggie wisely let it pass. She drove the next ball down the right field line, and the outfielder raced after it, but Hill knew it could easily have been a double.

"Nice hit. Can you do the same to the left?" the coach requested.

Maggie nodded and foul-tipped the next ball. A fraction of a second late to swing, but she adjusted well, and the next pitch bounced off the fence. She turned to see the coach smiling.

"Deep center?"

Hill nearly laughed when Maggie swung, and the ball crossed the centerfield fence with room to spare. The pitcher was obviously annoyed that a high school player just took her yard.

"Run this one out," the coach instructed.

Maggie drove the next pitch deep into leftfield and trotted into second base.

"Yeah, she's fast," Hill heard one of the scouts comment.

"Bring it in," the coach said.

Maggie trotted to home plate and picked up her bat to carry it to the dugout.

"Good job," the coach praised as she jogged past.

Maggie sat in the dugout and looked over at Hill, smiling.

Hill smiled and nodded to Maggie.

They watched as the rest of the players took their turn at bat, most failing to make solid contact with the ball. When the coach saw a food truck pull up in the parking lot, she called a lunch break. "Eat a good lunch, and we will have a scrimmage game after."

Maggie joined Hill in the parking lot. "Can you stay for lunch and the scrimmage?"

"The boss gave me the afternoon off with strict instructions for me to buy you lunch." Hill grinned.

Maggie shook her head. "Thanks, boss."

"You did very well this morning," Hill said as they approached the food truck. "I was tickled to see you knock that smug look off the pitcher's face."

"Did I look terrified?"

"Nope. You looked confident and prepared. I loved it when you took her yard."

"I think I actually closed my eyes on that one and swung with all my might," Maggie admitted.

Hill chuckled. "Should I call Anita and tell her I'll drop you home this afternoon?"

"Would you mind?"

"Not at all. I'm enjoying watching you perform."

They reviewed the menu while waiting in line.

"What sounds good to you? I think I'm having the double bacon cheeseburger and fries."

"That sounds perfect," Maggie said.

†

They carried their meal back to the bleachers and were eating when Hill saw the coach approach.

"Good job today. Is this your mother?" she asked Maggie.

Maggie looked at Hill and grinned. "As close to one as I have. This is Dr. Hillary McCall," she said to introduce Hill.

"Just Hill," she said and offered her hand.

"Nancy Smith. Your almost daughter has performed great so far this week. You should be proud."

"I am. Very much. She's so excited to be here. Maggie has worked all summer to make the money for this camp."

"I hope you've found the money well spent," Nancy said.

"Yes, ma'am. I've learned a lot already."

"You've been impressive, and I wanted to let you know my school would be interested in you if you choose to stay close to home. Those other vultures in the stands," she said, nodding toward the group of scouts, "are interested in you as well. We can't officially approach you until next spring, but I wanted to be the first to show you interest."

"Thanks, Coach," Maggie said.

"Enjoy your lunch, and we'll start back in an hour."

Hill waited for the woman to walk away before elbowing Maggie. "Well, aren't you the hotshot? Congratulations."

"Nothing written in stone yet, but it feels great to be recognized for all my hard work," Maggie said.

†

When the coach called the girls back to the field, they stretched and ran two laps around the field to warm up before she divided them into two teams. Maggie was chosen to play third and would start on the home team playing defense first. She caught a line drive and threw out a runner attempting to bunt. Maggie batted third in the line-up, and after she belted a home run on her first at bat, driving in two runs, she was walked on her subsequent two appearances. When she came up to bat in the sixth inning with the bases full, the pitcher had no option but to pitch to Maggie. She took the first pitch for a strike and, on the next pitch, she bounced a double off the wall, clearing the bases. Her team won eight to one, and the coach called them into a huddle, then released them for the day.

Maggie removed her cleats and loaded her gear into the bag before walking to Hill.

"Great game," Hill said.

"Thanks," Maggie replied. "It felt good to be playing again."

"Load up, and I'll drop you at home."

When Hill parked at the group home, Maggie smiled at her. "Thanks for coming today. It meant a lot to see you in the stands."

"Don't be surprised if you see me there again."

"We will finish out Friday afternoon with a doubleheader. That would be more exciting than watching us do drills."

"I'll see you for lunch on Friday then. I hope that truck comes back out. That burger was delicious."

Maggie grinned. "I'm pretty sure he'll be there. Thanks again, Doc."

"My pleasure."

†

Hill drove back to the farm and regaled Alice and Jess with Maggie's athletic performance for a half hour.

"I'd say you enjoyed your day," Alice remarked.

"I had a blast and plan to return Friday afternoon for the big finale."

Jess got up to pour a drink. "I bet Maggie loved having you there."

"She did, and I was able to sit close enough to a group of college scouts to catch their comments. Needless to say, they were pretty impressed. The coach from the local university that's running the camp has also told Maggie she would be interested in her if she wanted to stay local. I don't think Maggie will have an issue with college tuition if that's what she plans for her future."

Alice bumped shoulders with her wife. "Like you wouldn't do everything in your power to ensure she has that opportunity," she teased.

"I'll admit the girls have gotten under my skin. They deserve so much more in life than they've received."

"The orders from Amazon should have begun arriving today. I expect the girls will be totally wired when they arrive tomorrow." Alice looked at Jess. "We did a great job of ordering some really cool stuff."

Hill smiled. "That's great news. Are we all set for the Fourth of July celebration?" Hill asked.

"The barbecued pork butts have been ordered, and the invitations have been delivered. I ordered some tables and chairs for our guests," Alice answered. "We have assignments for the side dishes, so I think we are in good shape."

"I've ordered a large cake and a large order of brownies for desserts," Jess added.

"That's great. Let me know how much, and I'll reimburse you," Hill said.

Jess shook her head. "This is my contribution, but thank you."

"I just had an idea," Alice chimed in. "If the campground isn't full, we can use the firepit, have S'mores, and watch the fireworks. We are far enough away that the sound won't disturb the animals, but we can still see them light up."

214

"That's a great idea," Hill agreed. "Didn't Lou and Betsy say they would return that week?"

"Yes. Betsy's already agreed to make macaroni salad and a couple of gallons of tea," Alice answered.

"I'm getting hungry already," Hill replied. "Why don't you see if Blakely can join us at the steak place for dinner tonight? My treat," Hill added.

"She works until five," Jess said.

"Fine, we can meet at six. That gives us time to shower and get dressed."

"I'll text her now." Jess smiled at Hill.

"Speaking of text," Hill said, pulling out her vibrating phone. She opened the texts and laughed. "I think our packages have arrived." She read the text from Anita thanking them for the mystery boxes that had arrived today and showed them pictures of the girls opening the boxes with sheer delight.

More to come. Hill texted.

"Blakely will meet us at the restaurant at six." Jess smiled.

Hill looked at Alice. "Are you ready to roll?"

"Let's go. I'm hungry too," Alice replied. "See you at six," she told Jess.

†

"That was delicious. Who's having dessert with me?" Hill asked as she pushed her plate away.

"I'll split one of those brownie delights thing with you," Alice replied.

"Ladies?" Hill asked Jess and Blakely.

"Will you split a strawberry shortcake with me?" Blakely asked.

"I'd love to," Jess answered.

After finishing the dessert, Hill sipped from her coffee. "I'm pretty sure I will sleep well tonight after that meal."

"That was delicious. Thank you," Jess said.

"You're welcome. I plan to work it off you tomorrow." Hill grinned,

"What do you have planned for us?" Jess asked.

"I want to build a firewood shelter at the lake and remove some trees for the new campground."

"I'm off tomorrow if you'd like an extra pair of hands," Blakely offered.

Hill smiled. "If that's how you want to spend your day off, we always welcome help."

"I'd love to help. Just let me know what I can help with." Blakely smiled.

"I'll go to the store in the morning to purchase the lumber and supplies. I'd like to start around ten if that's not too early."

"The girls and I will take care of the animals and order lunch," Alice replied.

"I guess we have a plan. Will you load some tools for us?" Hill asked Jess.

"Sure. What do you need?"

"Post hole diggers, tape measure, nail gun, skill saw, extra battery pack, chainsaw, and supplies. It should fit in the wheelbarrow."

"Don't forget gloves and safety glasses," Alice stated.

"Those too." Hill grinned at Jess.

"I'll have it ready to roll," Jess said. "You want me to take it to the lake if you aren't back yet?"

"Sure. I will meet you there as soon as I can."

216

Hill paid the bill, and they went their separate ways after exiting the restaurant.

†

Alice was curled up in Hill's arms after they went to bed. "Maggie really made my heart swell today."

"By the way she performed?"

"That, too. When Maggie introduced me to the coach, the coach asked if I was her mom. Maggie told her I was as close to a mother as she'd ever had. I almost choked on my heart."

"Did that make you think about adopting? I know we never considered kids before," Alice said. "I know she has a special place in your heart."

"I don't even know if we could adopt or if that's what Maggie would want," Hill answered.

"Are you kidding? Maggie would jump all over the opportunity. We have room here, but are you ready for a hormonal teenager in the house?" Alice smiled and looked into Hill's sparkling eyes.

"Do you think we could handle it?"

"Hillary McCall, you should know we can do anything together by now. I'm surprised it's taken you this long. I was thinking along those lines after I saw how much fun you were having with Maggie getting her ready for camp."

"Would you mind talking with Anita when she drops the girls off tomorrow to see if adoption is possible?"

"I'd be glad to. When we find that out, we need to talk with Maggie."

"I'm like you. I think Maggie would jump at the chance of a permanent home." Alice leaned in and kissed Hill.

217

"I could talk to her after the games on Friday, or we could if you'd care to join me." Hill's subtle hint didn't elude Alice.

"I'd like that. If the conversation goes well with Anita. She may need to do some research."

"That's true. I love you," Hill said and kissed Alice goodnight.

ELLI (CHRIS PAYNTER)

CHAPTER FIFTEEN

KENIDI (PAIGE KINNEY)

Hill woke up with enthusiasm the next day. She was excited about starting to work on the new campground and possibly adopting Maggie. Hill had already decided that if they weren't allowed to adopt, she would still be there for

Maggie as a surrogate mom. She ate breakfast with Alice and kissed her before leaving to pick up the lumber she had ordered. "I'll see you as soon as I can."

"Drive safe," Alice teased, knowing Hill's excitement. She worried that Hill hadn't slept much the previous night.

"I will," Hill said and left the house.

†

When Hill arrived to pick up her lumber, she was excited that her order had already been pulled. A young man started loading as she went in to add some three-inch nails to her order. After the order was loaded, Hill sang along with the radio as she drove to the farm. Life was good, and today looked like a beautiful day.

Hill drove directly to the lake and found Jess and Blakely waiting for her. They were sitting on the picnic table. When they saw her moving to the other side of the lake, Jess jumped up and began pushing the wheelbarrow to join her. Blakely walked beside her carrying the post-hole diggers.

"Good morning, ladies," Hill said when they arrived.

"Morning, Doc. What's the plan?" Jess asked.

"Come with me."

Jess and Blakely followed Hill away from the lake.

"The area we have marked off already is where the campsites will go. I would like to build the bathhouse/laundry room over there." She pointed to a relatively level spot. "Where would it be best to place the firewood shelter?"

Jess surveyed the spot. "It would be best between the bathhouse and the last campsite. That would make it easy access for everyone."

"My thoughts exactly. I'll pull my truck closer, and we can get started."

Jess looked at the load of lumber in the truck bed as Hill backed it close. "How big is this going to be?"

"Eight feet long and two feet deep," Hill explained. "We won't cut any firewood bigger than that."

Jess turned around and looked at the proposed campsite area. "We will probably fill that up with wood we have to take down."

"If not, it will be close. Ready?"

"What do we need first?" Jess asked.

"A tape measure and the diggers. Have you ever used diggers?" Hill asked.

Jess shrugged her shoulders. "Well, no. I bet I'm about to get a crash course on them."

"You are so correct, my young friend. Let's go."

Hill and Blakely measured eight feet across. "Will you mark the ends with your diggers, please?"

Jess took a chunk of ground out of both spots Hill indicated. "Okay, Blakely, let's measure two feet back from each of them, and Jess can also mark those spots."

"Okay, now to dig," Hill said. "I'll show you how to dig the holes."

"I've got these, Doc," Blakely said, reaching for the tool. "My grandpa had a farm, and I've dug plenty of holes. How deep?"

Hill smiled. "I like this young lady," she told Jess. "Three feet, please. Jess, you come with me, and we'll unload the posts."

Jess unloaded and carried the four posts while Hill measured and cut several two-by-fours. She loaded the nail gun with the three-inch nails, and while Jess and Blakely dug the holes, Hill started felling some of the trees. Blakely was impressive. Hill quietly watched as she measured the first hole at three feet and then showed Jess how to ensure it was level and square before moving to the next post. *A girl after my own heart.* Hill chuckled at the thought and moved to the next tree. She cut until they had set all four posts and returned to the shelter.

"Good job." She grinned at Jess. "Can I trust you with a nail gun?"

"You can. After you demonstrate how to use one," Jess answered.

"Bring over the six cut sections I left on the tailgate and the nail gun." Hill explained that there would be three boards. "One on the top and bottom and another in the center. Make sure they are level and flush with your posts." Hill held up a board to demonstrate the positioning. "Blakely, will you hold this in place while I show Jess how to use the gun?"

"Sure, Doc." Blakely held the board in position after checking it was level.

Hill showed Jess how to drive a nail into the board and then handed the gun to Jess. "Make sure you keep the gun flush to the board, so the nail drives completely into the wood."

Hill watched Jess shoot a nail. "That was good. Two nails in each board. Then, you can do the same with three eight-foot boards across the back at the same level."

"Seems simple enough," Jess said.

Hill measured a piece of the plywood cut sections for the sides of the shelter and cut four more boards to be interior supports. She walked them through nailing the supports and then changed the nails to one inch. Hill held up the plywood with Blakely while Jess nailed it to the supports. Then Hill measured the inside of the shelter and cut four more boards to the correct length for the surface the wood would be lying on. She added the longer nails into the gun and handed it to Jess. Then, they attached the last piece to the roof. "Here we go. We can add a tarp covering for the front later and call it finished."

"What's next?" Jess asked.

"Do we need a water break?" Hill asked.

"That probably wouldn't hurt either of us," Jess said.

"Why don't you two take the truck and grab us a few bottles?" Hill suggested. "I'll start sectioning the trees."

"You go, and I'll stay to monitor, Doc," Blakely said. "You shouldn't use a chainsaw alone."

"She's got a point. I'll be right back." Jess walked to the truck and drove away.

Hill smiled at Blakely and handed her some safety glasses. "Ready?"

"Should I empty the wheelbarrow to place the wood sections in?" Blakely asked.

"That would be smart. Good thinking." Hill checked the saw and added some oil. "Let's do it."

Hill began trimming and cutting the first of the trees into two-foot sections. Blakely followed behind her and placed the logs in the wheelbarrow. They almost had it full when Jess returned with the water.

†

Alice invited Anita into the office for coffee when she dropped the girls off. She looked worried. "Is everything okay?"

"Things couldn't be better," Alice replied, handing her the coffee. "I wanted to ask you something personal."

Anita looked at her. "What's up?"

"Is there any barrier to Hill and I adopting one of the girls?"

"Not at all. Alabama has finally made it into the twenty-first century, at least on that account. You can petition for adoption just like anyone else."

"Do you think Maggie would be receptive to Hill and I adopting her?"

Anita burst out in tears, surprising Alice. She reached for a tissue and handed it to Anita. "I didn't mean to upset you."

Anita raised her hand. "Oh, my goodness, no. I'm not upset at all. Maggie would thrive with you two as parents. She's pretty much given up on being adopted and is waiting to age out in three years."

"We are very interested in providing a home for her if she's interested. Would it be okay if we talked with her about it Friday, after her games are finished and maybe take her to dinner?"

"Maggie would love that. She thinks highly of both of you. If you'd like, I can bring the paperwork to start the petition next week."

"I would like that, given Maggie agrees."

"I have no doubt she will," Anita said, dabbing at her eyes. "It would be a dream come true."

"How long will it take to finalize an adoption?"

"It's not a speedy process, but you could register to foster her until you are approved for adoption. A normal adoption could take four to six months at best. Fostering would help speed up the process."

"Will you bring the paperwork out for fostering and tell us what we need to do to be approved as foster parents? I'm sure there are courses and inspections we have to pass."

"I would be more than happy to, and I'll give you a raving reference for both. Your reputation in town is well known and shouldn't be a problem. Both Maggie's parents gave up legal rights to her years ago."

"We would appreciate your help in making this happen. Maggie is going to be so excited. We will both be attending her games on Friday. So, if allowed, we'll take her to eat and talk to her then."

"Absolutely. I've been forced to turn down girls who need placement, so it would allow me to help one more girl," Anita replied.

"That sounds like a win-win situation, then," Alice said.

The door opened, and Jess entered. She looked at the seriousness on Anita's face. "I'm sorry to intrude, but I must grab some water."

"That's not a problem, Jess," Alice said.

"I need to get started on the grocery shopping and go check for more mystery boxes," Anita said with a wink to Alice.

"Thank you. I'll see you later today," Alice said, walking her to the door.

Alice turned back around to look at Jess.

"Is everything okay? That looked kinda serious," Jess said.

"Can you keep a secret?"

"Yeah, I can."

"Hill and I will try to adopt Maggie if she wants to be adopted. I asked Anita about the process and if we would be allowed to adopt."

"OMG, she will be over the moon on that. I don't know a more deserving kid, either. I was wondering what has made Doc so happy today. She hasn't stopped smiling since she arrived."

"Mum's the word until we talk to Maggie on Friday."

"I promise your secret is safe with me. Can I at least tell Blakely later?"

"I don't see why not. Thanks, Jess, for all your support."

"My pleasure. So what are we getting for lunch today?"

"Does pizza sound good?"

"Pizza always sounds good. Lots of it, though. Doc's working us hard." Jess laughed.

"Lots of pizza. Got it," Alice said. "Don't let her work you too hard."

†

With Jess and Blakely's help, Hill cleared all the trees from the campground area, sectioned, and stacked them into the newly constructed firewood shelter. Hill wiped the sweat from her brow. The trees weren't giant and had a few limbs they couldn't use for firewood. Jess and Blakely carried them deeper into the woods to allow Mother Nature to reclaim them for the soil.

"I don't know about y'all, but I vote we call it a day. We got a lot accomplished today. Thank you for your help."

Jess nodded. "What are your plans for the stumps?"

"I thought we might pull them out with the tractor, but I think I've changed my mind. I think Tom and his crew can knock them out quickly and level the area for the campground and bathhouse."

Jess ran her hand through her hair. "Do you plan to provide picnic tables and chairs at the campsites?"

"Yes, I'd like to build a community firepit over there." Hill pointed to a spot. "Add some pea gravel around it for a border and fire protection and place some Adirondack chairs there."

"This is a longer-term campground, right?" Blakely asked.

Hill nodded. "Six sites to accommodate the larger rigs for people who want to stay for weeks or months."

"How big will the bathhouse/laundry room be?" Jess asked.

"Three toilet stalls, showers and sinks. I think one commercial-size washer and dryer will be enough. I'll ask Tom to develop the plan and discuss starting after he finishes the build-out for Haley's apartment." Excitement was written all over Hill's face. "Once we have the plans, the plumbing can be laid and concrete poured. We will drill a well and add some solar panels for power, too."

"There will be a small community back here," Jess replied.

"Speaking of which, have you picked a spot for your future home?" Hill asked.

Jess' eyes lit up. "I was thinking of the large open area beyond the dog park. I could still see the compound but also have some privacy."

"That sounds like a perfect spot," Hill agreed. "Did you know there's a small creek back there?"

"No, I didn't. I'll have to go take a closer look," Jess replied.

Hill's phone buzzed with a text. She smiled when she saw Alice was texting her.

Are you gals planning to camp out there tonight?
Sorry. Lost track of time.
Come eat. I'll have dinner set out by the time you get here.
Thanks. We're starving. Love you.
Love you too. Hurry.

"I hope y'all don't have plans for supper. Alice has a meal set out on the picnic table for us. All she's missing is the three of us."

"My stomach has been growling for an hour," Jess said.

"Let's place the tools and wheelbarrow in the truck bed. Blakely, are you okay to stay?"

"No plans, so yes." She smiled.

†

Alice had set up a hearty fried chicken dinner. "I thought I was going to need to set out candles before y'all returned," she teased.

"I'm sorry, love. We got into such a good rhythm I lost track of the time. We managed to get a lot done, though." Hill placed her hand over Alice's. "Thanks for providing such a good meal."

"It sounds like you've earned every bite."

"Jess and Blakely built the firewood shelter while I cut trees to fill it," Hill replied.

"You helped quite a bit on the shelter, cutting boards and giving instructions," Blakely reminded her.

"But, you two did all the heavy lifting. Alice, you should have seen this young woman with post-hole diggers. She was amazing."

"I'll walk down in the morning to see what y'all accomplished, but it sounds like a lot," Alice said as she passed green beans to Hill.

"I'd say we put in a good day's work," Jess said. "I don't think I'll have trouble sleeping after caring for the animals."

Alice looked at Jess. "The girls stayed a bit longer and helped me get everyone fed and watered before they left. All you need to do is shower and relax."

"Thank you. I'll thank the girls tomorrow," Jess said. "Maybe I'll run into town and buy some donuts and juice."

"I'll take care of that," Alice said. "You can get back to business as usual unless Hill has other plans for you."

Hill winked at Jess. "Maybe we'll walk over to that creek in the morning."

"I'd like that," Jess answered.

†

"Why don't you head home to shower while I help the girls store the leftovers," Alice suggested to Hill.

"Do I smell that bad?" Hill teased.

"No, but you are covered in sawdust, so please undress in the laundry room and not trail it through the house."

"Yes, boss," Hill answered. "I'll see you soon. Thanks again for all your hard work today."

"I had fun working with the two of you, and I hope I can help with other projects," Blakely said.

"Be careful of what you ask," Alice told Blakely with a grin.

"I'm sure I'll think up something else before long." Hill chuckled. She kissed Alice and walked to her truck.

"Dang. Hang on, Doc, we've got to unload the tools," Jess said and rushed to the back of the truck. "I'll get everything cleaned and put away."

"We can clean them in the morning. Just put them inside for now. Thanks, Jess."

†

Hill was drying off after her shower when Alice made it home. "Toss on a robe and meet me in the den when you get dry," Alice called from the kitchen.

Alice poured them a glass of wine and waited for Hill on the couch.

"That felt good," Hill said as she entered and ran her fingers through her hair. She sat beside Alice and took the wine she offered. "What's up?"

"I had a great chat with Anita this morning about Maggie."

"Yeah. How did it go?"

Alice chuckled. "Anita said Alabama has finally reached the twenty-first century when it comes to adoption, and we are welcome to petition for the adoption of a child. Given our stellar reputation in the community, she didn't think we would have any issues, but it isn't a quick process. It could easily take four to six months or longer."

"Well damn, that's a bummer."

"Anita did give me some advice that should help speed up the process. She encouraged us to become foster parents to

Maggie while the petition is being processed. That way, Maggie could begin living with us before the adoption is final."

"What do we have to do to become foster parents?"

"We would have to attend some classes, and the home would be inspected, but I don't see any problem. Regulatory hoops are necessary for us to jump through. After we've talked to Maggie, Anita will put together the paperwork for fostering and petitioning for adoption next week."

Alice saw the bright smile return to Hill's face. "We can really do this?"

"Yes, love, we can. Anita said that Maggie's parents had already forfeited their parental rights, which made the process easier."

"Wow. This is so exciting," Hill said.

"I told Anita that we planned to talk to Maggie on Friday and take her to dinner before discussing it with her. She was perfectly fine with that."

Hill took a drink of wine. "Now we need to figure out the best way to ask Maggie."

"We have all day tomorrow and Friday morning to devise a plan. I think keeping it simple is the best."

"I agree. We can sleep on it tonight and make plans tomorrow."

Alice drained her wine glass. "I'm going to run through the shower. I've already locked up for the evening, so you don't have to worry. Finish your wine, and I'll meet you in the bedroom."

"Thank you, Alice." Hill stood and kissed her wife.

†

Hill slipped out of her robe and climbed into bed while Alice showered. The exertion of the day and the calming wine made her drowsy, and Hill was already sleeping when Alice arrived. Alice smiled and turned off the lamps before snuggling into bed with Hill.

Sherpard (Donna Gross)

CHAPTER SIXTEEN

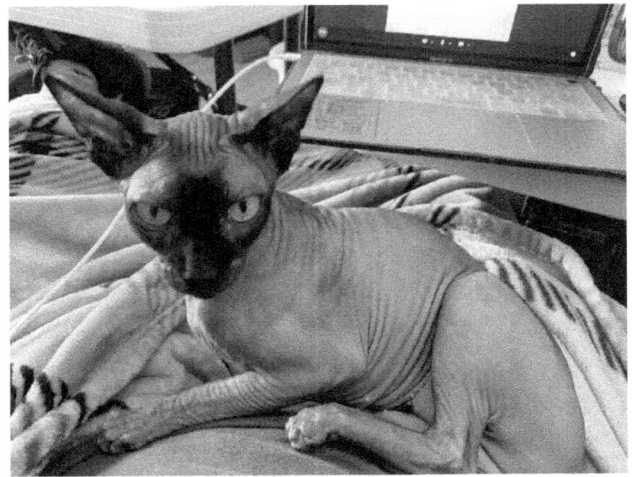

YAYA (DEB VICKERY)

Hill woke early the following day and returned to the shower to freshen up before dressing. Alice had begun to stir as Hill pulled on her boots.

"You are up early this morning," Alice said as she sat up and stretched.

"I've got a couple of things to do, and I thought I'd pick up the donuts and juice while I run errands. So, you can take your time. I've got this and will see you at the farm shortly." Hill leaned down to kiss Alice. "Any special requests?"

"You know how I love custard-filled donuts. Will you also pick up a gallon of milk?"

"Your wish is my command." Hill bowed and laughed. "I'll see you soon."

†

Hill's first stop was at a hardware store to get an extra set of their house keys made. Then, she was off to the grocery store to pick up juices, and then to the donut shop to pick out various donuts. She left with three boxes filled with the decadent sweet treats. The sugar aroma filled the cab of her truck, and when she arrived at the jeweler's, the store was still closed for ten minutes yet. Hill couldn't resist dipping inside one of the boxes for a cake donut. She was certain one wouldn't be missed.

Hill left her truck and walked inside when the open sign showed on the store.

"Good morning, Doc," the clerk greeted her.

"Good morning, Alicia. How are you?"

"Doing great, thanks, and you? I hear a lot of rave reviews about the new farm."

"It's been a dream come true. Come out and visit sometime."

"I will. What can I help you with this morning? Something nice for Alice?"

Hill smiled. "Not this trip, but soon, I'm sure. I need something special. Can you engrave?"

"I certainly can. What do you need?"

"This is a top-secret mission," Hill whispered, even though they were the only ones in the store.

"Oh, this sounds intriguing. What have you in mind?"

"Several young women from a local group home have volunteered at the farm since we opened. Great young ladies. Alice and I are planning to ask one of them, Maggie, a fifteen-year-old, if we can adopt her tomorrow."

"That is so exciting. So what are you thinking?" Alicia asked.

"I had another set of keys to the house cut, and I'd like a nice keyring engraved with her name and a fancy velvet box to put it in."

"I have just the right thing," Alicia said. She opened a drawer and removed a sterling silver key ring with a section designed for engraving.

"That would be perfect. Can you engrave it for me now?"

"Well, I'm not booming with customers yet," Alicia teased. "What style font would you prefer? I'd recommend something bold and not too frilly."

"Whatever you think will look best."

"Traditional spelling? Maggie," Alicia asked.

"Yes," Hill answered.

"Maggie McCall. That has a nice ring to it. I'll be right back. Pour a cup of coffee if you want one." Alicia disappeared into the back of the store.

Hill poured a cup of coffee and browsed the cases. She really hadn't thought of a gift to celebrate Alice's retirement. Maybe she was slipping in the romance department. Her eyes landed on a beautiful diamond tennis bracelet. As much time as they would spend at the farm, Alice wouldn't have much opportunity to wear the bracelet. But, she thought, she could wear a heart filled with diamonds around her neck. Hill smiled when she decided to kill two birds with one stone and buy Alice a retirement gift. She was still smiling when Alicia returned.

"Do you have the keys?"

Hill handed over the two keys and waited for Alicia to add them to the ring. "What do you think?" Alicia asked, showing Hill the keychain.

"That's perfect."

"Great. I'll box it up for you. Do you want it gift-wrapped?"

"That would be awesome. I have another purchase that you can wrap. I haven't gotten Alice anything for her retirement. I'd like the diamond heart on the gold rope chain, too, please."

"That's a lovely piece. Alice will love that," Alicia said. "Give me a minute, and I'll be back with both."

When Alicia returned carrying the two boxes, she slipped them into a bag for Hill. Hill handed her the card and watched her ring up the purchase. She noticed she didn't charge for the keyring."

"You forgot to add the keyring," Hill said.

"Consider it an investment for future transactions. I'm sure Maggie will get all kinds of jewelry from you and Alice in the coming years. Congratulations," Alicia said.

"She hasn't agreed yet, and we still have to go through the adoption process."

"Easy peasy. Any child would be blessed to have you two as parents. Bring her in soon so we can start setting her up," Alicia said as she handed Hill the card and receipt.

"I will. Thanks, Alicia."

"My pleasure. See you soon, Doc."

†

Hill placed the bag in the glove box. She would give Alice the necklace tonight when they got home. She was proud of herself for her purchases and hoped they would enjoy their gifts. She drove to the farm, and Jess met her at the truck to help carry the bags and boxes inside.

"I can't wait to get into these," Jess said.

"The girls aren't here yet," Hill teased.

"Yes, they are," Jess said and nodded toward the drive.

"What perfect timing. The temptation has been killing me all the way out here."

The girls piled out of the van, and Hill waved at Anita.

"Do you need some help?" Haley asked.

"Sure, you can carry the milk. I hope you ladies have room for donuts. Jess wanted to thank you for feeding everyone yesterday while she helped me."

"Are you kidding? We always have room for donuts." Haley smiled. "I'd like to show you what Rex has learned this morning if you have time."

"Absolutely," Hill replied. "Right after we devour these."

"Will someone go to the office for cups and tell Alice the donuts are here?"

"I'll go," Lara said, and raced inside.

†

Hill was amazed by the girls' gusto in attacking the donut boxes. She had worried she overbought, but it seemed none would go to waste. She reached for the last custard filled and looked at Alice. "Do you want it?"

"Go ahead, I've eaten way too many already."

Hill devoured the donut and finished a glass of juice. "I need a nap now until all that sugar kicks in," she groaned.

Hill inched it out of her pocket with sticky fingers when her phone rang. "Hey, Dan. What's up?"

"I need your help if possible. We had a mother dog give birth to a litter of mixed-breed pups, but we lost the mom unexpectedly. We've already lost one pup, but I remember the good job you did with Walter when he was injured. Are you up to trying to save three pups? The shelter doesn't have an overnight staff, and they must be bottle-fed frequently."

"We are having a team meeting." Hill winked at the girls. "Let me ask."

"Dan has three motherless puppies that will require frequent bottle feeding. Are we up for that?"

Jess was the first to respond. "Yes."

"It will mean many sleepless nights to come."

"I will help at night if you clear it with Anita," Haley said. "I'm sure Maggie would, too."

"Bring them on, Dan. We'll give them our best shot."

"Thanks, Doc. I'll see you soon and bring supplies."

"Thanks, Dan." Hill ended the call. "Operation puppy rescue," she announced. Hill looked at Jess. "Do you want to set them up in a run or your apartment for now?"

"Let me set up a bed in my living room. I'm sure Gabby and Buster won't mind some babies."

"Start on that while Haley and Rex put on a show for me." She smiled at Haley. "We can ask Anita about you staying overnight when she comes to pick you up this afternoon."

"Twins. Where are our twins?"

"Here, Doc," Lara answered.

"Start thinking about three names. I didn't remember asking about the gender of the pups, so pick both boys and girls."

"On it, Doc," Lara answered.

"Let's go see what Rex has learned. Alice, are you coming?"

"Yes. I'll create a feeding spreadsheet while you examine the pups."

"Great idea. Thank you."

†

Haley and Jess had moved the obstacle course from Rex's run to the dog park for more room. Haley worked with him almost daily and was ready for Rex to show off. "Let me throw a few balls to warm him up, and then we'll get to it."

Rex danced around Haley, waiting for her to throw the ball and give him a command. He raced after the ball and returned it, placing it in her hand. Rex sat in front of her. "Are you ready to run the course?"

Rex barked.

"Ready, set, go," Haley said. Rex took off like a shot clearing each of the obstacles, and when he reached the end, Haley waved her hand like she was twirling a lasso, and Rex ran the course in reverse."

"Oh, my goodness. That's fantastic. You two have worked well together," Hill praised. "You have got to show Dan when he arrives. He won't believe Rex is the same dog. I'll send him out before he leaves if you two want to practice a bit." Hill hugged Haley. "I'm very proud of you." Rex had returned and sat in front of Haley. He let out a woof. Hill knelt down to him. "I'm very proud of you, too."

"Watch this." Haley made a motion of throwing a frisbee, and Rex raced over to the toy container and rummaged until he found the frisbee. He rushed back to Haley and placed it at her feet.

"I swear he knows exactly what you say to him," Alice said.

"He's so smart. Ready to catch?"

Rex barked, and his whole body shook with excitement.

Haley let the frisbee fly, and Rex rushed to catch it before it hit the ground.

Hill and Alice clapped. "Good boy, Rex," Hill said.

Rex trotted over to her and dropped the frisbee at her feet.

"He's inviting you to play," Haley said.

"Lord, I haven't thrown a frisbee in years," Hill said as she bent down to pick it up. She looked at Rex. "Here goes nothing." Hill released the frisbee, and while it wasn't thrown as far as Haley's, Rex still caught it in mid-air. "Great catch, Rex."

He trotted back to Haley with the frisbee dangling in his mouth. "Go get a drink," she instructed, and Rex walked to the fountain for a drink.

"Amazing," Hill said. The approach of a vehicle caught her attention. "That's Dan. I need to care for the pups, but I'll send him out soon. Thank you, Haley and Rex."

"Thanks, Doc."

†

Alice and Hill walked over to the van to meet Dan. "What are the chances of all three surviving?" she asked Hill.

"Not good, but we will give it our best shot," Hill answered and walked over to Dan. "Let's see who we have here," Hill said, peeking inside the box. "I'll bring them inside if you carry the supplies," she told Dan. "Before you go, please watch the Rex and Haley show. I told them you would before you leave."

Dan waved to Haley. "I most certainly will."

Alice opened the door to the clinic as Hill carried the carrier with the pups, and Dan brought in boxes of supplies.

Jess walked into the clinic. "Hey, Dan."

"Let's see what you've brought us," Hill said as she opened the carrier.

"One boy and two girls. Mom was a shepherd mix, and I honestly have no clue what the pups are."

"I bet it is a Rottweiler," Hill said as she removed the first pup. "Based on these markings and the size of these feet."

"If they survive, I will return for them to see if we can adopt. With all the handling they are about to receive, I'm sure

241

they will have good dispositions and make good pets for someone."

"We will do everything we can for them. How often are you feeding them?" Hill asked.

"Every two hours. This one and the boy eat well, but the smaller female is my biggest worry. She's not as active or eating as well as the others."

"How much are they eating?" Jess asked.

"Two ounces for the others, but you're doing well to get an ounce into her." He nodded to the boxes. "I brought twelve bottles and several pounds of milk formula. If you need more, just let me know. I hate to dump these guys on you, but the shelter is very low on staff."

"We understand, Dan. We can take them from here, but call whenever for an update."

"I'll walk you out," Alice offered.

"Let's see what we have here." Hill weighed the puppy, and Jess took notes. When Alice returned, Hill looked up. "Will you get the twins?"

Alice returned with the girls.

"Okay, two girls and a boy," Doc announced. "What shall we call them?"

"That's Thelma," Lisa said.

"The other girl, naturally, is Louise," Lara added.

"And the boy?" Hill asked.

"Rufus," Lara said.

"Where did you come up with that one?" Alice asked.

"Don't know. It just popped into my head," Lara answered.

"Okay, Jess, do you have those?"

"Thelma, Louise, and Rufus. Got it."

"I'll go work up a feeding schedule," Alice said.

"They will probably be hungry again by then," Hill said. She went back to examining Thelma. "Strong heartbeat and her lungs are clear." She looked at the twins. "Puppies are often born with worms, but these are too young to de-worm, so wash your hands well before and after you feed them. They will also easily fall sick because they aren't receiving their mother's milk, so we must carefully handle them for now."

"No puppy kisses," Jess said. "I know you'll be tempted, but don't."

"Once they open their eyes in seven to ten days, you can begin to handle them more." Hill handed Thelma to Jess.

She removed the smaller pup from the carrier. "Louise, it is. You are going to have to be a fighter to catch up with your siblings," Hill spoke to the pup as she weighed her. "Almost a half pound less than Thelma." Hill listened to her heart. "Strong heart, but she's got a slight wheeze."

Jess broke out laughing. "I'm sorry, Doc."

"What's so funny?"

"Louise, with a wheeze, is going to be turned into Wheezy as sure as I'm standing here."

"That is funny, but I hope the wheeze is only temporary." Hill shook her head. "Wheezy. That's a good one." She turned to the twins. "Go wash up, and you can hold the girls while I examine Rufus."

They rushed over to the sink to wash their hands, and when they returned, Jess sat them in a chair and handed them a puppy. "Hold them close so they can feel your warmth and your heartbeat," she instructed. "No puppy kisses."

"Yes, Jess," Lara said.

"Well, aren't you a big boy," Hill said to Rufus as she placed him on the scales. "A pound more than Thelma. I guess we know who the good eater is." She winked at Jess. "Strong heart and healthy lungs."

Hill looked at the twins holding the pups close, whispering to them. Louise was the only one that concerned her at the moment. The pup's low weight and weak lungs could become problematic, but she hoped the pup would eat well. "Do you want to feed them here or in your apartment?"

"It's probably warmer in there," Jess said.

"I'll carry the supplies in and mix up a batch of formula. I want you to feed Louise to see if you can get more than an ounce in her. The other two will probably be the easiest for the twins to feed."

"Do you want me to carry the supplies?"

"Thanks, Jess. I've got this." Hill picked up the box and followed them to Jess' apartment. She placed the supplies on the counter and saw that Jess had brought in a case of puppy pads to line the beds. That was a good idea, and she was proud Jess thought about it.

Hill removed three tiny bottles and used a small funnel to pour the powdered mixture into each one. She filled a measuring cup with warm water and filled the three bottles, placing a lid on each and shaking them to mix the contents.

"Those look like Barbie doll bottles," Lara said.

"They aren't much bigger than doll size. Let's see if we can get these guys to eat. I want you to watch how Jess supports the puppy and keeps the head up so the puppy can eat safely without choking. Do you think you can do that?"

"Yes, Doc," Lisa answered. She held Rufus exactly as Jess demonstrated and wet his lips with the formula. When Rufus licked his lips, he opened his mouth for the small nipple and began sucking.

"Good job, Lisa."

Hill turned to Lara, who was holding Thelma, and handed her a bottle. Thelma began sucking right away. Hill nodded. "Remember to support their heads. They don't have good muscle control yet."

When Hill turned to check on Jess, she saw the frown on her face. "Is she taking any?"

"She doesn't seem to have much interest in it."

"Do you have some syrup in the fridge?"

"Yes, I do."

"Let me add a few drops to see if that will help. The sugar might give Louise some energy."

"What about honey? Is that a good alternative?"

"No. You should never give a puppy or grown animal, honey. Botulism may be hidden in honey. You don't want to give that to pups, especially if the immune system is compromised."

"What are other acceptable products?" Jess asked.

"Cane or Karo syrup can be used safely as an additive. Let's see how she does with Log Cabin." Hill smiled and returned the bottle to Jess.

"Come on, baby girl, eat for Jess," she said softly, stroking the top of the pup's head and placing the nipple between her lips. "That's it. Good girl," Jess whispered.

Hill looked over at the twins. Both pups were almost finished with their bottles. "Good job, girls."

"Can they have more?" Lisa asked. "Rufus has sucked his right down."

"Not yet. We'll keep Rufus at two ounces every few hours for now. We don't want to overfill them either."

Gabby and Buster came into the room to see all the activities. Gabby rubbed her body into Jess and sniffed Louise. Hill recognized the mothering instinct in Gabby. Buster couldn't care less about the tiny squeaking critters and ran to the kitchen to check his food bowl.

A knock on the door sounded, and Haley stepped inside. "How are they doing?" she asked as she sat beside the twins. "They are so tiny."

"Those two have eaten well, but this little girl is a bit more stubborn," Jess said.

"Now for the fun part, girls." Hill smiled. "You need to burp the puppies."

"Like a baby?" Lisa asked.

"Just like a baby. When they nurse, they suck in air, too, which makes their bellies swell. "Hold them in your hand like this and gently pat their backs until you hear or feel them burp."

Lisa leaned close to Rufus and listened until he let out a burp. "That's too funny." She giggled.

"Thelma's not burped yet." Lara frowned.

"She may not have taken in much air or burped more quietly than Rufus. You know how boys are," Hill teased. "Give her a few more taps."

"There it is," Lara said. "You're right. Not as loud. Now what?"

"Nap time. Put them close together on the bed. They will move closer until they touch to share warmth."

"There we go. Keep Louise at one ounce?" Jess asked.

Hill nodded. "For now. See if she'll burp and then put her down for a nap."

They all listened until Louise let out a soft burp. Jess stood and placed her on the bed with her siblings.

"Can they have a toy?" Haley asked.

"Sure," Hill said.

"I'll be right back," Haley said. When she returned, she was carrying a purple stuffed snake.

"That's perfect. Wrap it around the pups, please," Hill said. "There. I bet they sleep for two hours before it's time to eat again."

"We can help while we are here," Lisa said.

"Can I sit in on the next feeding to see how it's done?" Haley asked.

"That would be great. I can show you how to mix the formula, and Jess can teach you how to feed them."

"Thank you."

"Was Dan impressed with Rex?"

"He couldn't believe how smart Rex is."

"You've done an amazing job with him. You should be proud," Hill said.

†

"Are you sure you're up for this?" Hill asked Jess when the girls left.

Jess nodded. "I'll have help during the day and some at night. Blakely has offered to help when she gets off work."

"Well, that's an added benefit." Hill grinned.

Hill saw the heat creep up Jess' neck. "I certainly won't complain."

"Are you good for Haley spending a night or two on your couch to help?"

"Yes, Maggie too, if we need her."

"Alice told me she shared our plan with you."

"I think it's a wonderful idea, and Maggie deserves parents like y'all."

"I hope everything goes well and we can make it happen."

"Have faith it will." Jess turned at the sound of the pups squeaking. "Will Louise make it?"

"Only time will tell. I'm worried about her lungs."

"Is there anything I can do if she stops breathing?"

"Lay her on her back in your hand and rub her sternum. Other than that, just pray she will be strong enough."

"I know they are brand new to us, but I think it would crush the twins if we lost a puppy."

"Probably so, but that's all part of life. It's a hard lesson, but not one we can spare them from." Hill shrugged. "I don't cherish that thought either."

Alice opened the door and walked in. "Here's your schedule. I hope this will work for you," she said, handing it to Hill.

"This is perfect, darling. Thank you."

"We can spend the night to help whenever needed," Alice told Jess.

"Let's see how it goes," Jess said.

"It can be a long two weeks," Hill warned.

"Good thing I'm young then." Jess smiled.

"Do you want to catch a nap while the girls are here?" Hill asked. "There's not much left to do."

"That's probably a good idea."

"We'll be quiet when we come in for the next feeding and let you sleep as long as possible."

"Thanks, Doc."

Hill placed the schedule on the counter and followed Alice out of the apartment. She set the alarm on her watch for ninety minutes.

†

After lunch, Hill called the girls around the table. "We must work together to ensure everyone gets fresh food and water before you leave today. Haley will mix the formula and supervise you for the next feeding at two. Just remember to be quiet so Jess can sleep. It's going to be a long night."

"What else do we need to remember to do before and after?" Haley questioned them.

"Wash our hands," Lisa and Lara answered.

"That's right," Hill said. "I'll take the dogs to the park with the twins if you will wash out the runs," Hill said to Haley.

"I can help with that," Alice offered.

Haley shook her head. "I've got this."

"Why don't you check the bathhouse for supplies? You can join us at the dog park after," Hill suggested.

"I'll see you in a bit then." Alice left the compound.

"Ready girls?" Hill opened the first gate.

†

Hill sat on the bench and threw balls for Hank and Rex. She missed JR, but he was doing great at his new home with the girls. Maybe she would ask them to bring him out to play sometime. The girls played with the smaller dogs and were getting lavished with kisses. Hill smiled as Jax climbed into Lara's lap. He had survived his bout of pneumonia, and she held out hope for Louise. She looked at her watch, still forty-five minutes before the next feeding. Hill knew she had placed a lot of responsibility on Haley's shoulders, but if Haley was going to help out at night, she would need to know how to do everything. Hill had every confidence Haley would be just fine.

Alice arrived and sat beside her. "Lou called. They will arrive on Saturday morning. She said she can't wait to be back."

"If she and Betsy are still planning to winter here, maybe we should consider hiring them as campground managers."

"Free lot fee for keeping an eye on things?" Alice suggested.

"That's not a bad idea, and it would give you an extra pair of hands if needed," Hill said. "We can talk to them when they get here."

"I didn't have a chance to ask this morning before the puppies arrived, but do you have a plan for tomorrow with Maggie?"

"I have it covered." Hill grinned.

"Would you be disappointed if I didn't go tomorrow? Jess will need to get some sleep if she is up and down all night. If both of us are gone, the girls will be alone."

"That's a good point. Will you join us for dinner after the girls go home?"

"I can definitely do that," Alice said.

Hill saw Rex take off at full speed and turned to see Haley approaching. "It's hard to tell which of them is happier, the girl or the dog."

"I'd say it was a toss-up," Alice answered.

"Everything's washed out," Haley said.

"Thank you."

"Doc, would you monitor me for one more feeding to ensure I have everything right?"

"Sure," Hill said. "You got this, but I'll be there if you have questions. It's getting close to time. Do you want to play with Rex while we put everyone else up?"

Haley shook her head and grinned. "He had a good workout showing off for everyone this morning."

"Let's do it then." Hill stood and whistled. "Let's go dogs."

The dogs followed them out of the park back to the compound and walked into their runs. "When everyone is secured, it will be time to feed the pups. After, we will feed the cats and clean the litter pans."

"We've already cleaned the litter, so we must feed and water. Lisa and I can do that before we leave for the day."

"Thanks for all your help. I appreciate how y'all have stepped up today."

Lisa smiled up at Hill. "No problem, Doc. We'll do what we can."

†

Hill and the girls crept into the apartment to prevent waking Jess. The twins headed right to the pups, lazily stretching in the bed. "Are you ready to mix the formula?" Hill asked.

Haley nodded, took three clean bottles, and filled them with formula before adding three drops of syrup to Louise's bottle. She ran the water in the sink until warm and filled the measuring cup. She filled the bottles and shook them to mix the formula before taking them to the puppies. "Did everyone wash their hands?" Haley asked.

The twins both nodded and picked up their puppies. "Let's do this," Lara said.

Hill leaned against the kitchen counter and watched with pride as the three girls fed the pups. They carefully burped them as she had instructed. "Good job," she said. Hill rinsed the bottles in hot water while the girls petted the puppies. "Okay, go wash up in the office," she said, holding the door for them. "You did good," she told Haley. "I knew you would."

"Thanks. It was nice to have you observe. I didn't want to make any mistakes."

"You can supervise another feeding before you go. Then I will take over until it's time to wake Jess."

"Would you mind if I ask Anita if I can stay over tomorrow night?" Haley asked.

"That would be helpful," Hill said. "Thank you."

†

They finished a feeding right before Anita came to pick them up. Haley rushed out to talk with her to explain about the puppies and to request permission to stay over tomorrow night.

Anita was hesitant but consented when Hill assured her Jess would also be on-site.

"They've been a huge help today," Hill told Anita as the girls entered the van. "Thanks again for all your help today."

"We will pray for Thelma, Louise, and Rufus tonight," Lisa said.

"That's an excellent idea." Hill smiled and closed the door.

She walked inside to find Alice in the office. "I want to stay later tonight to give Jess some rest. "I'll be home after the eight o'clock feeding."

"Can I at least bring you something to eat?" Alice said.

"Only if you stay and eat with me." Hill smiled.

"I know it's not Tuesday, but how about tacos? I'll go home and iron an outfit for us for tomorrow. Some dress shorts and a polo for you?"

"That would be perfect. Thank you, my love."

"Is there anything else you need from town while I'm gone?"

"I think I'm good. I will catch up on some charting while you're gone."

Alice stood and walked over to Hill. "I won't be gone long then. I love you."

"Love you too," Hill said, walking her to her car.

As she returned to the compound, Hill saw the sun slipping behind the trees, preparing for a beautiful sunset.

†

After dinner, Alice stayed to help Hill with the next feeding. "I'll see you when you get home," Alice said when she left for the night.

253

"I promise I won't be late," Hill said, kissing her.

Hill set the alarm on her watch and settled into the recliner in Jess' apartment to watch over the pups. She had drifted off to sleep when she heard the door open and was startled awake to find Blakely walking inside.

"Hey, Doc. I didn't mean to startle you. Jess called me earlier and told me about the puppies. I thought I'd bring her some dinner and stay with her tonight if that's okay."

"That's very thoughtful of you."

"Did you eat something?"

"Yes. Alice made a run to town, and we had some tacos."

Blakely placed the bags on the counter and walked over to the puppies. "They are so tiny."

"Be sure to wash your hands before and after handling them. They are too young to be wormed yet, and I don't want to take risks. There are also gloves if you would prefer to use them."

"I will wash well. How are they doing?"

"So far, so good. The smaller female, Louise, is at the most significant risk. She's got some fluid in her lungs and doesn't eat as well as her siblings, so she's underweight."

"Do you think she'll make it?"

"The next few days will tell. If she continues to eat, there's a better chance. That's all we can hope for. Why don't you wake Jess to eat while the food is warm, and I'll head home for the night."

†

Blakely walked down the hall and gently woke Jess.

"Hey, baby," Jess said as her eyes opened.

"Hey, yourself. I brought you a burger and some onion rings. Doc says to come eat while it's still warm, and she'll head home."

"What time is it?"

"Seven thirty. Enough time to eat and get ready for the next feeding if you get a move on," Blakely teased.

Jess crept from the bed and ran a hand through her hair. "Do I have drool on my face?"

"Dunno, I better check," Blakely answered. She leaned in and kissed Jess. "Nope. You're all good."

"Thanks," Jess said with a chuckle.

They walked hand in hand down the hall. "Hey, Doc," Jess said.

Hill smiled as they approached. "Hey, there. Did you get some rest?"

"I slept like a rock."

"Good. I'm going to leave you to it then. I'll be back at seven to take over with the girls until Alice takes over while I'm gone to watch Maggie."

"Tomorrow's the big day, huh?"

"The first step of many to come," Hill said.

"That's so exciting," Blakely said. "Good luck."

"Anita has permitted Haley to stay over tomorrow night to give you a break."

"That's good. I know Haley will do a good job. I'll be here if she needs me."

"Try to get some rest tonight. Do you work tomorrow, Blakely?"

"Not until ten."

"I'll see you in the morning then. Goodnight, you two. Call me if you need me."

"Will do. Thanks, Doc."

"Everything is locked, and I'll shut the gate behind me."

†

When Hill arrived home, she opened the glove box, pulled out the gift for Alice, and walked inside. Alice was in the kitchen setting up the coffee pot when she entered.

"Welcome home. You're earlier than I expected."

"Should I go out and ride around for a bit?"

"No, silly." Alice smiled.

"Blakely came out to bring Jess dinner and to spend the night, so I came home. I wanted to share something with you that was interrupted today."

"It did turn out to be a busy day. What do you need?"

"To share this with you. I realized I hadn't given you anything to celebrate your retirement this morning." Hill handed Alice the box she had hidden behind her.

"Being with you daily is gift enough for me," Alice said.

"I guess I could take this back then," Hill teased.

"Well, since you made an effort, I should at least look at whatever you bought." Alice removed the gift wrapping and opened the box. "Oh, Hill. This is beautiful."

"I thought a necklace was more practical than a bracelet since you work at the farm daily."

"You made a great choice. I can wear this even on the tractor." Alice grinned. "If I can get it back from Maggie, that is."

"She is getting good on the tractor, isn't she?" Hill smiled.

"Must be the great teacher she had." Alice chuckled. "Thank you, sweetie. This is beautiful."

256

Hill smiled and fastened the necklace around Alice's neck. "It looks good on you."

"I was serious before. Working beside you daily makes me a happy woman. I never knew a farm could be so much fun."

"We've been lucky to have such good support. I feared we would be doing all the work when we first had this dream."

"That would have been okay, too, but we wouldn't be nearly as far along as we are now." Alice took Hill's hand. "Are you excited about tomorrow?"

"I am. Nervous too. We'll make great parents, right?"

"Yes, we will. I have no doubt. Do you plan to go in early again?"

"I told Jess I would be there by seven. I'm hoping she can rest."

"Go take a shower, and we'll hit the sack. I have our clothes pressed and ready to go," Alice said. She reached for Hill and flipped the light switch to turn off the lights.

Micro (Rosie Stetler)

CHAPTER SEVENTEEN

SHAKIRA(ROBIN HASPIEL)

Alice handed Hill a travel mug of coffee. "I'll bring out some blueberry muffins when I come since I know you are in a rush. You look very handsome, too, by the way."

"You dress me well," Hill said. "I just hope I can stay clean until it's time to go to the games."

"I have faith in you, but would you like me to bring another outfit just in case?"

Hill hugged Alice. "If you wouldn't mind, we never know what will happen. I'll try my best, though."

"That's not a problem. I love you."

"I love you too. I'll see you later."

†

Hill knocked on the apartment door when she arrived. Jess opened the door, smiling and looking well-rested. "Good morning, Doc."

"Good morning. Is Blakely still asleep?"

"No, she's in the shower, so we don't have to whisper. She should be out in a minute."

"Do you still want to walk to the creek this morning?" Hill asked.

"Yes. Do you mind if Blakely joins us?"

Hill laughed. "I assumed she would. How did the pups do last night?"

"Louise is doing much better. She ate well during the last two feedings."

"That's great news."

"Grab a refill while I check on Blakely."

Hill poured a fresh cup and walked over to the pups. They were snuggled into the stuffed toy Haley had given them. She thought Rufus was dreaming as he kicked his back legs like running.

"You're not even walking well yet, but you're running in your dreams." Hill chuckled and stood as Jess and Blakely arrived. "Ready."

†

They walked beyond the dog park and another four hundred yards before they could hear the trickling of the stream.

"I never would have guessed the stream was here," Jess said.

"I found it the first time I walked the property," Hill replied. "This would make a beautiful homesite, and we could provide you private access off the road."

"This is such a beautiful spot," Blakely said.

Jess sighed deeply as her eyes surveyed the spot. "One day, you will be home," she said. "Nothing too big, but big enough for two, maybe three. It won't be until after I graduate and get some money coming in, but I appreciate you reserving this spot for me."

"This would have been the spot Alice and I would have built a home, but I think we will stay in town if you are determined to make this home."

"I am, but I can choose another plot if you intend to build here."

"With you on-site, I wouldn't need another home. It's a win-win for both of us."

"Thanks, Doc."

"Thank you for making another dream come true. I hope y'all haven't eaten yet. I see Alice coming down the driveway,

260

and she's bringing blueberry muffins. I saw two mixes on the counter when I left."

"My favorite," Blakely said.

"Let's go then. The muffins may still be warm," Hill said.

†

After examining the puppies, Hill prepared to go into town to have lunch with Maggie before the games started. She called the group together at the picnic table for a quick meeting.

"I'm heading out for the rest of the day, but I wanted to give you a report on the puppies. Thelma and Rufus have both gained two ounces and are doing well. Louise has gained an ounce, and her lungs sound much better today. All three formulas can be increased by an ounce, but Louise's syrup stays the same. Y'all are doing a terrific job, and I'm proud of all of you."

"Thanks, Doc. Have fun today, and wish Maggie good luck for us," Jess said.

"I will. Call me if you need me," Hill replied.

Alice walked Hill to the truck. "Relax and have fun today. I will see you at four-thirty for an early dinner."

"Sounds good." Hill climbed inside and drove to the ballpark.

†

The girls were still out on the field when she arrived. The food truck hadn't opened for business yet, so they continued

261

their drills. Hill could smell food cooking as she walked to the stands and nodded at the scouts, who continued to take notes on the players. Maggie caught her eye and waved before scooping a ground ball and firing it to second base.

The coach pulled the girls together when the vendor's window opened to begin taking orders. "Eat some lunch and be ready to start warming up at one-thirty," she instructed.

Maggie jogged to the dugout to place her glove in her bag and then walked across the field to meet Hill.

"How's it going today?" Hill asked.

"Great. I knocked three out of ten over the fence this morning." Maggie grinned.

"I guess Firefly has some pop to it," Hill replied. "Hungry?"

"Starving, but may I buy today?"

Hill hesitated for a second. "Sure, same order as last time. That burger was to die for."

"Sit tight, and I will be back in a few minutes," Maggie replied, jogging over to the food truck.

Hill watched as Maggie waited in line and chatted animatedly with a tall, brunette player. She was all smiles as they moved slowly through the line. Hill turned toward the field when she saw Maggie rushing back with a bag and two bottled sodas. The young woman Maggie had been talking with joined other teammates for lunch.

"I sure hope this vendor sets up for all of your games. These burgers are delicious."

"There are usually one or two food trucks in the parking lot during the games," Maggie answered. "We usually play on the same days as the baseball team, so there's a decent enough crowd, and the school doesn't have to worry about a concessions stand."

"That makes good sense. We always struggled to find someone to work concessions back in my day," Hill replied.

"Haley told me about the puppies," Maggie said. "If it's okay with Anita, would it be okay if I stayed over this weekend to help at night? I'm sure Jess will need a break."

"I don't have a problem with that," Hill replied. "I examined them this morning, and all three are doing well."

"That's great news. I know you are worried about the little one."

"If she survives, she's going to be a strong pup. She'll probably be the runt of the litter, but that's often the best dog."

Maggie took a drink and looked up at Hill. "Would it be possible to adopt a dog and pay you to board them in the future?"

"If you are talking about you, then no." Hill watched the change on Maggie's face. "There would be no charge for you. Let me know when the right one comes along, and we'll make it official."

"Thanks, Doc."

The coach walked past and looked up at Hill. "Maggie's having a great camp. You should be proud."

"I am, and thanks for coaching her this week."

The woman chuckled. "I hope I will be able to coach her in the future."

Hill shrugged her shoulders. "You never know."

Maggie waited until the coach passed. "I would love that. I could play locally and still work at the farm."

"Yes, you could, but education needs to be a top priority. Do you have any idea of what you want to study?"

"If I can keep my grades up, maybe a vet. I would like to open a clinic with Jess one day."

"Have you discussed this with Jess?'

"Only jokingly," Maggie said.

"Are your grades good?"

Maggie beamed. "All A's last year. I will take more advanced classes this year, but if I apply myself, I should do well."

"That sounds like a good plan." *It would be nice to have another Doc McCall in the family.* "Alice should arrive at four-thirty, and we plan to take you out for a steak dinner to celebrate your camp's success. I told Anita we would bring you home later. If you want to go."

"Heck yeah, I do. I'll try not to get too dirty." Maggie grinned.

"Play hard, and if you need a shower, we can go back home, and you can freshen up. It's a fairly casual restaurant, but it's your choice."

"We'll see how the afternoon goes."

†

The first game was close for a few innings before Maggie's team pulled out a seven-to-two win. Maggie had two hits, a double and a homer before the opponent started walking her. She cleanly fielded every play that came her way and had a gem of a play tracking down a fly ball. When the first game was over, the coach instructed them to hydrate while she changed around some players. The tall brunette walked over with Maggie between games. Maggie introduced her as Lexie.

She was the shortstop for Maggie's high school team and would pitch the next game.

"Do you enjoy pitching?" Hill asked.

"Not really, but I'm good at it. Coach only used me when we got in tight spots. I prefer playing the field."

"I can understand that," Hill said. "I think this coach wants to show your arm off to the scouts," Hill said, nodding to the nearby group.

Lexie's face lit up. "I didn't think about that."

"You should try using my Firefly, too, during the next game, to see if you like it."

"What? You will let me touch your magic bat?" Lexie teased.

Maggie's face grew scarlet. "Yeah, but only for you. If you strike out, I'm revoking your privileges," Maggie teased. "I can't have bad juju on my bat."

"Oh, I see how you are," Lexie said and playfully punched Maggie in the shoulder.

Hill enjoyed the teasing banter between the two girls and wondered if a bit of crushing was happening between them. *It certainly wouldn't be the first romance to bud on a softball field.*

"It was nice to meet you, Doc. I need to start warming up my pitching arm," Lexie said.

"I'll be right behind you," Maggie said.

When Lexie was out of hearing range, Maggie leaned in toward Hill. "Would inviting Lexie to the Fourth of July party be okay?"

"Sure. We have plenty of food. I can pick her up if you need me to."

"No need. Lexie's sixteen and already has a car."

"That's fine with me. Invite her."

"Thanks, Doc." Maggie left the stands and began warming up for the second game.

†

Hill stretched and settled in for the next game. Alice texted to let her know everything was fine without her and that Louise had eaten two ounces. This was turning into a great day. Maggie's team was the visitor for the second game, so they started off batting.

Lexie batted third, and Maggie batted cleanup, so Maggie handed Lexie the bat. "Remember, no bad juju." She smiled.

Hill saw the exchange and grinned. *Definitely some flirting going on there.*

The first batter walked, and the second popped out. "Go get 'em, killer," Maggie said to Lexie.

Lexie stepped into the batter's box and took the first pitch for a ball. The second was down the middle of the plate, and she drove it deep and bounced it off the left-field line, scoring two. Maggie picked up the bat and approached the box. After the first two pitches were wide, Maggie worried she wouldn't get a ball to hit. However, on the next pitch, the pitcher left the ball too close to the plate, and Maggie hit a line drive over the right field fence. She jogged around the bases and collected high-fives from her teammates. "So, what do you think of Firefly?"

"I think I will be getting one soon," Lexie said. "That felt really good."

"It was a hard decision between the Firefly and the Ghost for me," Maggie said.

"Maybe I'll get a Ghost then, and we can have shared custody."

"That works for me." Maggie smiled.

At the end of the first inning, Maggie's team was up five to zero, and Lexie mowed down every batter she faced, with only a popout to mar her streak of strikeouts.

After five innings, they were ahead twelve to two, so the coach called the game.

The Coach called the group together and complimented everyone on their performances during the week. She handed out several shirts for the most improved and most outstanding players. Hill watched with pride as Lexie and Maggie received a shirt for the top-performing players. When the coach ended the session, Maggie returned to the dugout to change her shoes and gather her equipment before walking to Hill.

Hill looked at her watch. "It's a little past three if you want to shower and change clothes."

"That works for me," Maggie said, tossing her bag in the back seat. "I won't take long."

"I'll chat with Anita while you get ready."

†

When they arrived at the home, the van was gone. "I have a key," Maggie said.

"I'll wait for you here then," Hill said. "I need to check my messages anyhow."

Maggie exited the truck and carried her bag into the house. Hill was checking emails when Anita pulled up a few minutes later.

"Sorry, I had to run to the store."

"No problem. Maggie finished early, so I brought her to shower and change clothes."

"Come on in. You don't need to wait out here," Anita said.

"Do you need help carrying anything?" Hill asked.

"No. I hadn't realized the girls had wiped out the milk this morning. I swear it would be cheaper to buy a cow," Anita replied. "You can see all the goodies you sent and check on JR, too. He's such a great pet for the girls."

"Any problems with him?"

Anita laughed.

"What?" Hill said.

"JR is a conspirator with the girls who don't like vegetables. I catch them feeding him under the table, especially when it's broccoli night."

"At least it's good for him. You can train him to stay in his crate until everyone has finished eating," Hill suggested. "Hey, boy," she said as she knelt down to pet him. "And remind the girls, people food is not good for him."

"Ah, that's a good point," Anita agreed.

"Wow, that didn't take long," Hill said as Maggie entered the room. Maggie was wearing jeans and the Top Performer T-shirt she had just received.

"I told you I would be quick." Maggie grinned. She turned to Anita. "Would it be okay for me to stay at the farm with Haley this weekend at night to help with the pups? I've got catching up to do."

"Is it okay with you, Doc?"

"I'm sure Jess would appreciate a whole night's sleep for a change. The puppies still need to be fed every two hours. I'll ensure the girls have plenty to eat and drink this weekend."

"Okay, you can stay tonight and tomorrow night if that helps. Go pack some clean clothes."

"Thanks," Maggie said and dashed down the hall.

"Are you all set to pop the big question tonight?"

"Yes, I am. I'm excited about the possibility."

Anita chuckled. "She will be so excited she won't sleep tonight anyhow, so this is good. It gives her something else to think about."

"That's a good point."

Maggie rushed back into the room with a small gym bag. "Thank you. I'll see you in the morning when you drop the twins."

"Have fun tonight, and do well feeding those puppies."

"I will." Maggie looked at Hill. "Ready?"

"I'm just waiting on you," Hill replied. "See you tomorrow, Anita."

"Goodnight," Anita said as they walked to the door.

†

It was four-twenty when they arrived at the restaurant, and Alice hadn't arrived yet. "We can get a table while we wait for her inside," Hill said. She reached into the glovebox, pulled out the plastic bag, and carried it inside.

They were seated in a corner booth and had drinks delivered when Alice arrived. "I hope I didn't keep you waiting."

"We just sat down and ordered drinks," Hill replied as Alice sat next to Maggie.

"Are you two as hungry as me?" Alice asked.

Hill looked at them. "Appetizers then?"

"The onion peels look good," Maggie said.

"They are delicious. Let's get some."

Hill smiled at Alice. "You must be hungry. Remember to save room for dessert."

Alice turned to Maggie. "They have the most delicious brownie and ice cream dessert. The strawberry shortcake isn't bad either."

"Have you been dreaming about dessert all day, my love?" Hill asked Alice.

"Pretty much," Alice admitted.

"What do you recommend for dinner?" Maggie asked Hill.

"I usually get the boneless ribeye, street corn, and a salad. The steak has two sizes, so if you're hungry, get the big one. You can always take leftovers to the farm."

"Are you staying the night with Haley?" Alice asked.

"Yes. Anita said I could tonight and tomorrow night," Maggie answered.

"Maybe we should send some shortcake back with you then. The ice cream on the brownie won't last," Alice suggested.

"That's a great idea." Hill ordered the appetizer and a glass of tea for Alice.

"When the waitress returned with Alice's drink, she took their orders. Hill placed her order and looked at Maggie. "How do you like your steak cooked?"

"I've never had one," Maggie said.

"Let's start out with medium then. You can try my medium rare, but stay away from Alice's hockey puck."

"I just like my steak well done," Alice said in self-defense. "Not still mooing."

"Okay, one medium rare, one medium, and one hockey puck," the waitress joined in on the teasing. "What sides?"

"Street corn with a salad and honey mustard for me," Hill said.

"Make that two," Maggie replied.

"Might as well do three," Alice said.

"I'll have your onion peels out in just a minute," she said, leaving the table.

"So, how did the games go today?" Alice asked.

"Great. My team won both games," Maggie said.

"She was awesome. She hit one ball a country mile," Hill teased.

"Yeah, I don't think they will find that ball." Maggie glowed with Hill's praise.

When it arrived, they dug into the appetizer, and the salads and bread followed right behind it.

"I'll get refills on the tea. Is there anything else I can get right now?"

"Some honey mustard for dipping, please. The dip is spicy tonight," Alice remarked.

Hill grinned at Maggie. "More for us."

Alice cut everyone a slice of bread while they ate their salads. "Do you want butter, Maggie?"

"Just a little, please," she answered.

They were almost done when the steaks arrived with ears of street corn. "Those look huge," Maggie said as the server placed the platter before her.

"Dig in, everyone," Hill said, picking up a knife and fork. She took a bite and moaned. "Oh, this is heavenly."

Maggie took a bite, and her eyes went wide. "This is the best thing I have ever tasted."

"It's good, but not as good as those Hill cooks," Alice said. "Maybe we'll do a cookout soon."

"Definitely before everyone starts back to school," Hill replied. "If not sooner."

†

After the meal, they ordered desserts. Hill nodded at Alice and then handed the bag to Maggie.

Maggie's face was filled with confusion as she took the bag. "What's this?"

"Alice and I would like to ask you something very important tonight. You don't need to answer immediately, but we wanted to ask. Open it."

Maggie took the gift-wrapped box from the bag and removed the wrapping paper. Hill held her breath when Maggie opened the box with the key chain and keys. She looked at Hill with curiosity.

"Maggie, Alice, and I wanted to know if you would allow us to adopt you. Those are keys to our home."

Maggie and Alice both broke into tears. "Are you serious?" Maggie asked.

"Very much so. We would love for you to come live with us," Alice stated through her tears.

Maggie wiped her hand across her face. "I don't need time to think about it. It would be a dream come true to finally have parents."

Hill smiled with tears in her eyes. "It won't happen right away, but we needed to know if you were interested before we proceed with the paperwork."

Maggie hugged Hill's neck. "I don't care how long it takes as long as I know I can call you my parents one day."

"We will start as foster parents as soon as we get approved. You can move in once we've been certified. It will take a few months to finalize an adoption once we have petitioned the courts."

"That sounds too good to be true," Maggie said as the tears flowed down her cheeks. "Are these really keys to your house?"

"No, they are keys to our house," Hill answered. "Once we get the paperwork started, we want you to come over and see your room, and we can discuss furnishings."

"As long as it has a bed, I don't care what's in there," Maggie said.

"You'll need more than a bed. A television, a desk, and a laptop for doing schoolwork. You and I will do some shopping for school clothes, too," Alice said.

"Can I have an Alexa?" she asked.

"That's easy," Hill said. "I want to get a couple for the farm, too."

"Will I still be able to work at the farm on weekends once school starts?"

"I don't see why not," Hill answered.

The waitress returned with their desserts and saw the tear-stained cheeks. "Did I pick a bad time to deliver these?"

"Oh no," Maggie said. "Can I tell her?"

"Go ahead," Hill replied.

"They are going to adopt me," Maggie announced.

"That's fantastic news, and you know what? I think you need pictures of this event. Congratulations to all three of you."

"Great idea." Hill handed her the phone, and she took several photos and handed it back to Hill to check. They were all smiling broadly in the pictures.

Maggie split a brownie dessert with Hill and helped Alice finish the strawberry shortcake. "They were both delicious," Maggie said.

"Will you box up four more strawberry shortcakes to go?" Hill asked.

"Sure will. Is there anything else?"

"A couple of take-home boxes and the check," Hill said.

Hill paid the bill, and Maggie hugged her. "Thank you for my first steak and offering to be my parents. I promise I won't let you down."

"We hope to not let you down, too. This is new for us as well," Alice said. "I'm sure we can figure things out together."

†

Alice pulled their leftovers from the bag, handed them to Maggie, and kissed Hill. "I'll see you at home later."

"I won't be late," Hill promised.

When Maggie settled into the truck, Hill looked at her. "You realize that Alice and I are lesbians and legally married, but that may not prevent some harassment for you at school. Are you sure you can handle that?"

"That doesn't bother me at all, and truthfully, I've been harassed about being a retard living in a group home all my life. The idiots don't know an orphanage from a hole in the ground, so I don't let their opinion affect me."

"I'm sorry that has happened. People can be so cruel."

"Not just the kids. Adults tend to look down their noses at us, too."

"The ones that should know better." Hill sighed and started the truck.

Maggie cleared her throat. "If I can be honest, I have feelings for another girl."

"Lexie?" Hill asked.

"Is it that obvious?"

"To me, it is. I see how you look at one another and the way you interact. It's delightful to watch. Has she voiced her feelings to you?"

"No. I think Lexie's scared to admit them. Her parents are well-to-do, and she's afraid they will ship her off to private school if she doesn't follow their strict rules. She's voiced that threat more than once."

"That's even more pitiful," Hill said. "It shouldn't matter who you love as long as you're happy and treat each other well."

"Only two more years and she can be out from under their rules. That's why we both work hard to get scholarships, so we can openly be our natural selves."

"I hope you know that you don't need a scholarship to do that around Alice and me."

"I do, and I appreciate how to respect everyone no matter their age or circumstance."

"That's how we roll," Hill answered with a chuckle. "Do you want to break the news to everyone?"

"Is that okay? I don't want to jinx anything."

"That's entirely up to you. I don't think it will jinx the process." Hill pulled into the farm's driveway and parked. "Besides, you're bringing a sinful dessert to them."

"I see why you said to get four now," Maggie said when she saw Blakely's car next to Jess'.

"Another young love unfolding," Hill said, turning the truck off.

†

Jess was cleaning up from the latest feeding when they entered the apartment. "Hey, you two," she said.

"I'm bringing you another assistant for the next two nights so you can get some rest, and she comes bearing gifts."

"So I see. What do you have there?" Jess asked.

"Strawberry shortcake for everyone," Maggie said, placing the bag on the counter.

"In that case, I'll grab some spoons," Jess said.

Hill walked over to the pups. "How are they doing?" she asked Haley.

"Good. Louise is even beginning to get more aggressive with feeding."

"Let's see how they do tonight. Maybe we can adjust the volume and slow down the frequency."

Maggie handed out dessert containers, and Jess gave everyone a spoon. "I'm starting to get used to two-hour naps," she teased.

"I bet. If the pups can tolerate a higher volume, we might be able to back the feedings to every four hours. I'm not worried about Rufus or Thelma as good as they are eating."

"That would be nice," Jess replied.

Hill stood and stretched. "I'm going to head home. Call me if you need anything. I'll see you in the morning." Hill was walking to the door when Maggie called to her.

276

"Thanks again, Doc."

"You're welcome," Hill smiled and left the building. She closed the gate behind her and drove home.

†

"Welcome home," Alice said. She was reading a book in bed while she waited for Hill to come home.

"Thanks, sweetie. How did you think tonight went?"

"I think your plan was perfect. What a great idea. Maggie was shocked."

"I can't imagine a fifteen-year-old never having a steak. I guess it shows how much we take our upbringing for granted. We didn't eat steak often, but we did have them."

"I think there's a lot we take for granted."

"I talked with Maggie about us being a married lesbian couple and warned her she may be teased. Do you know what she said?"

"What?"

"That she was used to teasing. Kids had always teased her about being a retard in a group home."

"That's so cruel. Maggie's a smart young woman."

"She also admitted she has feelings for Lexie, one of her teammates."

"Really?"

"Lexie apparently comes from an influential family who threatens her with the private school if she doesn't follow their rules, so they are keeping their feelings low-key until they graduate."

"That's even more inexcusable," Alice growled.

Hill's phone pinged with a text from Jess.

Congratulations. Maggie just gave us the good news. She is over the moon excited.

Hill smiled and responded to the text.

Thanks. We are, too. Hoping we can help make this happen quickly. Enjoy your night with Blakely, but get some rest. 😊

I will. Goodnight, Doc.

"Maggie shared the news with the group, and she was so excited."

"Just like us?" Alice teased.

"Just like us," Hill said and climbed into bed. "What time do you expect Lou and Betsy to arrive?"

"You know they'll be early. They are so excited to return."

"No sleeping in tomorrow, then?"

"You can, if you want," Alice offered.

"Heck no. Where you go, I go," Hill said, kissing her goodnight.

TIO (RENEE WHITESIDE TAYLOR)

CHAPTER EIGHTEEN

KATIE (JULIE MEACHEN)

Hill chuckled when she recognized Lou's RV following them down the farm driveway. "It looks like we got here just in time," she told Alice, who looked in the sideview mirror.

"I told you they were excited to return here," Alice said.

"You weren't kidding."

Lou pulled the rig into the same spot as before and parked. When the door opened, Toby was the first out, and he raced toward Hill and Alice. Hill thought she was about to be mobbed, but Toby flew past her and into Maggie's open arms.

Hill turned to watch the reunion. She hadn't seen Maggie's arrival, but Toby was on target to greet her first.

"Hey, there, Toby," Maggie said. She picked him up and twirled him around as he covered her face with kisses.

"He's been pacing the RV for a half hour since he heard your name," Lou said. "He knew exactly where we were heading."

Betsy walked up beside Lou and tossed Maggie a tennis ball. "He's been waiting for a strong arm."

Maggie placed Toby on the ground and tossed the ball toward the dog park. Toby raced after it. "Good morning, everyone, and welcome back," she told Betsy and Lou.

"Thanks, Maggie," Lou said. "It's great to be back. You all have been busy."

"Yes, we have," Hill replied. She looked at Maggie. "How are the pups?"

"They had a good night. Haley is prepping the formula now. I heard a vehicle, so I came out to investigate."

"Go play with Toby, and I'll help Haley with the pups."

"Thanks, Doc," Maggie said and jogged to the park with Toby.

"Pups?" Lou asked.

"Three newborns lost their mom, and the shelter asked if we could bottle-feed them. Of course, we said yes. Maggie and Haley have been helping us with a two-hour feeding schedule."

"Ah, I see. I will gladly help if you need a second pair of hands."

"Why don't you and Betsy get settled in? Then, we can share some coffee in the office and update you. We have a lot to catch you up on." Hill grinned.

"That sounds good. We'll see you in a bit," Lou answered.

"I'll get some coffee started while you help with the pups," Alice offered.

Hill turned to look at Maggie and Toby, smiling as she entered the compound.

†

"Wow. Adoption. That's a big step, but I know you two will make great parents, and Maggie is a great kid, much deserving of a forever home." Lou smiled at Hill.

"She really is, and we are excited to welcome her into our family."

"That is such great news," Betsy said. "How long will it take?"

"We plan to apply as foster parents until the adoption petition can be processed. I hope we can be approved quickly and bring Maggie to live with us in a few weeks," Alice answered.

"I bet Maggie is super excited," Lou said.

"She is, and we are, too. We plan to start prepping a room for her as soon as we finish the Fourth of July party," Hill said.

Lou grinned. "That's just a few days away. Is there anything we need to help with?"

Alice shook her head. "Nothing other than the sides Betsy has agreed to make. It should be an enjoyable event."

"Other than adding the dog park, what else have you been up to?" Lou asked.

"Let's take a walk, and I'll show you," Hill said.

"I'll be back soon," Lou said and kissed Betsy.

"Take your time. Alice and I have to catch up, too," Betsy answered.

†

Hill and Lou walked out the rear of the compound and headed to the lake. The morning was beautiful, and the humidity had remained low. "Jess, Blakely, and I have been doing some clearing."

"Blakely?"

"Jess' girlfriend," Hill replied. "She's studying to be a nurse practitioner. She's a fabulous young woman and is smitten with Jess."

"Ah, young love," Lou answered.

"Their relationship has really blossomed this summer. Blakely spends several nights a week here and has been a great help on projects."

When they reached the edge of the lake, Lou stopped. "Wow, you have been busy."

"We've done some basic clearing for the campground," Hill pointed to the large clearing. "We built a firewood shelter and added the trees we cut down for firewood," Hill explained as they continued to walk. She pointed to a smaller, cleared section. "That will be the combination bathhouse and laundry facility."

"Great idea," Lou responded.

"I want this area to be a community fire pit with some Adirondack chairs around it," Hill stated. She looked at Lou. "Do you and Betsy still want to winter here?"

"That's the plan. When we leave for home, we'll be gone for a few weeks as we place some things in storage. Some friends will move into the house while building a new home. Then we will be back here as fast as we can."

"I have a proposition for you to entertain then."

"I'm listening."

"Would you and Betsy be the supervisors of the long-term campground as residents so Alice can focus on short-term campers? We will give you free rent if you oversee things. Let us know when we need to address any issues."

"We will gladly do that, but we insist on paying rent. It's already in our budget. You can use it for upgrades or anything you need."

"I'll get Tom and his crew working on the final clearing and leveling to have the concrete poured. He will also build the bathhouse for us. We will have a well dug and solar panels installed."

"You have planned well, and the project should be well underway by the time we return," Lou said.

"Just think about the proposal and let me know if you have additional recommendations."

"The only thing I can think of right away is to fill the path to the lake with gravel for easier travel for larger rigs."

"See, I hadn't thought of that." Hill grinned. "Tom will also be building another apartment next to Jess. When Haley ages out of the home after graduating high school, she will join us here. Mrs. Thompson has created a foundation to fund her college education, and she will work here for a small stipend."

"You have been busy, my friend," Lou said.

"It's been an amazing summer," Hill agreed.

"Sue and Tina will be rolling in a few weeks, so we'll have extra hands if needed. They are so jealous that they can't spend the winter here." Lou chuckled.

"We never turn down help."

"How are the adoptions going?"

"Several cats and a few dogs," Hill said. "We all enjoyed the pictures of Toby you sent. Maggie's room at the group home is plastered with his photos."

"I noticed you had some of them posted on a bulletin board, too. Toby's been a great dog, and all three of us are happy together," Lou said.

"All of our adoptions have gone to great homes, and we look forward to seeing pictures of their adventures. Especially the kids, who get attached to the animals so quickly," Hill stated.

"That appears to have been a great relationship with the group home. They learn about responsibility and love, and you get extra help."

Hill nodded. "I praise the day Anita came to visit." She smiled. "Wait until you see what Haley has trained Rex to do. It's amazing. We'll ask her to give you a demo later."

"That sounds good," Lou said. "Do you still do a special lunch on Saturdays?"

"Yes, I think today is pizza day," Hill said. "You and Betsy are welcome to join us."

"Can we buy today?"

"You'll have to take that up with the boss. She handles the pizza ordering."

"Got it," Lou said. "I'll catch up with you later then."

Maggie and Toby were still playing as Hill walked into the dog park. "He looks good," Hill said as she sat on the ground next to them.

"He's still such a sweet boy," Maggie said as she stroked Toby.

"Did you get any sleep last night?"

"Yes, I did. I set the alarm to wake up for the feedings but returned to sleep afterward. We stayed up a while with Jess and Blakely talking. They were all so excited by my news."

"That's great to hear. How are you?"

"I'm still on cloud nine. It hasn't really sunk in yet," Maggie said. "I've hoped for a real family for so long. It's hard to wrap my head around that you are there for me."

Hill's watch beeped. "I think it's time for a feeding. I can handle it if you want to stay with Toby."

"Naw, I think I've worn him out. He may need to nap." Maggie chuckled.

"Let's go then."

†

The crew worked on chores until it was time for lunch. Hill had examined the pups and shared with the group that they could increase the volume and cut back to four hours. "You have done a tremendous job with them," she praised.

As they sat at the tables eating pizza, Haley looked at Hill. "I know Monday is the Fourth of July holiday, and we have the party in the afternoon, but we've decided to come out as usual and get all the work done so everyone can enjoy the day."

"We appreciate all your extra effort," Hill said.

"Jess told us we could use her bathroom to shower and dress for the party," Haley explained. "So, we'll all bring extra clothes."

"That sounds like an excellent plan," Hill replied.

"Blakely is going to stop at the bakery for the cake and brownies on her way out," Jess said.

"I'll need to go pick up the smoked butts," Alice chimed into the conversation.

"Betsy and I can help out as needed. She will have her sides already made, so let us know what we can help with," Lou offered.

†

Later that afternoon, Hill looked at Jess. "You have everything under control here, so I think Alice and I will head home early today. "We'll see you in the morning."

"I'll be out tomorrow to mow and make sure everything is fresh for the party," Maggie said.

"Am I ever going to get my job back mowing?" Alice teased. "I miss my tractor."

Maggie chuckled. "Once school starts, she's all yours unless you want me to mow on the weekends."

Hill shrugged. "Why mess with a good thing? Maggie should be able to keep everything fresh cut until the grass goes dormant."

"Yeah, yeah. But I'm not giving up my John Deere hat," Alice teased.

Hill looked at Maggie. "I'll get you one of your own."

"Thanks, Doc," Maggie said.

"Tom is coming out in the morning to discuss the campground projects if you want to be a part of it," Hill told Lou.

"I'll be up and caffeinated by the time you get here," Lou replied.

"See you tomorrow then," Hill said, walking Alice to the truck.

†

"It seems strange being home before dark," Hill said as she hung her keys by the door.

"I think we work harder now than before the farm, but it's so worth it," Alice replied.

Hill pulled her into her arms. "I would have never imagined what it has turned into six months ago. It's more than just a farm or home. It's also like a sanctuary."

"That's true on so many levels. I'm happy we were able to do this project."

"Me too. So what are we to do with ourselves this evening?" Hill asked.

"Dinner, a hot shower, and some loving?" Alice suggested.

"You know I could go for some of your French toast and bacon," Hill answered.

†

Alice and Hill made love deep into the night. "It's been a while since we've done that," Alice said. "Maybe I should cook French toast more often," she teased.

"I think we were both overdue for some attention. We've been working so hard on the farm that we neglected our needs. We should work harder on that."

"I never feel neglected, but tonight was spectacular," Alice said, curling into Hill's arms.

"I agree completely. I need to meet Tom in the morning. Do you want to go with me or stay home and relax?"

Alice lifted her head to look at Hill. "Go with you, of course."

"Good." Hill turned out the light and snuggled with Alice.

†

Sunday morning began with overcast skies, but the weatherman had confidence that the skies would clear mid-morning. Hill was excited to see the forecast for the Fourth, which would be clear and sunny. "It sounds like we will have a great day for our event." She reached for Alice's hand. "I am so excited."

"I'm sure it will be a great day and everyone will have a wonderful time. The girls are incredibly excited, according to Anita. "They plan on spending today getting all their sides prepared. Did you dig out the ice cream maker?"

"I did. It's in the back of the truck," Hill answered.

"If you don't need me, I'll run to the store for ice cream supplies while you meet with Tom. I'd like to get a variety of toppings since we are going with vanilla ice cream.

"Don't forget some dry roasted peanuts," Hill replied.

"They are at the top of my list, baby." Alice grinned.

†

When Hill parked, Tom had already arrived at the farm and talked with Jess. She climbed out of her truck, pulled out the ice cream maker, and handed it to Alice. Hill reached out her hand to welcome Tom as Lou arrived at the group.

"Tom, this is Lou. She will be helping to manage the long-term campground, so I asked her to join us this morning," Hill explained.

"Pleasure to meet you, ma'am," Tom said, extending his hand to Lou.

"Likewise. I'm excited to participate in this project," Lou answered.

"Let's get started then. Jess, do you want to join us?" Hill asked.

"I've got pups to feed," Jess said. "You can catch me up later."

"Everyone okay this morning?" Hill asked.

"Ha! Rufus is eating anything we place in his mouth. I think his eyes will open soon."

"A little early, but not unusual."

"Are you bottle feeding a litter?" Tom asked.

"Dan from the shelter brought us three that lost their mother," Hill explained as they started walking. "Jess and the girls have been taking shifts feeding them, first every two hours and now every four."

"That's got to be hard on sleep cycles." Tom chuckled.

"I'm glad the youngins can handle that. One short night was enough for me."

"You've got a good bunch working here," Tom agreed. "I should be ready to start on the apartment in the next few weeks unless the campground takes precedence."

Hill nodded. "We won't need the apartment until spring, so let's do the campground first."

Tom nodded. "You're the boss."

"We'd like to start with a gravel pathway to the campground to make it easier for large rigs to navigate," Hill said.

"We will be using some heavy equipment, so that should pack it down well, and we can place gravel on top. Do you need me to arrange for a well to be dug?"

"Yes, if you already have contacts. That would be great. I'll use the same company for the solar system. Will your team be able to handle the concrete work, or do we need to sub it out?"

"It's just as cheap to hire concrete professionals. I've got a great plumber who can lay the plumbing for the bathhouse and laundry, and run water wherever you need it once the well is dug. You just tell me when to start."

"After the holiday?" Hill asked.

"I can get the well dug and sit down with the plumber next week. Do you have a rough idea of what you want?"

"Three shower stalls, toilets and sinks, and one commercial set up for laundry. Do you think one laundry station will be enough, Lou?"

"It should be. Even if the campground is full, we should be able to rotate schedules," Lou answered.

"I'll go ahead and run the wiring and hook up for another set if needed," Tom said. "It's easier to add them now versus later."

"Go ahead," Hill said. "We envision the bathhouse to be here." Hill pointed out a clearing. "Six RV pads will go here. We've already cleared the trees, but we'll need stumps removed and some leveling."

Lou cleared her throat. "The long-term campers are mostly going to be larger rigs like mine. Would adding a gravel pull-through lane that circles back around the bathhouse be possible?"

"That's a great idea. We shouldn't have anyone backing into the lake then," Hill teased.

"That will be easy enough to add," Tom said. "Do you want to go with cinderblock and a metal roof for the bathhouse?"

"With a great ventilation system so it doesn't get too hot or muggy running the dryers and showers," Lou said.

"That's an excellent point. We also need to add some heating and AC to the building. It won't need a big unit," Tom added. "Since we will have equipment out here, if you will mark out your location and size for a fire pit, we can dig that too."

"I'll take a look at some inserts tonight if you want me to," Lou offered.

"That would be great. I'd like to surround it with pea gravel to reduce the chance of sparks catching fire," Hill stated.

"We can run a water line right out to it as well," Tom said.

"This is getting exciting. How long do you think it will take to complete the project?"

"Barring any issues, I'd say three weeks to a month," Tom estimated. "We need to get the well dug before we start construction." He ran his hand through his hair. "October is usually a slow month for us. Would you mind if we started the apartment then?"

"That would be perfect," Hill answered.

"I'll get some plans and costs drawn up and bring them out this week for both projects. If I can start the well drilling, will that be a problem?"

"Not at all. The sooner, the better," Hill replied.

They walked Tom to his truck when they reached the compound. "I'll see you next week. Have a happy Fourth."

"You too, Tom."

†

"Coffee?" Hill asked Lou.

"Sure. I can't pass a coffee maker," Lou teased.

When they entered, Alice and Betsy were sitting at the table chatting. "Do you ladies need a refill?" Hill asked.

"I'll take one," Alice replied, handing Hill the cup.

"I'm good for now, thanks," Betsy said.

"How did the visit go?" Alice asked as Hill poured coffee.

"Good. Tom will draw up plans and cost estimates for the campground and Haley's apartment this week. He will contact the well driller to get him started before anything else."

"Too bad Karen isn't here. You know she'd insist on doing all of the plumbing," Alice said. "She was extremely helpful with the dog pool and fountain," she told Betsy.

"That's true." Hill smiled.

Lou sat down at the table and took a sip of coffee. "Have you considered a garden plot?"

"I'm not the one to ask about that since I have two brown thumbs," Hill said.

"It could be a community garden, and the girls would probably enjoy growing things," Alice replied. "Fresh vegetables would be much better than all the processed ones."

"I bet your campers would help tend one as well for a share of the veggies," Lou said. "This used to be an old chicken farm, right?"

"Yes, about ten years ago," Hill replied.

"I bet there are several spots beyond the compound they used to dump manure that would probably make a prime garden spot. Reclaiming it may take some work, but nothing difficult."

The gears were churning in Hill's head. "We could also build a few mobile coops and have free-range eggs."

"That would make it a true farm," Alice said.

"I just don't want anything that would take us away from our original mission for the animals," Hill said.

Alice smiled up at Hill. "I'm pretty sure you and Jess have things well covered in that department, so why don't you let us cultivate a garden plot?"

Lou nodded. "A few rolls of chicken wire, wheels, and a bit of lumber, and we can make the mobile coops."

Hill chuckled. "Create a list of what you'll need, and I'll order the materials."

"Nope," Betsy said. "We've got this."

"It probably wouldn't hurt to purchase a roto-tiller, though," Lou said. "We can set up an automatic watering system, so once we get planted, we just maintain the crops."

"Once we return, it will be time for a fall garden, which would be perfect timing."

Hill lifted her hands. "I can't argue with that plan. I bet Maggie and Blakely would love to use a tiller. Maggie never shies away from anything, and Blakely's grandfather farmed."

"The twins would be perfect for chickens," Alice added.

The door opened to the office, and Maggie walked inside. "I'm ready to mow unless you need me to do something else."

"You can take a walk with Lou and me first," Hill said. "We are hunting for the old manure field from the chicken farm. These ladies are convinced we need a garden."

"That would be great. I think I know the place you are talking about precisely. I've been mowing it, but it has the greenest grass on the property."

Hill and Lou stood. "Take us there."

As they walked, Hill also told Maggie about the chicken coops. "The twins would love chickens," Maggie stated. "What doesn't get eaten could be sold in town."

"Ask Anita to start saving her egg cartons then," Hill replied.

After walking about two hundred yards beyond the compound, Maggie pointed out a large clearing. "This is the spot. See how green the grass is?"

"I do believe you have hit the jackpot," Lou said. "Are you up for some building projects and learning how to use a tiller?"

"Heck yeah," Maggie said. "I mean, yes, ma'am."

"When you mow back here, keep it close. That will make it easier when we start tilling," Lou said.

"I'm on it," Maggie said. "I'll mow around the compound first and cut this area next."

"Thanks," Hill replied. "I need to go examine the pups. Jess says Rufus will eat us out of house and home if he keeps going."

"There's nothing wrong with his appetite," Maggie answered.

"Speaking of appetites. I'm grilling hamburgers if you want to join us," Lou said.

"We can't pass on a good hamburger," Maggie said. "Can we, Doc?"

"Nope," Hill replied.

Lou smiled. "I'll check with Jess and Blakely and see if they will join us, too."

"Haley's here too. She was going stir crazy at home."

"The more the merrier." Lou smiled at Maggie.

Hill nodded. "I'll call Anita and tell her I'll bring you home later."

†

Hill took each one of the pups into the clinic to examine them and administer a dewormer. Now that they all showed signs of survival, she didn't want them competing with a parasite for nutrition. Rufus had gained nearly a pound, and his eyes were cracked open.

"I can already tell you will be a handful when your eyes open and you get your feet under you," she said as she held him close. "I'm giving them all a dewormer today," she told Jess when she returned Rufus. "Be sure to keep a puppy pad under them. It should work quickly."

"Got it, boss," Jess said.

"We can move them to a run if you're ready to have your apartment back," she offered.

"Let's wait until they have their eyes open and start to move around a bit more," Jess replied.

Hill nodded and took Thelma to the clinic. She, too, had gained weight, and Hill could see deep blue eyes emerging.

"You won't be far behind your brother." Hill chuckled as she stroked Thelma's head. "Now for the big reveal." Hill walked back and exchanged Thelma for Louise. "You feel like you've gained some weight," Hill told the pup as she carried her to the scale.

She smiled as the weight popped up on the screen, and showed Louise had gained over a quarter pound. Hill held the puppy to administer the meds. "It won't be long until you start catching up with your siblings. Keep fighting, little girl."

When Hill examined her lungs, she was delighted to hear they were clear of fluid. Thelma had dodged a dangerous bullet. "You will make someone a great pet one day."

She carried Louise back and handed her to Jess. "She's gained over a quarter pound, and her lungs are clear. You and the girls have done a great job with them. I am very proud of y'all."

"Thanks, Doc. It's been a great experience for all of us," Jess answered.

†

When Hill walked out to check on Maggie, she found she had finished mowing the campground and dog park areas. She waved her over and handed her a bottle of water.

"You've got this place looking good," Hill praised.

"Thanks, Doc. I'm going to mow the garden spot next."

"Finish that spot and call it a day. You've done well today."

Maggie smiled and placed the cap on the water bottle before driving away.

Hill found Alice sitting at one of the campground picnic tables with Lou and Betsy. They were busy making some sort of plan as she walked up.

"You all look like you are deep into planning," she teased.

Alice smiled up at her wife. "Betsy and I are planning the fall garden, and Lou is drawing up plans for the chicken coops."

Betsy looked up. "May I get you a coffee or something?"

"I'm good, thanks," Hill answered. She looked at the drawing Lou was working on. "That looks more like a condo than a coop. Are you planning satellite TV, too?" she teased.

"Hey, I didn't think of that." Lou grinned. "What do you think about adding a water catchment system on the back of the coop to catch rainwater?"

"That's not a bad idea, but we're going to have to run a water line to the garden anyhow," Hill replied.

Alice's head popped up. "Do I get to run the Ditch Witch this time?"

"Yes, dear, you do." Hill laughed.

"I also had an idea about the fire ring for the campground. Instead of buying something, why don't we find a tractor-trailer rim? It will be solid steel and the perfect size."

"I know the perfect place to get one. One of my customers owns a trucking company." Hill grinned at Lou. "I'll give him a call."

Lou nodded toward Betsy and Alice. "I hope you have plans for a pumpkin patch event. From what I'm hearing, they are planting quite a few."

"It's all good. What doesn't get used, we can supplement the dog's food and the local wildlife, so nothing will go to waste," Hill stated.

"That would be fun to host a pumpkin patch for the local kids," Alice said. "It would add more exposure to the farm as well."

"See. There's a method to all your madness," Hill teased.

†

Hill looked into the review mirror while driving the girls home and saw Maggie's head drooping. She had worked hard today, and now, with her belly full, all she needed was a hot shower, and she'd be ready for bed.

Maggie's head jerked up when Hill pulled to a stop. "Thanks for all your help today, ladies. We'll see you tomorrow."

"Thanks, Doc. Have a good night," Haley said.

"You too."

Hill waited for the girls to be safely inside before driving away. She looked over at Alice. "Maggie was so cute dozing in the back seat."

"She worked hard today," Alice reminded her.

"Yeah, she did. I think she loves the farm almost as much as we do."

"That could be possible," Hill said with a smile.

TUCKER (DANA HOLMES)

EPILOGUE

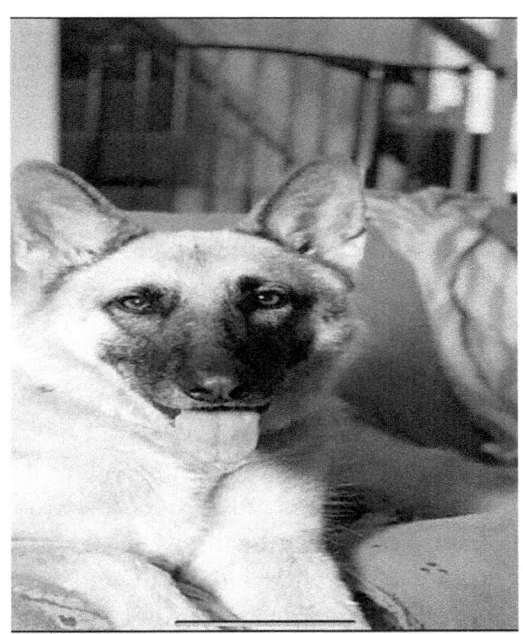

JULIET (BRITTANY WILSON)

The Fourth of July Bash turned out wonderfully. No one went hungry, and even the dogs were wowed by the brilliant fireworks the city put on.

"It's so nice to see them without the disturbing noise," Alice said.

Hill chuckled when she realized how much they had overestimated the food, but they had leftovers to send back with the girls, Lou and Betsy, and they kept plenty for lunches for the coming week. Alice's sundae bar was a huge success, and it quickly became a competition to see who could make the largest and most creative dish. Jess won hands down when she brought bananas and made splits for her and Blakely.

"Oh, that does look good. You win, but do you have more bananas?" Alice asked.

Jess raised her hands in celebration and walked inside her apartment for more bananas.

Lisa, Laura, and some younger girls started to doze in their lawn chairs.

Anita looked at Hill and Alice. "I think I'd better get this group home before I need to carry them all inside. Thank you for another great day."

"Thank you for coming to visit us a few months ago. The girls have been vital to the success the farm has experienced thus far. We couldn't have done it without their help."

"They have all grown so much since they started here. I hope we can have a long relationship with the farm."

"I don't see any issue with that," Hill said.

"Will you both have time to sit down and discuss some paperwork tomorrow?" Anita asked.

Hill beamed. "Absolutely."

†

Hill and Alice passed the coursework and inspections to become a foster home. They were approved three weeks after the Fourth of July gala, and Maggie moved home.

As they sat around the table eating dinner on the first night, Maggie looked at each of them. "Is it now okay for me to call you both Mom?"

Hill looked at Alice, who also had tears in her eyes. "We would like that very much."

†

Lou and Betsy had returned home after the Fourth and wrapped up their business quickly to return to the farm. When they pulled back into the campground, Maggie rushed to meet them.

"Welcome back. You won't believe our progress," Maggie excitedly told Lou and Betsy.

"Show us what is going on," Lou said as Toby jumped out to greet Maggie.

The campground was nearly finished. The garden had started being tilled, and the supplies had been delivered to build the chicken coops.

"You weren't kidding about the progress. We arrived just in time to get to work," Lou told her.

†

The farm continued growing, and Hill was excited one night when they returned home to find a summons in the mailbox. They all sat around the kitchen table as Hill read the notice. Their petition to adopt had been approved, and on October tenth, they were required to be in court to make everything final.

They were all eager for the day to arrive, and when it finally came, they were joined at the courthouse by Anita, Jess, Blakely, Lou, and Betsy for the event. When the bailiff announced their case, Maggie, Hill, and Alice were called to the Judge's bench.

"I understand you wish to become a McCall," the Judge stated.

"Yes, sir, I do," Maggie answered.

"I know you have chosen wisely and will become an asset to our community." He looked at Hill. "You have chosen wisely as well. Are we ready to make this a done deal?"

"Yes, please," Maggie replied.

The Judge turned a piece of paper to her and handed Maggie a pen. "We just need everyone's signature."

Maggie's eyes filled when she saw her name, Maggie McCall, on the paper, and then she took her time to enter her new signature proudly.

She smiled up at Hill as she handed her the pen. "Moms, you're next."

Hill smiled and signed her signature, and Alice added hers as well.

"There is only one thing left to do," the judge told Maggie. The judge handed her a large stamp and pointed to a spot on the document.

Maggie pressed the stamp solidly on the paper, and when she lifted it, she read the words, "Officially Adopted."

"Congratulations to the McCall family," the judge said.

They went to lunch, and when they returned to the farm, Maggie was surprised by a party that congratulated her on her adoption. A smile never left her face as she cut the cake and served the guests large slices.

Hill looked at Alice and lifted her glass of punch. "Here's to another happily ever after."

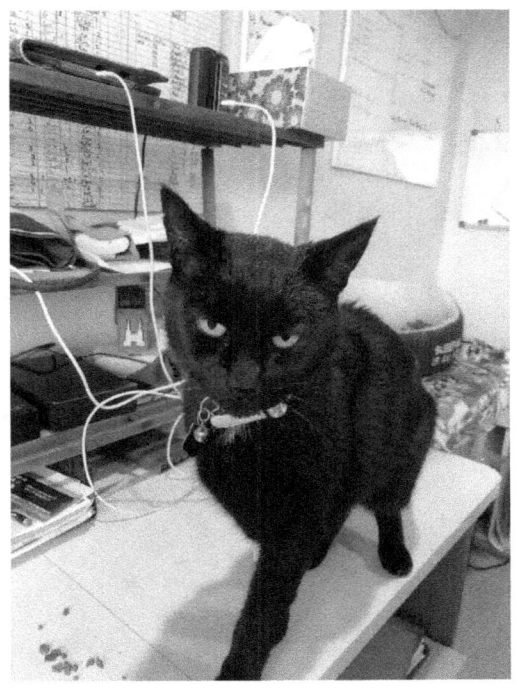

MAXWELL (HE ENJOYED HIS HAPPILY EVER AFTER)

ABOUT THE AUTHOR

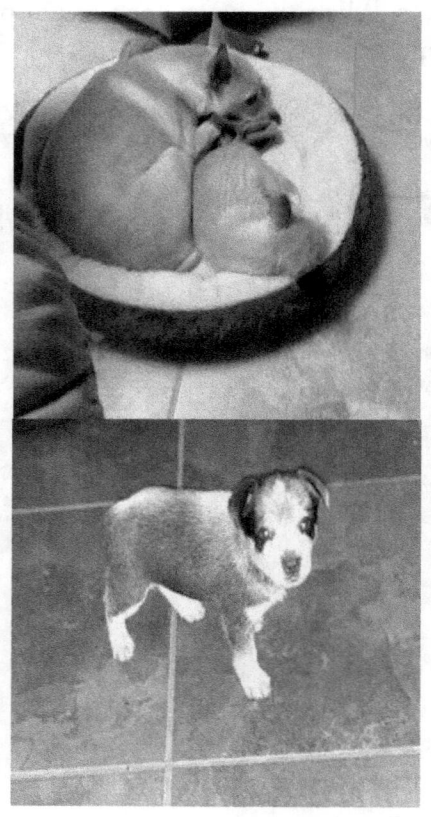

Casper and Punkin & Baby Cruz

Ali Spooner lives in beautiful northwest Florida with several fur babies. Ali's writing began as a hobby, and with the assistance of the Affinity Rainbow Publishing team, her love of storytelling has advanced to a new level.

Ali's characters are primarily everyday people, from cowgirls to psychics. Ali also has created a few supernatural characters in her paranormal series. Several of her thirty-plus books have been Amazon-rated number-one choices and always include a happily ever after. Ali's hobbies include photography, reading, travel, college sports, and spending time with family and friends.

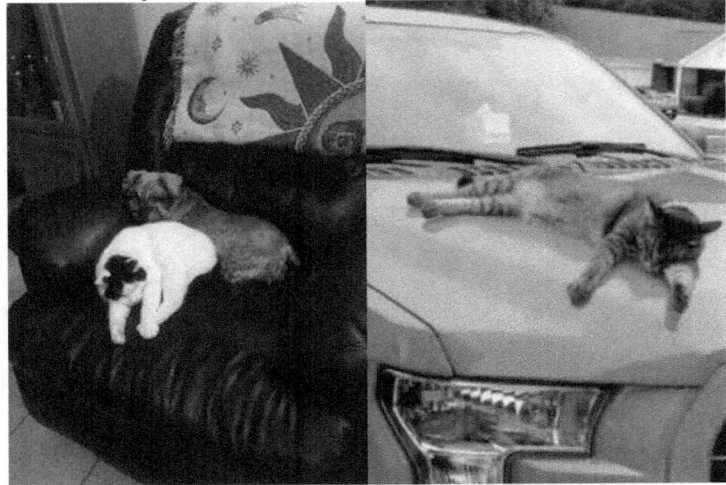

Maggie and Oreo-Rascal

Ali Spooner

OTHER AFFINITY BOOKS

Coal and Easter

The Love Demand by Annette Mori

In the dazzling realm of reality television, where love and drama entwine in a complicated dance as old as time, a groundbreaking series emerges that transcends the ordinary. *The Love Demand* is not your typical reality show. Lacey Fellows isn't sure she wants to subject herself to further humiliation, however, on the off chance her girlfriend may agree to accept a second marriage proposal, Lacey reluctantly consents to participating in the new reality show. What she doesn't count on is meeting a kindred spirit—one she can't seem to shake from her thoughts. Jaimie would do almost anything for her girlfriend, including following her to the ends of the earth and participating in a conniving television show that puts her in front of a camera, which happens to be her least favorite place. Her girlfriend, Sabina, hasn't met a camera she doesn't like. They couldn't be more opposite, but Jaimie still hopes Sabina will want marriage, kids, and the whole shebang. The last thing she expects is to fall in love with someone else. Let the games begin.

Humbug: the Ultimate Lesbian Christmas Carol

Ebban Scrage, the formidable CEO of Scrage Financial, has built her empire by sacrificing everything—including love and compassion. But as Christmas approaches, Ebban is tormented not by ghosts but by relentless nightmares that peel back the layers of her hardened heart.

At the center of her turmoil is Barbara Craig, her talented yet overworked top employee, and Barbara's daughter, Tammy, a resilient young girl battling bone cancer. In her nightmares, Ebban is forced to return to the painful memory of losing her first love, a casualty of her relentless ambition. As Christmas approaches, the dreams grow darker, shifting to Tammy. In these chilling visions, Ebban witnesses a tragic outcome to Tammy's upcoming surgery, igniting a flicker of empathy she can no longer ignore.

As reality and nightmares blur, Ebban must decide if she will continue down a path of isolation or embrace the chance to change—not just her own life, but the lives of those she unknowingly holds dear.

Sullivan's Trace by Ali Spooner

Micah "Sully" Sullivan has settled into a solitary life at the family horse ranch after her father's death. When her long-term vet, Doc Barton, plans to retire, his granddaughter, Bryn, arrives to take over his practice. An attack on one of Sully's prized horses throws Sully and Bryn into a whirlwind as they fight to save the young animal. Just as Sully is becoming comfortable with her growing attraction to Bryn, tragedy occurs, and her brother and his wife are killed in an accident. Sully's solitary life drastically changes when a family of three is born.

Love Sins by Annette Mori

Jessica Green's life is predictable and boring. As the chief engineer for Solar Flair, her career is right on track. Her love life, not so much. The last thing she expects is a call from her estranged father's attorney. Too curious to ignore the message, she can't resist meeting with him and discovering more about specific instructions related to his estate, as well as the letter her father left for her. Rattled by what she finds at her father's home, she promptly dials 911.

Special Agent Amanda Forrester is perplexed by a call to join a homicide investigation until she arrives at the scene and learns the victim is not only a serial killer but an elite assassin the authorities have been after for years. To Amanda's increasing irritation, the daughter recognizes a picture of the last target and insinuates herself into the investigation. As the case takes a surprising turn, Amanda finds she has landed smack dab in the middle of a complicated and dangerous situation. The facts lead her to a puzzle weaving together the recent suicide of a wealthy businessman with the activities of several prominent politicians. Amanda must join forces with a mysterious organization and the persistent woman she finds increasingly hard to resist. Her instinct to protect the alluring and vulnerable Jessica Green kicks into high gear, taking the reader on a roller-coaster journey for the last book in *The Next Generation* series.

A Wild Moon Rises by Jen Silver

Successful author, Malory G Holmes, has had a rough year. Wounded by an emotional breakup and writer's block she returns home after eight months travelling to discover the startling results of a DNA test. Apparently, through her mother's side, she is related to a baronet with an estate in Briarbay, Northumberland. She decides to visit the place to find out more about this unknown side of her family.

Selene Wylde is content with life, running a bookshop in the small hamlet of Briarbay. She also looks after her father, Reginald, who is grieving over the recent death of his husband,

Sir Alan Guyatt. Reginald is worrying about his claim to stay at Briarbay Hall as the Will of Sir Alan has not yet been found.

With the arrival in her shop of a very attractive, well-known writer, Selene's world begins to tilt alarmingly. Malory and Selene become entangled in a web of secrets and deceptions with the added complication of a rapidly growing attraction.

The Wolf and The Unicorn by Ali Spooner (Erotica)
Ready to explore a steamy, passionate, and tantalizing erotica romance....

Keagan and Celeste have built a solid relationship on trust and independence. A successful surgeon, Keagan understands Celeste's supercharged libido and her desire to experience a variety of sexual encounters. Everything changes when Sky, a new doctor, arrives at the hospital, and Celeste is immediately drawn to the younger woman. Keagan is surprised when she is also attracted to Sky, who shares common interests with Celeste and her. When more than a physical attraction develops, the three women discover a loving relationship beyond the bedroom.

The Blank White Page by Ali Spooner
Tatum Chastain, Corporate Officer of Chastain International, her family's real estate empire, accepts the challenge her father, Charles, has set forth. Charles has tasked Tatum and her brother, Charlie, to survive in the wilderness for six months to prove their skills in taking over the family business once he retires. Charles fails to realize that Tatum would fall in love with the southeastern Alaska cabin he has chosen for her to test her resilience and creativity. Tatum

prepares for life in the bush, and shortly after she arrives, Poe, a beautiful raven, becomes her companion and guardian. When River Foster, a designated hunter for her village, crosses Tatum's path, she finds a different kind of love awaits her.

Love Hacks by Annette Mori

Joy Stiles is adrift. Having finally finished her graduate degree at the National Defense University, the only thing keeping her interest is an ongoing feud with a fellow hacker to gain access to sensitive information. Against all odds, the person snuck their way into her tech and kept leaving taunting messages. It's driving Joy crazy. She doesn't have time for this. Operation Elephant Bites isn't working as The Organization thought it would when they started down that path two years ago. Now they have a new worry. Someone is desperately trying to find out more about The Organization, believing they are behind the attacks on the mines. Whoever that person is has not only ties to the Chinese and Russian governments but also members of the US Government. Top secret files at the NSA call their unknown group The Crusaders. Joy's efforts to uncover the identity of the enemy lead The Organization to a lot more than evil plans, and it's up to The Next Generation, with support from senior members of The Organization, to thwart the inevitable trajectory, perhaps with the assistance of Joy's irritating foe.

Strength Within by Mia Barnes

Samantha Wilson is an award-winning freelance writer with a passion for being the voice of others. Despite vowing never to go back, she returns to Milwaukee, Wisconsin, for an assignment. Her return awakens memories that force her to confront her sad and lonely childhood, including the violent attack she'd rather forget. Moving away and making a quiet, successful solo life for herself, leaving the life she knew behind cannot keep Sammie from facing her past.

Fortunately, her best friend, Zoë, flies in from New Mexico to be by her side while she confronts the demons of her past. Sammie has a knack for helping others find their happy endings. Will she finally let Zoe help her become whole again and maybe discover her happy ending in the process?

Mom's Last Wish by Charlene Neil

After fifteen years away from home, Lucy Donald receives an email from her mother's personal assistant, Cameron Bishop, compelling her to return. Soon after Lucy's arrival, threatening letters start to appear, and Lucy realizes her life is in actual danger. She seeks comfort in the arms of the alluring Cameron Bishop, but can Cameron really be trusted?

Lucy's return home and the events that unfold lead to an intense and suspenseful atmosphere.

Left to uncover the mysteries by herself, she finds herself grappling with the dilemma of not knowing whom to trust.

The Next Generation by Annette Mori

Despite Toni's legendary brilliance, even she could not stop the march of time. After learning her daughter, Joy, and Joy's two best friends, Pepper and Alina, attempted to deceive the senior agents in The Organization with a bogus Spring Break cover story, she convinces her wife it's time to let the Next Generation take over.

The last thing Pepper Maggio expects after agreeing to lead a mission is literally running into the woman she's followed for years. Not only is Grace Turner beautiful, but she's a passionate crusader for the same innocents that The Organization vows to protect. Along with her two best friends, the three young women embark on an adventure to save the day. But the mission quickly gets out of hand as the human traffickers target not only Grace and her film crew, but also the young Mexican woman who managed to catch Alina's eye. Maria might be the bravest of the bunch as a survivor of one of the Mexican mines, but she's a sitting duck if they don't intervene. They might be the Next Generation, but they'll need the full support of The Organization, including Pepper's lethal mother, Val, to get out of Mexico alive.

Turn the Page by Ali Spooner

Continue the journey with Whit and Eli in this final installment of the Cast Iron Farm series. The brilliance of their twins, Mack and Zack, rapidly develops, challenging Whit and Eli to keep up with their education. Their sensitivity to others and kindness are far beyond their youth and a testament to the family's efforts to help them grow into young adults. In addition to more adventures, a budding romance, and wedding bells ring for the Fortner family once more as a new generation begins life on Cast Iron Farm.

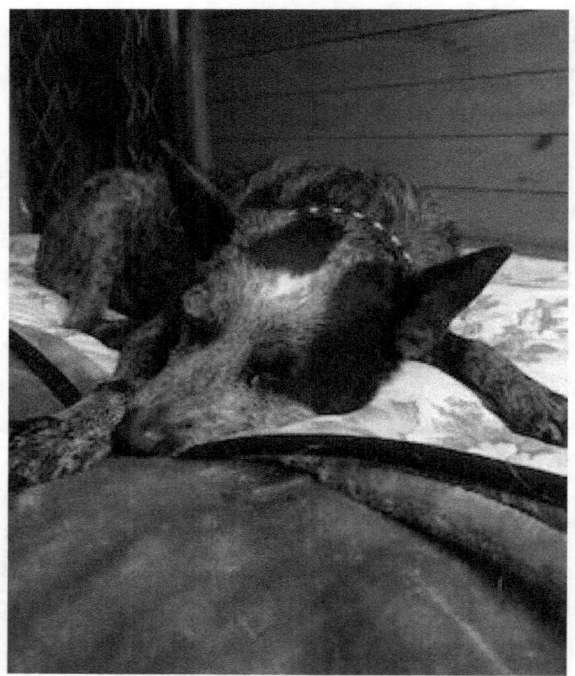

Kiwi (Ali Spooner)

Affinity
Rainbow Publications

eBooks, Print, Free eBooks

Visit our website for more publications available online.

https://affinityebooks.com/

Published by Affinity Rainbow Publications
A Division of Affinity eBook Press NZ LTD
Canterbury, New Zealand

Registered Company 2517228

www.ingramcontent.com/pod-product-compliance
Lightning Source LLC
Chambersburg PA
CBHW070045030726
47506CB00002B/351